Praise for
The Catch

"[A] warm and funny debut novel . . . perceptive, wry and witty."

> —*The New York Times*

"I laughed, I cried, I thought about life. I now want to read whatever Alison Fairbrother writes."

> —SUSAN MINOT, author of *Why I Don't Write:*
> *And Other Stories*

"In this wonderful, wholly absorbing family drama with a mystery at its beating heart, Alison Fairbrother asks, What are we owed by the people we love? The answers she provides are funny, sad, complex, and always surprising. I loved this book and you will too."

> —MEG WOLITZER, *New York Times* bestselling
> author of *The Female Persuasion*

"An affecting, often funny debut."

> —*People*

"Sparkling . . . [Fairbrother's] narrative voice percolates with poetry. . . . A complex portrait of a father-daughter relationship for us lucky, lucky readers."

—*The East Hampton Star*

"Confident and assured."

—*Pittsburgh Post-Gazette*

"Fairbrother's debut is characterized by its elegant yet comfortable prose—readers will feel at home with Ellie as if experiencing the story's events along with her. The mystery drives the plot, but Ellie's personal growth is the heart of the novel. . . . This layered coming-of-age story will appeal to fans of Jennifer E. Smith's *The Unsinkable Greta James*."

—*Booklist*

"In Fairbrother's perceptive debut, a young journalist is left reeling and looking for answers after her father's sudden death."

—*Publishers Weekly*

"Punctuated by sharp, spot-on observations of journalism ('They can comment after we publish') and Washington life ('Sometimes it seemed as if people in their mid-twenties did all the work in D.C.'), informed by the author's own decade reporting in the capital . . . Pack this for your next long weekend—it's fun!"

—*Kirkus Reviews*

"*The Catch* is about the mysteries left behind in death but, importantly, it is just as much about the mysteries of living and the discoveries made while aching and searching and loving. This is a satisfying and wise novel by an author I will happily follow anywhere."

—RAMONA AUSUBEL, author of *Sons and Daughters of Ease and Plenty*

"*The Catch* is an intimate family drama about secrets and what we are willing to do, or hide, from those we love most. Alison Fairbrother's writing makes her characters, with all their flaws and weaknesses and desires, feel like people you know. Set against the vibrant backdrop of Washington, D.C., *The Catch* unfurls in entirely unexpected directions and had me utterly engaged from the very first page."

—ANTON DISCLAFANI, author of *The After Party*

THE CATCH

THE CATCH

A Novel

Alison Fairbrother

RANDOM HOUSE

NEW YORK

2023 Random House Trade Paperback Edition

Published in the United States by Random House, an imprint
and division of Penguin Random House LLC, New York.

RANDOM HOUSE and the HOUSE colophon are registered
trademarks of Penguin Random House LLC.
RANDOM HOUSE BOOK CLUB and colophon are trademarks
of Penguin Random House LLC.

Originally published in hardcover in the United States by Random House,
an imprint and division of Penguin Random House LLC, in 2022.

LIBRARY OF CONGRESS CATALOGING-IN-PUBLICATION DATA
Names: Fairbrother, Alison, author.
Title: The catch: a novel / Alison Fairbrother.
Description: New York: Random House, [2022]
Identifiers: LCCN 2021034300 (print) | LCCN 2021034301 (ebook) |
ISBN 9780593134313 (trade paperback; acid-free paper) |
ISBN 9780593134306 (ebook)
Classification: LCC PS3606.A365 C38 2022 (print) |
LCC PS3606.A365 (ebook) | DDC 813/.6—dc23
LC record available at lccn.loc.gov/2021034300
LC ebook record available at lccn.loc.gov/2021034301

Printed in the United States of America on acid-free paper

randomhousebooks.com
randomhousebookclub.com

2 4 6 8 9 7 5 3 1

Title page image: © iStockphoto.com

Book design by Dana Leigh Blanchette

For my mother and father

THE CATCH

One

My father, a minor poet, celebrated holidays out of season. He couldn't get custody of all four of his children at once, so he moved the fall, spring, and winter holidays to the heat of summer. A man who had fathered four kids with three different women was unusual in our Maryland town. Neighbors gossiped and strangers commented. My father struggled financially, and I suppose he could have resented the way we tethered him, but he didn't. Over and over, he brought us into his world.

The first holiday I remember was Summer Christmas. I was seven, shy and compliant. Our neighbors swam in the Chesapeake and grilled hot dogs; we sat inside and heaped a fake fir tree with tinsel and chains of cranberries. We knew Christmas in summer was odd, but we didn't care. In fact, we liked it. Or at least I did. Getting to celebrate with my father in the wrong season was far superior to not celebrating with him at all. He was the kind of parent you wanted to be with, and on a holiday he took such pleasure in the details. Once, he lifted one of my baby half-sisters up to press a snowman cookie cutter into a roll of dough, and in that moment, when her shirt rose and her arm stretched out, and everyone was oven-hot and overexcited, I thought that if I ever had children, I would scramble up the holidays too, not because I would need to, but just because I could.

Dad's second wife, Barbara, the woman he married after he divorced my mother, would go upstairs after dinner to give my two half-sisters a bath and put them to bed. She was like the head nun at a nunnery, a grim tactician, her hair always in a bun, and she absented herself from me as much as possible. Because I was the oldest and she wasn't my mother, and because my real mother was then far away in Philadelphia, I was allowed to stay up late with Dad. I sat by his knee and listened to him strum his guitar and sing "Jimmy Crack Corn," which I later learned was racist.

Easter came in summer too, in July. Dad bought PAAS dye kits from Walmart and we dropped colored tablets into plastic cups, adding vinegar and watching the dye swirl through the water. He was so enthusiastic about the whole thing, as if he were a scientist trying to get his children interested in his chosen field. There were a few happy years of Easter-egg hunts, our cheeks fat with chocolate, Barbara wiping my sisters' mouths with wet napkins, until the year of Dad and Barbara's divorce, when he lost patience with the flimsy egg holder and dunked his egg directly into the cup, staining his fingers iridescent purple. My half-sisters, then four and three, paced our father's new place, sniffling and listing all the things they missed about their mom's house, the stuffed animals that hadn't made the half-hour trip to visit Dad and a favorite bedtime book called *Randy the Hippopotamus*. I didn't miss Barbara at all. I thought of her alone in the bathroom I would never see again, removing pins from her bun, drawing herself a bath, and letting the water out at 7:45 P.M. exactly. Dad and I let my sisters splash in his new tub as long as they wanted, until their skin was mushroomy and they'd finished soaping all their Easter rabbit figurines. After they were tucked in bed, exhausted and pink, their eyelids fluttering because of chocolate or dreams, Dad put his purple fingers on my shoulder and said, "You bring out the best in me, Ellie."

The first time I met Colette, who would become wife number three, was the following year, at Summer New Year's. We all wore oversized blue-glitter sunglasses, and we painted signs that read, SO LONG 1999! Dad made razzleberry fring frongs—juice and ginger ale with a raspberry floating on top. I am certain he named them. The grown-ups' fring frongs were topped with gin. If Colette was nonplussed that we were ringing in the millennium four months earlier than everyone else, she hid it well. When you were married to my father, or when you were one of his children, you got with the program, because that was what everyone else did. And the program was always exciting, so you never really minded. Colette, though, did she mind? She must have known what he was like. The word *boyish* was frequently in play, and it was an appealing description, because how many women had married older divorced men, only to find themselves soon taking care of them in ways they had never anticipated? But a boyish man, a perpetual *boy*, would last a long time. He could grow older with the beautiful girlish woman he loved. And together they would have a family, and together they would have a life.

Colette—did she think about any of this? I remember how

she spread newspapers on the kitchen table and made Popsicle-stick picture frames with my half-sisters, the family she had inherited. She asked with genuine interest whether I had a crush on anyone at school, and I told her about Ronny Devine. I tried to hate her for encroaching on my territory as Dad's closest confidante, but mostly I didn't take her seriously. She had slim Irish looks and dark wavy hair; she knew which plants to mash into pastes and boil into tea, but she didn't read books and never knew where her keys were. She was like a medieval village herbalist. I didn't think she would be around long. This was before Dad and Colette had Van, before it was revealed that Van was deaf, before they were bound together not just by their child but by Van's particular needs.

That first Summer New Year's with Colette, after the five of us clinked our razzleberry fring frongs and thought about the enormity of a millennium, Dad put on Van Morrison's "Brown Eyed Girl" and pointed the speakers out the window. We danced out the back door and into the night, following Dad's lead, sliding over the dark grass. "Happy New Year!" we cried, and Dad kissed Colette, and my half-sisters jumped up and down, and crickets sang long after the music ended, and under the full moon we all seemed to glow.

Our final holiday out of season was Summer Thanksgiving in 2012. I had finished college by then and moved to Washington, D.C., to take an entry-level journalism job at a news website called *Apogee*. It was a fast-paced, hard-drinking kind of job, and keeping up required long hours at the office and socializing with other young journalists at happy hours and brunches on weekends, all of which I could barely afford. Obama was in the White House. It felt inevitable that we—the youthful, educated, diverse residents of D.C.—would inherit the halls of power. All we had to do was work and wait.

I hadn't been home to my father's house in Maryland in months when I asked my boss, Jane Ostrawicz-Jones, for time off for Summer Thanksgiving. "Summer Thanksgiving?" She'd arched an eyebrow that was already too pointy, since she drew them on as upside-down V's. From the moment I'd met her at the job interview, where she was terse and cryptic, I'd thought of her as *angular* in all ways, and I'd even imagined her house as being filled with furniture with sharp edges that could cause small injuries if you weren't careful.

"Family tradition," I said.

"Be on your phone," Jane answered.

When I got off the train with my overnight bag, the air was stewy with moisture. The train to Maryland had seemed a lot larger the summer I was nine, the first time I traveled alone from my mother's house to my father's, but Dad had been waiting for me by the track every visit since then. I was currently twenty-four and paying down the interest on my student loans; I had a good job, for which a scarily sexual-sounding holding company called Fantasia XSP deposited money into my checking account in two-week intervals; I owned a vacuum cleaner. I was the most adult I'd ever been, but, then again, I'd been playing an adult even when I was nine, holding myself stiff with maturity, coaxing my father to talk about marriage, money, and responsibility.

"Hey, you," he said on the platform. "Good trip?" I had

barely answered before he said, "Colette is making a million dishes. I didn't even know our kitchen cabinets held so many medium-sized casseroles."

"Live and learn," I said. I always felt as if I had to respond or he would be disappointed. We had somehow, during my upbringing, developed a banter that was, if not witty, definitely our own.

"Then we'll get cozy and decorate the tree later," he said.

"The tree already? It's only Summer Thanksgiving."

"Who knows when we can lure you away from Washington again?" He put his nose in my hair and snuffled. "You even smell like that city."

"What does D.C. smell like?" I asked. "Record humidity?"

My father stepped back to look at me. "Like power and pleasure," he said, hands on my shoulders. His voice sounded funny.

I wondered if he had intuited something. I'd met Lucas at Union Station early that morning, before my train. We'd held hands in the corner of the basement food court, drinking coffees and smiling at each other over the lids of our cups. Most of the food stands were shuttered at that hour, but two cooks in hairnets behind the counter of Wok n Talk were cutting gristle from bone and throwing chunks of meat into fryers. It seemed impossible that life could go on around us while I sat there with Lucas, leaning forward so he could kiss me across the sticky table, brazenly, at one of the few places where we didn't worry about anyone we knew seeing us, observed only by workers rhythmically splashing chicken into grease. There was the pleasure and there was the power.

My father and I started across the parking lot together, arm in arm, our faces damp with a fine summer mist, as if we were exotic plants getting a greenhouse spritzing.

"I have to make one quick stop. Need anything, fancy D.C. girl?"

"I'm not fancy."

"You're fancier than me. I mean, look." We reached his patched-together 1996 Jetta, unlinked our arms. Van Morrison's "Astral Weeks" played on the tape deck as we slid into our seats, which meant he had the stereo system working again. "I'm proud of you for getting that job," he said, shifting the car into reverse, "even if you do have to live in that sybaritic city of bloviating assholes."

"Really, Dad, do you have to use such predictable words?"

He swung us out of the lot a little too fast. Pollen swirled in the air around the car, the universe responding to my father's pitch. I sat back, relishing the brief time I got to be alone with him before we got home to Colette and his other children. My phone dinged. It was Lucas saying he missed me; I knew it would be. It dinged again.

"Who's blinging?" He glanced over at the phone on my lap.

"Nobody. It's work." I flipped it over.

"Not that Lucas character, I hope."

"Dad!"

"I don't want you to get hurt, Ellie. I can't bear the thought of you in pain."

I put my hand on top of his on the gearshift. "I know. But let's not talk about him, okay?" The first and only time I'd

told him about Lucas, Dad hadn't understood. I didn't want
to get into it again. It was better to keep my thoughts about
Lucas to myself, where no one could interfere.

He made a motion like zipping his lips. "Next stop, Super
Food Emporium, Ice, and Tackle."

We nosed around the dairy aisle, which was separated from
live worms by frozen vegetables. Super Food Emporium, Ice,
and Tackle was my father's favorite store. His most anthologized poem, "The Catch," had a line that was an homage to
the place, about tossing a ball back and forth on rainy summer afternoons in "dusty store aisles." Four times a year Dad
would get a tiny royalty check as anthologies containing
"The Catch" were sold to high school and college classrooms.
It was a mournful poem about having to leave someone you
loved. I knew without his telling me that the poem was about
me. He'd written it the same year he and my mother divorced,
the year of my earliest memories, the year that I was three
and he taught me to play catch.

Dad always joked that getting royalties for poems was the
equivalent of being paid for saying, "Maybe." Poetry was a
way to be decisive about nothing, to ask endless questions, to
be open to everything. He supplemented this indecision by
teaching classes each semester at Chesapeake College.

We doubled back toward the ice cream. "It's kind of insane to think a supermarket would carry eggnog in June," I
said.

Dad flagged down a local kid in a white paper cap crouching in front of a display case of sunblock. "Harris, where do you keep your eggnog?"

"Hiya, Jim. What are you looking for?" Harris pushed his cap farther back on his wide forehead.

"Eggnog. Creamy caloric beverage served around Christmas?"

Harris glanced at his watch. "It's June first."

"Your watch tells the date?"

"It's broken. Don't know why I looked at it."

"Probably could use a new battery. Give her here." I watched my father examine the watch and shake his head. "No, this is broken. But you need a watch. Take mine." He removed the black Casio from his own wrist—he'd worn it for as long as I could remember—and handed it to Harris.

"I can't accept this," Harris said formally, bowing his head.

"Nonsense. I don't need it! My wife and I got phones that have clocks in them."

"Flip phones," I clarified.

"I'm never supposed to be without mine." He dug into his pocket and produced the phone. Harris shrugged shyly and they shook hands, Dad's wrist now bare.

That was my father. Uncommonly generous. My entire childhood, toys were always disappearing. The moment any of us stopped playing with things, Dad would give them to another family. He believed objects should go to people who needed them, that they should rightfully belong to whoever would use them the most, and so while he was always buying us things, he was forever taking them away too. The only ex-

ceptions were his most prized possessions, the things he cher-
ished beyond their usefulness—his Van Morrison records,
the oil painting of the Patuxent River that hung in the living
room, his lucky baseball. I was especially glad about his lucky
baseball, which sat on a shallow dish above his desk and was
the very first thing I could remember holding in my hands.
We'd all played endless rounds of catch in the backyard on
lazy afternoons. If he ever gave that away, I would kill him.

As we made our way to the exit, Dad turned and gave Harris a wave. "A good employee should never be without a
watch," he called.

I froze. It was a tone that I recognized as judgment. When
I turned around to see Harris's expression, he was pinching
the watch with two fingers, looking down at the screen,
oblivious. I walked slightly behind my father as we left the
store. Maybe it hadn't been judgment at all but a statement
of fact, a sincere offer of guidance. A good employee should
never be without a watch.

The rain began in earnest now, drops falling hard and
warm as pennies. Relieved, I ducked to run to the car, but he
was proceeding slowly across the parking lot, undeterred. I
could pick him out of a crowd from far away because of his
walk. When he swung his left leg forward, it hitched before
coming down again, as a cellist must interrupt the progress
of the bow across a ringing string in order to strike a new
note. With each step he made his own music.

It was Colette's policy to get Van out of the kitchen during
the cooking for Summer Thanksgiving. She would enlist my

two half-sisters and me, wiping sweat from her face and opening the screen door. Sadie, Anna, and I would race across the lawn to the cool, dark shade of the woods, and Van would chase us, playing the part of the younger brother who couldn't keep up, as we acted out the older sisters who could never be caught. Being pursued was the easy part. Once we stopped running, we didn't know what to do with him. Only Dad, Colette, and Van were fluent in sign language.

This year, when Colette asked Sadie and Anna to play with Van, it was clear immediately that my sisters had aged out of games of tag. Possibly games of all kinds. They were eighteen and seventeen, sprawled on the floor in various stages of teenage distress. The heat had made Anna's eczema break out, and she was picking at little blotches on her chest and sighing. Sadie was typing furiously into her phone, cycling through a baffling number of facial expressions as she read messages from her friends, barking laughter one minute and then growing silent the next, scrunching her shoulders up when she read something she didn't like.

"Girls?" Colette was balancing a salad bowl on her hip.

"Can I just finish this." Sadie's eyes skimmed back and forth across her screen.

"One minute," Anna echoed.

Sadie and Anna would never have said no to Barbara, their own mother. I'd seen Barbara stand over her daughters with a list of French vocabulary words to memorize in one hand and a primer on cursive in the other, for when they had sufficiently conjugated the verb être. Because Sadie and Anna never got to act out with her, they stretched their contrarian muscles with Colette. When you were a child of divorce, you had to be two versions of yourself, one at your mother's house and one at your father's. But neither one was your real self, because your presentation at one house was forged in opposition to whatever parent was currently off-duty. I felt this made divorced children like me especially fit for the adult art of dissociating.

"I'll help," I told Colette, and she gave me a grateful smile.

Van was at the kitchen table, lifting and lowering the brim of his Orioles cap as he pored over our father's baseball magazines. He was ten, young enough for his pastimes to be inextricably wound up with our father's.

"Van, do you want to go outside?" I swept my arm to the door. Van peeked at Sadie and Anna to see if they were coming. "They're being teenagers. They don't want to play." Van was good at lip-reading simple phrases, but Dad or Colette usually translated anything complicated. "We could take a walk to the woods. Or go down to the creek?"

Van glanced at Colette, who began to sign and then became distracted by a pot spitting on the stove.

"Van the man," Dad said, from the window seat. He lifted his hands and asked Van if he wanted to play catch. I didn't know much sign language, but their shorthand for playing catch mimed the act itself. Dad's arm went up above his ear, hinged at the elbow, and swan-necked to the point of release. On the other side of the table, Van reached up and caught the imaginary ball.

Dad swiped his lucky baseball from the shelf above his desk and they headed outside. As I stood on the threshold, my chest had a scraped-out feeling of exclusion. He hadn't asked whether I wanted to play too.

I wondered if he had lumped me into the category my sisters were currently occupying: apathetic, closed off, a little bit selfish. Or maybe just female. I looked back at Sadie and Anna, the redheaded beauties from Dad's second marriage, still on the floor where it was cooler, leaning against the couch. I realized I barely knew them.

The turkey was making the kitchen unbearably hot. Outside, Colette's vegetable garden was in full verdant bloom. Inside, it was 400 degrees, and she was cooking with canned pumpkin while wearing a bathing suit. I took an ice cube from the freezer to suck on and went into the living room, plopping onto the window seat Dad had vacated. He and Van were on the lawn, between the sweetgum trees, the lucky baseball blurring between them. Dad shot the ball high, pressing it against the blue sky like a summer moon. It fell back to earth, into Van's mitt, which was open in a clamshell above his head.

I thought of texting Lucas, but it would be a long weekend away from him. I didn't want to text too much and seem needy—or worse, wait a long time for his response and have to wonder what he was doing. Instead, I cracked open my notebook, running my fingers over the ink-textured paper. I carried this notebook everywhere I went; in it I wrote down the first lines of every book I'd ever read. It was a comfort to skim the familiar lines without their context.

Dad had taken great interest in this notebook when I'd started it, a few years after Sadie and Anna were born. My visits to his house had become infrequent as he juggled the demands of his new family. I'd started reading my eyes raw and falling asleep at night with the worlds of the books like kaleidoscopes across my vision. I favored books about horses, endless permutations of girls and horses and their irrevocable bond. A horse found its way back to a girl after she had moved three thousand miles away! A horse diagnosed a girl's foot cancer by repeatedly nudging her foot, saving her life! When Dad called, he'd say, "What's new in the notebook?" And I'd read him a sampling of first lines, which he would dissect. " 'The orphaned copper filly stamped her hoof,' " he'd repeat. "See how that's giving away too soon the most important detail, about the horse being orphaned?" I didn't tell him that I disagreed.

The lucky baseball thocked between mitts like a clock ticking too slowly. I considered going out and asking to play catch too, but I felt hurt and as if I'd be intruding. Skimming ahead in the notebook, I found pages that were filled with the first lines of what my father called "real books." When I was nine, one of my teachers recommended I see the school psychologist. In our first session together, she asked whether I liked to read. Yes, I responded promptly, and proceeded to tell her the story of a rascal named Tom and his friendship with a boy called Huck, how they witnessed a murder and ended up saving their small Mississippi town.

The psychologist took off her glasses, which fell from a beaded chain onto her bosom. "You've read *The Adventures of Tom Sawyer*?" she asked, leaning forward in her chair.

I nodded. I had not, in fact, read *The Adventures of Tom Sawyer,* but it was one of my father's favorite books. I'd heard him call Mark Twain "the greatest genius to come out of the vituperative American South." I repeated this line to the school psychologist, and before the lunch period, half the teachers

in the school were looking at me with admiration. I began
reading to keep up with my reputation.

There must have been a time when Thanksgiving came in
autumn, before the stepmothers and half-siblings, when it
was just my mother, father, and me. But I don't remember it.
I can imagine how the meal went, my mother carefully scooping a pat of stuffing in a quarter-cup measure, placing a slice
of dry turkey on a food scale, avoiding the gravy. My entire
childhood, my mother kept a marbled notebook next to the
kitchen telephone, where she added numbers of calories in
columns she drew with a ruler. There was no reprieve for the
holidays; she would have been calculating her calories even as
she heated my bottle, while my father turned up his favorite
Van Morrison record and made gravy for one, humming
along to the music, pouring so much of the thick, dark fat
over his Thanksgiving plate he'd eat it with a spoon.

After he left us and I was old enough to swim, my mother
brought me to her aqua-aerobics class on Saturdays. I did
grapevines in the water with old ladies in rubber caps. My
mother was a secretary then at the office of Boris Gettleman,
MD, whom she would go on to marry, but she taught aerobics on the side for the extra money and because she wanted
to exercise anyway. I stood in the locker room after those
classes, dripping chlorinated water onto the brown tiles,
watching my mother peel off her suit and step on the kind of
scale used in doctors' offices, which made a rocking sound as
the balance adjusted to your weight.

The special treat after aqua aerobics was a trip to Bagel
Alley. Before we spread the cream cheese, we "de-breadified
the bagels," which involved taking the mushy insides out of

the bagel and leaving the husk. The mushy parts had to be put in my mother's palm, and she would ferry them to the garbage can.

Colette poked her head into the living room, holding a steaming potato with an oven mitt that was shaped like a lobster. In the other hand she balanced a white platter.

"Do you think I should use this dish or the ceramic one for the potatoes?"

"That one's nice."

"It's coming together, finally." Colette rested the platter on the coffee table and sat on the window seat near my feet. She looked glamorous in her bikini and somehow dry, whereas my thighs were mashed together and there was a damp pocket of sweat at my back. The rainstorm had passed but it had done nothing to cut the humidity.

"They've been out there a long time." I pointed my chin at Dad and Van in the field.

"It's a language between them." Colette nudged the potato onto the platter.

How many languages do they need? I thought.

Colette said, "The bird's almost done. Why don't you go call them in."

I went out the back door and walked through the warm spikes of grass. Endless arcs in the air, the ball's laces spinning. It was a country life; there was no cell reception in the field. Mothers sent their children as messengers and sentinels. Stepmothers too. I found the two of them in the throes of their meditation. The ball curved against the sky, the porch light, the dark squares of windows. It took a few moments before they saw me, before the ball began its last descent into Van's glove.

We had a tradition of getting dolled up for the Summer Thanksgiving feast. Sadie and Anna jockeyed in the mirror, pouting as they lined their mouths with pencil and smeared their eyelids in blue.

"You wore that dress last year." Sadie curled her lip. She was going to fashion school in New York in the fall and was increasingly critical of other people's clothes.

"I did not. That wasn't a halter. Mom got this dress for me for homecoming," Anna said.

"Stop lying!"

"You both look beautiful," I said. My strategy with them was usually tepid distance. To fight like sisters, you had to have grown up in the same house, and Sadie and Anna had lived by one set of rules under their mother Barbara's roof, while I'd lived in a different world with mine. My sisters were their own tightly controlled unit of drama, love, and reproach.

"Do my arms look fat? See how they poof out?" Anna poked the flesh of her biceps.

"You look perfect," I said. "That's not fat." When you were a size 12, like me, you had to live with thinner women complaining about their bodies all the time. But women had tunnel vision when it came to disparaging their own bodies. It never occurred to them that to call themselves fat at size 6 might aggrieve the size-12 sister standing beside them. Mostly,

I didn't mind. Ever since I was a teenager, I had rebelled against my mother's de-breadifying; you might say that whenever possible, I breadified.

"Anna! You pushed me!" Sadie cried, cradling a palette of eyeshadow.

"You pushed me first," Anna said matter-of-factly. She nudged her elbow into Sadie's ribs, forcing her to step sideways.

"Stop it!"

Would I even like these people if we weren't related? I wondered. I had no reason to stay in the bathroom listening to them, sitting on the edge of the tub in the humid fog of my family's ablutions.

In the living room, I found Dad sitting on the window seat, crunching through a bowl of Utz pretzels and onion dip. His version of dress-up was clean jeans and a button-down tucked in. He kept his blond hair cut below his ears, a boyish length that went with his tall, stooped frame. I remembered seeing his high school yearbook, and in the photo of him with the rest of the staff of the literary magazine, he had essentially looked exactly as he would as an adult. But it was unclear if he looked older then or younger now. Unlike most people, he'd had only one way of looking, maybe one way of being, his entire life.

"Colette always does this," he said. "She makes these delicious meals but lets me fill up on dip right before we eat."

"If she didn't, you'd complain there was no dip."

"True. She probably expects me to have self-control. As if one could exercise restraint around her onion dip." He balanced a crumpled napkin under his mouth as he took another bite.

Sadie shrieked in the bathroom. "Fighting again," I said.

"They used to get along so well," Dad said. "It's like a switch has been flipped. And it's always Sadie initiating, yelling at Anna. Calling her out on something."

"Nothing that ten or twelve years won't fix," I said, rustling in the pretzel bowl for a small piece.

"Do you think I should talk to them about it?" he asked.

I looked at him for a few moments, considering. Then I shook my head. "They're probably chafing at each other because Sadie is going away to college, and they've never been apart before. I bet the distance next year will help."

He made a happy sound in his throat, impressed with me. "You're absolutely right. Though I don't understand why Anna just takes it. She doesn't stand up for herself."

But that wasn't quite true, I thought. I'd seen Anna in the bathroom, snaking an elbow into Sadie's side. I felt a little flare of disappointment that my father was oblivious to the theater of power among sisters, even as it was performed right in front of him.

"Anna has her own way of sticking up for herself," I said.

"I never had this trouble with you."

I smiled slightly, trying to mask my secret pleasure. I liked it when he criticized them and praised me. It made me feel like the favored daughter. What I didn't say, but what I knew, was that he'd seen me less than he saw them; if I'd misbehaved, if I was rude or unkind or juvenile, it was my mother who dealt with me. Having children in separate households had split him up into different-sized father pieces, and I felt as if my whole life I had been competing for the biggest piece. A divorced father put his children in competition with one another; the catch was that no one could ever win. Though I wasn't the youngest, or the prettiest, or the thinnest, or the child who saw him the most, I had compensated by being mature, thoughtful, considerate, and literary, and he had responded with unusual openness. My natural inclination toward bookishness had coincided with his own interests; in our daily phone conversations he often spoke to me as though I were a peer. It was a way in, and maybe it was calculated on my part, but it worked. I tried never to disappoint him.

"Yeah, I was a *model* child," I said, with a little sarcastic laugh.

"You were," he agreed.

When we'd settled around the table in our good clothes, Dad motioned for us to hold hands. He had tears in his eyes. I grasped Sadie's nail-polished, jeweled hand on my left and went for Colette's on my right, only to find it padded with a lobster.

"Not that speech again, Dad," Sadie said.

"Dad, you have to do the speech!" said Anna.

He held up his hands, entwined with Van's on one side and Colette's on the other, squeezed, and dropped them so he could sign for Van. "All right, girlies. Let me have a moment. We don't all get to be together very often, and I want to thank everyone for being here. And special thanks to each of you. Van, for his unbelievable right hook. Anna, for her perfect sense of humor. Case in point, she's the only one of my children who appreciates the comedy of Jerry Lewis. Sadie, for being the most gorgeous and stylish of women, who will come home from fashion school every weekend, right?"

Sadie snorted. "Yeah, right, Dad!"

He turned to me. "Ellie, for coming from D.C. to grace us with her brilliance. Colette, for this extraordinary pavane of fall colors."

Dad shaped an additional phrase for Van, maybe the meaning of the word *pavane,* as though it would be useful to a child whose primary interest in life was the batting averages of Orioles infielders. Colette jumped up and flitted around the table, spooning mounds onto Van's plate. She had changed into a slinky black dress.

"Hon? Do you want to sit down?" Dad asked.

"One sec, let me get Van some turkey."

"He's ten. He can get his own turkey."

Colette sat back down, shook out a linen napkin. "What about the eggnog?"

"I forgot to tell you, they didn't have any at the store. I'll have to google how to make the noggle."

"Why does he have to call it noggle?" Sadie moaned under her breath.

"To make an imperfect rhyme with google," I said.

Dad tapped his wineglass with his fork. "Attention, family!" He brought his fist to his mouth like a microphone.

Anna laughed, anticipating Dad's signature speech. She was only seventeen but she had a laugh like a lifelong smoker, three gravelly "heh"s.

"Again," I signed to Van, rolling my eyes toward our father. Van gave me a thumbs-up.

When he had our attention, Dad gestured to Colette to sign while he spoke into his fist microphone, doing the trick with his voice where he sounded like an echo across a stadium of ten thousand people. "Today-ay-ay-ay I-I-I-I consider-ider-ider myself-self-self the luckiest man on the face of the earth." It was Dad's version of the speech first baseman Lou Gehrig gave to a sold-out crowd at Yankee Stadium before he died of a disease named for him. Dad did an impersonation of this speech every year at Summer Thanksgiving. Even though he hadn't eaten anything yet, Dad swallowed hard, like he was pushing something down. He lifted his wineglass, which caught the last flare of orange as the sun dropped into the hills. "Now let's eat!" he said.

Five days later he was dead.

Two

Father Gary waited a respectful amount of time for Colette to stop crying. When she didn't, he said, "The sign-language interpreter will arrive shortly, at eleven-thirty. We'll end the service by playing Van Morrison."

"'Astral Weeks.'" I pulled the album from my purse. "It's track one."

Father Gary was the priest at Dad's Catholic church. Colette and I were talking with him in what I assumed was the rectory, but it may have been an office. I didn't really know, since my Jewish mother hadn't exactly encouraged church-going, and Dad only went to mass when his kids weren't around. Father Gary was unruffled and patient, and I thought I smelled incense on his breath. But, then, did priests swallow incense? I wondered, while my stepmother wailed.

"And the casket won't be open, Father?" Colette said. She twisted a tissue between her fingers, flecks of white drifting to the carpet. "My husband thought that was kind of— I don't know—icky?"

"Odious," I supplied.

"The service will be a fitting tribute to Jim," Father Gary said, rising to his feet, and then went on to add something Jesus-y, which I didn't follow.

I hooked my arms under Colette's armpits and gently helped her up. "Here we go," I said, unfolding her like a camping chair. I imagined it was what Dad would have done.

Over the past two days, I'd called and emailed everyone he knew, asking them to distribute the details of the service. Because there was almost no money in Dad and Colette's checking account, I'd put the deposit for the funeral on my credit card. I felt that if I stopped organizing, I might die too. Nobody was acting normal. Van was playing on his phone from morning to night, and Sadie and Anna blitzed themselves with television. Colette spent hours on the couch under an afghan blanket, reading my father's high school yearbook as if it were a novel. Later, when she fell asleep, I saw that she'd left a mug of tea on top of the yearbook, *The Castle Hill Moat*. When I picked it up to wash it, there was a ring of damp encircling the word *Moat*.

While she napped, I had tiptoed upstairs to Dad and Colette's bedroom. Colette's bedroom now, possession shifting even as I passed the dresser and the bed, the wooden rocking chair, the chest with Van's baby clothes, the fan rotating slowly on its axis. I grasped the knob of his closet door in my hand until it jiggled loose in its joint. The door had been shut firmly, and in chafing the old wood against the frame and yanking, I knew I was acting out violence.

Inside, his sweaters were folded on shelves, shirts hung from hangers. His shoes were lined up in pairs like schoolchildren. As I stood before his clothes, marked by his familiar smell, a groan welled up and burst from my throat. It felt as if the air in the closet contained him. Nutty, sweet, laced with the clean breeze of his cologne. I touched the leg of his one suit, kept for formal events and graduations, the suit he would have worn to his funeral had he lived to attend it.

Once, when I was three or four, I had been with him in a crowded room and lost him among the legs of strangers. When I heard his voice behind me, "Ellie, here I am"—the warmth with which he said my name—I had clasped myself against his knee, the rough material of his suit against my cheek. Flooded with a child's uncomplicated love. My father!

I said aloud, "Here I am, Dad." My lips trembled. I closed his closet door and opened it again. The air inside was dull, swimmy with dust. I couldn't smell him anymore.

When my mother called to tell me, two days earlier, I had been at an office party at the editor-in-chief's house. My *Apogee* colleagues and I were seated in Steve Glanz's living room, balancing plates of quiche on our knees. Steve had insisted we come over for brunch before spending the afternoon in a "working session."

My mother never called at random times; our calls were scheduled in advance via emails with subject lines like "From Your Mother." I knew instantly that something was wrong.

"Ellie? Terrible news. Your father is gone," she said. I excused myself and took my phone into the bathroom.

I almost asked where he went.

My mother went on. "I'm so sorry, honey." When she spoke again, her voice was anguished. "I can't believe it. Your father is gone."

I looked up and saw myself in the mirror. I was clutching a fork, which I had accidentally taken with me. Bits of egg were stuck to the prongs. Blood thudded in my ears. My mother was still talking. ". . . Colette needs your help. I don't think she's much with details."

"How do you know?"

"Know what?"

"My dad," I said.

"Colette called me. She thought it would be better if I called you."

"Mom?"

"I'm going to have Boris drive me to the airport. He found me a direct flight to D.C. I'm coming," she said. "Hang on, I'll be there soon."

I managed to leave the bathroom and find Jane, my boss, the sole adult in a room full of millennial reporters. "Jane," I said. "My dad died." I watched her face drop from surprise to concern. Why did concern always seem to collect at the corners of mouths? Concern collection, I thought. My father is dead. Where was he? I had to get to him. How would I get to him?

"Oh my God, Ellie, I'm so sorry," Jane said.

"I have to go."

"Go," she said, whisking me toward the door. The angularity of her body, her mind, was now like an arrow, shooting forward, helping me.

"But Steve." I doubted the editor-in-chief of *Apogee* would take note of my absence from his brunch; he was like a machine that turned small talk into social capital.

"Don't worry about Steve."

I turned. I couldn't feel my feet on the ground; it was as though I were walking on fog.

"How are you getting home?" Jane asked.

"I have my bike."

She pulled out her phone. "I'm calling you a cab. You can't be biking in this state. I took the Metro here, otherwise I'd drive you. My father died when I was seventeen, and not a day goes by when I don't think of him," Jane said. "I'm really—"

"Okay," I said, unable to listen anymore. Jane's talking like this was making the news seem true. I opened the door and walked out into the hallway, which still smelled like the bacon we'd eaten for brunch.

What I later learned: Dad hadn't been feeling well and had stayed in bed later than usual that day. Colette, an early riser, heard a crash while she was in the kitchen making coffee and ran upstairs to find that he'd fallen to the floor in his blue pajamas, clutching at his chest. She called 911 and performed CPR for as long as she could, breathing air into his lungs and beating her hands against his chest. When she couldn't do it any longer, she woke Sadie. They leaned over him. They asked him to come back. My sister's red hair fell into her eyes as she pressed down on the hollow space between his ribs. She leaned into him with all her strength. "Dad, don't go!" she cried. "Dad!" It took seventeen minutes for the ambulance to make it to their door. By then, he was gone. An hour south in D.C., I slept soundly.

———

Outside it was a brilliant day, the sky safe and blue, clouds the color of milk. People began arriving through the open doors with somber expressions, and by ten minutes to noon, the chapel was packed. My mother had flown in from Florida, where she lived with her husband, Dr. Boris Gettleman, an allergist who allowed me to call him Boris, but whom all my friends had to refer to as Dr. Gettleman. I saw with relief that Mom had refrained from wearing anything the color of passion fruit or mango, which had dominated her wardrobe since she'd followed Dr. Boris Gettleman to Tallahassee, "the city for all seasons." Like me, she was very tall; unlike me, she had zero percent body fat, and looking at her in her brown suit with her silvery bangles and dangling earrings, I thought she looked like an ornamental tree. Barbara, wife number two, had chosen to sit in the third row, clutching a black raincoat on her lap, her hair in its usual tight bun.

I recognized my father's colleagues from Chesapeake College, as well as various local businesspeople and neighbors. I wondered crossly if they had come just to see all three wives in the same room and realized my sadness was making me uncharitable, sullen. Colette's artsy friends occupied one of the side aisles. High school friends of Sadie and Anna clustered in the middle rows, wearing short black party dresses that they hadn't expected to need for an occasion like this, and Van's friends milled around looking bewildered and formal in shiny shoes. Two of them found Van at the front of the room and signed something before enveloping him in a hug. I pulled out my phone and tapped out a quick text: *I'm so glad your friends are here.* Van was better at using a cell phone than anyone I knew; it was an essential tool of communication in our family.

I greeted Bruce, a homeless Vietnam vet who often occupied the faded green bench in the center of town, serenading passersby with a chewed-up voice. Dad would sometimes join him for a rendition of "The Battle Hymn of the Republic" on his way to get his morning paper. I was touched to see that Bruce was wearing a button-down shirt, his hair ridged with comb lines.

I glanced at the text Lucas had sent me earlier, using it now to calm myself. He'd written, *I'm picturing you now, reading your father's poem at the service. You'll be wonderful. He would be so proud of you. I mean he was so proud of you. And so am I.*

When the service started and Father Gary summoned me, I walked to the pulpit with my back to the bodies, hearing rustling, cough drops being unwrapped, the hush of people settling into pews. I opened the notebook where I'd transcribed Dad's poem and leaned over the microphone, a little red light pulsing on its base. I knew the poem by heart but worried I would stumble. But no, I would be wonderful; Lucas said I would. I would find a way to summon a reasonable voice, not a sob. I was seconds away from having to speak, but I still didn't know how that would happen.

Next to me, the ASL interpreter shifted, waiting for me to begin. The whole town peered up at me, eyes bright. Dad's poem "The Catch" began with the line *but, if time could kneel* . . . I wondered how the ASL interpreter would translate that line. Colette once told me that conjunctions worked differently in sign language, though I couldn't recall how. Maybe she'd said that there weren't words for *and* or *but* in sign language. Could that be it? It made no sense to me, because *and* linked ideas together, whereas *but* implied a contrast to what had come before.

In "The Catch," nothing came before *but*. The reader had to guess what the speaker had relayed before the poem began. The great absence at the beginning was the mystery. I took a breath and began to read.

> but,
> if time could kneel, as a catcher
> shifts to his knees when the pitch is wild
>
> For the summer we played in ruffled green grass,
> or indoors if the sky shivered with rain,
>
> Tossing the ball from end to end
> in dusty store aisles.

A door clicked at the back of the chapel, echoing across the room to where I stood. Someone had entered and was leaning against a column behind the pews. The figure removed a gauzy black scarf that had been wound around her head, letting loose a mass of dark hair that fell against her pale skin. From where I stood, she looked beautiful and darkly mysterious, like a lagoon. Who was she?

I steadied myself, studying the glass chandelier that swooped from the ceiling. There was the ancient smell of church, the treated-wood beams, damp plaster, and the smell of grief from the front row. The smell of not me not me not me from the rows beyond. I continued reading.

> **Would the solid walls still echo with the hollow**
> **slaps of our hands to leather mitts,**
>
> **Or would I leave you there**
> **your arms outstretched**
>
> **as if to receive me.**

When I finished the poem and looked up, the woman who had come in during the service had taken a seat. She was holding a tissue to her nose, and her shoulders were shaking. What was a strange woman doing crying at my father's funeral?

From the first row, Colette smiled at me, her chin trembling. Beside her, Anna was pressing her fists into her cheeks. Sadie held Van's arm. The sign-language interpreter's hands came to rest by her sides, a symphony conductor in the beat before the applause. But there was no applause, of course. I stepped down from the pulpit, my public celebration of my father done. I imagined him sitting in the audience, holding a video camera, proudly taping my performance, as he had for my childhood musicals and readings and ball games. When a sob rose up through my throat, I let it come.

Colette's friends had supplied dishes laid out neatly on the kitchen table at my father's house—thick ham slices with grainy mustard, deviled eggs sprinkled with paprika, pickled onions and gherkins, little white cakes laced with filigrees of pastel icing, a mound of potato salad with plastic spoons sticking out of it like shovels from a grave. I scooped food onto a plate and moved through a sea of people, floating. Their heads were enormous. They said, "Your father bailed me out of jail—twice—when he didn't have any money to spare." They said, "Your dad saved me." They said, "You're a lucky girl to have had a father like Jim."

Lucky, lucky, lucky girl. Beautiful speech. What a tragedy. Here's some cake. Here are some words. I took a forkful of potato salad and chewed it too many times, until it slimed down my throat. Harris, the young guy from the grocery store, swam up in front of me. "Sorry for your loss. He was a nice man," Harris said.

"Fifty-two," I said. Had Harris asked me how old Dad was? Harris was balancing a plate of ham and a glass of juice in one hand. I strained to see if my father's watch was on either of his wrists, but they were covered by the sleeves of an extra-large suit jacket that had clearly been borrowed for the occasion.

Harris sipped from his juice. "If it's okay to ask, how'd he die?"

"Heart attack."

Dad was gone in less than than five minutes, Colette had told me. She was trying to be comforting, but I wanted to know everything about his death. What color was his body? What expression was on his face? What did it look like when his soul left? What does a body look like when the soul is gone?

"I wasn't here," I told Harris. "It was Summer Christmas

Eve, and I always come home for Summer Christmas, but I wasn't here." Lucas had invited me to meet at the last minute; I'd made an impulsive decision to be with him, telling my father that I had too much work to come home.

"Oh, okay. Summer Christmas. That's why you guys have a tree up." The tree stood in the corner, accosted by the air conditioner in the window behind it. People kept bumping into it in search of a cool spot. Ornaments were on the floor, a string of cranberries loosed from the branches.

"I didn't know he was going to die," I said. My voice cracked and I did nothing to smooth it over.

"I'm sorry." Harris darted forward to touch my arm, jerking quickly away. Looking down, I spied my father's watch in the dark cavern of his jacket sleeve. *Give it back!* I wanted to say. I needed every one of my father's possessions, the number of which would only now diminish, never grow. My tongue was dry in my mouth. I swallowed.

"You can eat," my mother said, suddenly at my side. She was holding a plate with half of an orange and four almonds on it and peering at the heaps of mayonnaised salads on mine.

Your father is dead and you can eat.

Your father is dead but you can eat.

Your father is dead so you can eat.

She took an almond off her plate and bit it in half. "I wish there was lighter food. All this heavy stuff isn't good when you're having emotions."

"An almond is a bite-sized food, Mom. Just put the whole stupid thing in your mouth."

"There's no need to get testy, Ellie."

"You're complaining about the buffet at Dad's funeral."

"Sweetheart, I'm trying to help you." She put her plate down and wiped her hands together as if wicking the feeling of food from her fingers. "I know how it is. When my father died, I couldn't eat for weeks. Then slowly things got a little better, and I started eating, but only the foods I remembered him loving. He used to eat a lot of borscht, which I've never liked, but those months after he left us, I had no taste for anything else. Do you remember when I used to make those pots of borscht? I called it purple soup. Let's see, you would have been six or seven. It turns out borscht is very slimming."

As my mother talked, I searched the crowd. A group of heads moved off toward the drinks table, and in the gap they made, I spied Colette at the sink with Van, blotting at his tie with a wet paper towel. A couple who lived down the hill pounced on Colette as she held Van's tie in her hands. "Such a tragedy," the woman said.

Someone had propped open the back door, and people were emptying out onto the lawn for fresh air. The sounds of the party there were less constrained; there was laughter, voices raised. I strained to see the strange woman in her long black scarf, the woman who had come late, but there were only ordinary townspeople stuffed into church clothes. That woman hadn't looked like she belonged in this town my father had loved, where little kids pressed their noses against glass cases of saltwater taffy and you could say hi to the teenage clerk at the grocery store and know his grandmother and know his name.

Next to the buffet, I found the guest book from the funeral and skimmed the names and addresses, looking for anyone

unfamiliar. My eye caught an entry near the bottom for a
Linda T., who listed an address in Lucknow, Maryland. I
whipped out my phone and snapped a photo.

"Water?" My mother pressed a cup into my hand. "I've
been drinking eight cups a day, especially now. We need to
stay hydrated. Having intense feelings is very taxing."

"You don't have to be here if you find it taxing."

"Sweetheart, Boris and I would like you to visit us later
this summer. He's putting a small dipping pool in the yard by
the orange tree, near where I planted those Drift roses last
year? It's going to be lovely. We'll figure out some dates and
run them by you."

"Sure, Mom," I said. I had no idea what she was talking
about. I'd been to visit her in Florida only twice. Any break
I'd had during college, I preferred to go home to see Dad.
Anyway, later in the summer was lifetimes away. I had a job in
D.C., and I wanted to be around for when Lucas was free.

Barbara was on the other side of the kitchen, still holding her raincoat, swiveling slowly while looking around the
room. Sadie came in through the back door and I tried to
catch her eye, but she walked straight across the room to
her mother, who dropped her coat and took Sadie into her
arms.

So this was how it would be. Our father dead, we would
go to our separate mothers for comfort. A lozenge of pain
clogged my throat; faltering, I leaned against my mother's
shoulder.

"Ohh!" She jutted her chin out. "That Barbara has always
been an unpleasant woman. So sharp you could use her to
cut butter."

———

Five of us now. Colette, Van, Sadie, Anna, and I sat in the living room among sweating, half-empty glasses. The air conditioner had given a final few chugs and puttered out, unequal to the task of cooling a three-hour funeral reception. All my manic energy was gone, and my face ached as though I'd been struck. I thought to rouse myself to put a load in the dishwasher, to breathe in hot lemony soap, but I couldn't move. The truth was I hadn't been cleaning up for Colette or my siblings. I'd done it for my father. Now that the funeral was over, he was seeping away: All the dishwashing in the world couldn't prevent it. Tomorrow I would be on a train from Maryland back to Washington, and Sadie and Anna would relocate to their mother's house. I'd overheard them saying that they wouldn't need to come to Dad's house as much anymore. Van and Colette would remain here; six would become five would become two.

"Here's one nice thing," Colette said. Van's feet were resting on her knees as he thumbed his phone. Sadie and Anna, curled together on the sofa, no longer at odds, had been reading old children's books aloud, regressing in their sadness. A ragged copy of *Randy the Hippopotamus,* their childhood favorite, was open on Anna's lap.

"Your dad didn't have much money to leave us, obviously," Colette said. "And that's something we'll have to figure out. But we'll be good soldiers, won't we?" She patted Van's leg, telling him to watch her while she signed. "The good thing is that he left instructions about things he wanted us to have. Special objects he felt would be meaningful to each of us."

"What are they?" Anna asked.

"He listed them in his will. I can give them out in the morning," Colette said.

"I want mine now," I said, thinking of Dad's lucky baseball, how it would be some small comfort to keep with me always. From where I was sitting, I could see the ball across the room, a bright spot on the shelf above his desk, the flecks of grass and mud that textured it, worn into the leather over decades in his hands.

"Upstairs," Colette was saying. "Get the folder on the bed."

I went upstairs and pushed the bedroom door open. There were two patches of evening sun on the unmade bed, separated by the shadow of the window casement. On the nightstand was a biography of Bruce Springsteen, the jacket flap holding the last page Dad had read. If there was a father-aged white man in America who wasn't obsessed with Bruce Springsteen, I had yet to meet him. But even this bit of contrivance was endearing—my father obsessing over an obvious musician. I knelt on the floor on Dad's side of the bed, where he had fallen. The floor was scuffed and uneven, with dark slats where the boards didn't quite line up. *He clutched his chest,* Colette had said. I straightened up and my head went fuzzy, the tree outside blurred yellow in the window, and the bed was one white wash. Then my breath hitched, and my eyes sought the manila folder lying on the comforter. "Last Will and Testament—James Adler" was written on the folder's tab in Dad's handwriting. On my way downstairs, I peeked inside at the typed pages of legal jargon but couldn't make anything out.

Colette seemed to know exactly which page to turn to. She started with Van, the youngest, her own child, who got all of Dad's Van Morrison records. Van dragged them out of the cabinet under the TV and sat on the floor, flipping through them, running his fingers over the album covers. He signed to Colette, rubbed his wrist across his forehead; he looked pleased. Van was, after all, Van Morrison's namesake, and even though he couldn't hear the songs, Dad had taught Van all the lyrics in sign language. I imagined he would display the record covers in his room. We could frame them for him so they'd never deteriorate, preserve them behind glass like pinned butterflies.

Dad had left Anna his box set of Jerry Lewis movies. They shared a love for slapstick and would watch *The Bellboy* on lazy weekend afternoons, drawing the shades to produce a murky light ideal for immersing themselves in the physical comedy of Jerry Lewis, who, dressed in a bellboy's uniform, juggled the four rotary phones that rang angrily at his desk under a fake palm.

"Thank you, Colette. Thank you, *Dad*," Anna said, brushing aside *Randy the Hippopotamus* to take the films on her lap. Her eyes were shining; she'd gotten what she wanted; Dad had known her so well.

Instinctively, I began to feel afraid. Sadie stood up and paced from Dad's desk in the corner to the bay window. She glanced down with each step, as though to confirm that everything was still there—her pert little breasts, her flat stomach, freckles smashed across her arms two shades lighter than her hair. What had he left her?

I looked around the room at the things my father had spent a lifetime acquiring: the brass lamps, three bookcases crammed full of books, an old barn door repurposed as a coffee table, an armoire loaded with CDs, the oil painting of a pastoral landscape done in rich, dark colors.

"'For Sadie, I'm leaving my hats,'" Colette read. Sadie leapt up and emerged from the hall closet with a plastic bin stuffed with baseball caps and fedoras in various patterns and hues. "I never knew a man who could pull off a fedora until I met your father," Colette said.

"If he pulled it off, then he wouldn't be wearing it," I said without thinking. It was the kind of thing I would've said to my dad, and he would have laughed.

"What?" Colette asked. "If he pulled it off . . . ?"

"Never mind," I said.

Sadie picked up a dusky-purple fedora, slid the brim through her fingers. "I'm going to sew a ribbon onto this one." She looked up at us, her face bright. It wasn't what I would have done, repurposing Dad's clothes, but Sadie had an eye for bold design, and I knew that whatever she did with his hats would be impressive and, more important, that Dad would have been pleased.

"And for Ellie—" Colette flipped the page over and cleared her throat. "It says here Ellie will get the glow-in-the-dark gingerbread-man tie rack."

"The glow-in-the-dark gingerbread-man tie rack," I repeated.

Colette nodded. She flipped the page over again, squinted at it, flipped it back.

"Let me see," I said.

I took the pages from her and scanned for my name. *For Eleanor, the glow-in-the-dark gingerbread-man tie rack.* "What is that?"

Sadie shook her head. "I think I know. Hold on." She went upstairs and came down a few moments later with a clump of ties Dad never wore, shucking them off like bananas from a tree. "Is this it?" Sadie held up a plastic gingerbread man with a bulky red smile. Hooks stretched down the length of its torso and arms. The whole thing cast a greenish light, like glow-in-the-dark stars pasted above a bunk bed.

"The baseball," I said hoarsely.

"I don't think I've ever seen that before," Colette said. "I guess it's always been covered with ties."

"Did Dad tell you anything about why—" I stumbled.

"He didn't say anything," Colette answered.

"I talked to him the day before he died," I said. "And every day before that." I took the gingerbread man from Sadie. On its face were two close-set black eyes shaped like gumdrops.

"I know you did, honey. You were so close."

For a moment we were still, gazing out the window. The creek rustled and frogs sang from its cold, reedy water. There were bees humming among the tomato plants. Van's red bicycle was on its side in the grass. A stranger passing along the road might have thought we lived happily, that we lived well.

"Don't take this as a referendum about his love for you," Colette said.

I sat up straight. "You mean indication. A referendum is a decision made by many people." I was aware of my pedantry but did nothing to soften it. My father would never have made such a mistake. "I assume this was not a decision made by other people?"

Colette shook her head.

"What did you get?"

"I got the painting," she said softly.

The oil painting of the Patuxent River hung on the wall between two ladder-back chairs. The river curved around a bend of grassland in a pink dusk. On the bank were two goats and several sheep, a wild turkey, a pair of speckled white ponies. A thin brown boat held a fisherman in a wide cap, and some distance away, a fish arced out of the water, its scales reflecting the pink sky.

We used to pose in front of this painting for our yearly family photo. I would sit on the far right underneath the fish, and next to me was Colette, who sat next to Dad, who posed next to Anna and Sadie. Van, the youngest, sat in the middle, on a low stool. Everything, everyone, in its place. Did my father put me on the end? Or did I put myself there?

With sudden force I shot up from my seat and snatched the baseball from the shelf above Dad's desk. "I want his lucky baseball. He never wrote a poem without it. Remember? He'd sit at his desk and toss it up and down. He put it in my crib when I was a baby."

Colette looked down at the floor. "Your dad actually left the baseball to someone else."

"Who?" I said. "Is it Van?" The two of them had played catch in the yard on Summer Thanksgiving.

"Not Van. L somebody or other." Colette ruffled the pages of the will. "Here. L. M. Taylor."

I closed my fist around the ball. "That doesn't make sense."

"I'm sorry, Ellie." Colette tapped her foot. With each strike of her shoe, a sword rose up through my throat. I sank back on the sofa and brought the baseball swiftly to my nose. It smelled of grass and hide and my father's hands.

"Who's L. M. Taylor?" Anna asked.

Van waved at us, asking what was happening, and Colette signed something that caused him to swivel toward the glow-in-the-dark gingerbread-man tie rack. He shook his head slowly, baffled. In that moment, I loved him.

"Who's L. M. Taylor?" I repeated.

Colette shrugged. "I'm actually not sure. Maybe a friend from college?"

I put the glow-in-the-dark tie rack down on the sofa next to *Randy the Hippopotamus*. I knew without looking that the first line of the book was *Now, where to begin*.

"What should we do for dinner?" Colette asked. "Any requests? What about tuna fish and crackers?"

"Yum," Sadie said. "I'm sorry, Ellie." The four of them stood and walked off toward the kitchen, holding my father's gifts. Tuna fish and crackers was his favorite. He used to salt each individual bite and nibble on a pickle in between.

"Ellie, come be with us?" Colette called.

"Right there," I said, unmoving.

"Want some, Anna?" I heard Colette ask through the open door.

"I'll have a few," Anna said. "With less mayo than last time."

I heard a clack of bowls set out on the table, the scraping of a fork. These sounds traveled from the kitchen as though they had occurred years ago and had only just arrived in the air above the sofa where I sat.

Van appeared beside me, holding out a cracker, a shy smile on his face.

"Thanks," I signed, trying to return the smile.

I looked down at my hand, still clutching the baseball in a white-knuckled claw. The hand of a lesser child.

Three

The next morning, I sat alone on a commuter train heading south to Washington, the wheels groaning as they spooled over the track. Heat rose in a haze from the trees as we passed little-used stations, buildings that were once hubs of commerce back when trains had the energy of America onboard. How many times had I taken a train to and from my father's house in Maryland, feeling that I was the daughter he loved? The smell of diesel, the mothy flutter of fluorescent lights in their narrow overhead tracks, the snap of the conductor's hole punch that wore grooves into thin slips of ticket paper— all this was my father.

I saw now that none of it was.

My phone buzzed and I thumbed it open, hoping it was Lucas with an invitation to meet him that night. We'd go to some dim bar, where we could drink whiskeys, our knees touching, and I'd tell him about what happened until I cried and he took my face in his hands. But it wasn't Lucas. It was a weekend; he rarely texted on weekends. It was my roommate Katherine, saying again she was sorry about my dad, and with a reminder to send her money for the electric bill.

My stomach plummeted in disappointment, and I got a floaty, pins-and-needles feeling. Lucas was never spontaneous. He couldn't be, because of his wife. Our time together was carefully choreographed based on her schedule.

What I had to look forward to was a sad Sunday with my roommates in 1938 House, the once-grand, now-grimy three-story group house we shared. Mallory and Adrian would be playing loud go-go music and arguing about capitalism. Nick would be cooking lentil mush and jotting his random ideas on the wall we'd covered with whiteboard paint, and afterward he'd fill the crusty lentil pot with soapy water and leave it in the sink, where it would sit for days. At some point Katherine would breeze in with individually wrapped chocolates or a bouquet of flowers left over from an embassy event she'd run. She'd want to sit on the couch after her grueling day as the social secretary at the Moroccan embassy, her long legs tucked up under her, and speak at length, as usual, about the ambassador's annoying, interfering mother-in-law.

Their normal world now seemed bizarre, untouchable, heartless. What was abnormal—my father's home without him in it—was suddenly appealing, even comfortable. Colette was there, and Van, my community in grief. What was I doing on this rattling train, moving out of my father's world, where a man could die suddenly in his own bed, going into one where twenty-somethings argued over who ate the last of the jalapeño-flavored potato chips? My life felt pointless.

The door at the front of the train car opened, and a girl hurried in, wearing a strapless orange dress that showed off the inky-blue tattoos on her back and arms, a frieze of sea creatures. She threw a small purse onto the seat across from me. Why, on an empty train, had she chosen to sit so close? I watched her peek over the seat in front of her, then duck and scrunch down so that her face rested against the window.

The car door opened again, carefully this time, and a foot appeared in a worn sneaker, followed by a man with a sunburned nose and an undershirt that was stretched out so the chains he wore around his neck were visible down to the crosses. "This is better," he announced, positioning himself in the aisle beside the girl in the orange dress. "How far you going? I have a cousin down in Richmond, said I could come stay."

The girl murmured something with her head turned away. The man mentioned the beers he had in his backpack. He commented on the humidity. He bemoaned his lack of chewing gum. He said he was tired of northern women, ha ha. The girl responded with a few benign words, and I saw she had decided that her best strategy to get away from him was light conversation. It was the nonconsensual version of many terrible dates I'd been on. A week ago, witnessing this would have made me angry, ready to fight for her, but today I felt nothing: It was just another man stalking another woman. I watched it from a distance, from the inside of a cloud.

Pain was what I needed—or pleasure. A hand brushing against my neck, my hips arching upward. I needed to narrow my focus, to feel something, anything at all. It was a weekend, and Lucas clearly wasn't going to be available or thinking of me. The last time I'd heard from him was right before the funeral.

Since I met Lucas, I hadn't been on ErosAble, the popular

dating app. It now seemed urgent that I set up a date for tonight, especially if it meant I wouldn't have to wander around
the house while my roommates went about their Sundays.
Maybe I could have the kind of casual, wild sex that would
poke through this fog, and I could make Lucas jealous at the
same time, which might result in seeing him sooner. I logged
on to the app.

The man in the undershirt had taken a seat and gotten
busy on his phone, facing away from the girl in the orange
dress. From where I sat, her eyes looked closed. In the new
quiet, I scrolled through dozens of men, as uncomplicated as
skimming my hand over racks of silky underwear at a department store.

Almost instantly, there were two messages in my inbox.
One included the caption *Heyyyyyy there* under a photo of
an engorged penis sticking out of boxers printed with sheep.
The second was from This Cyclocross Life, who had written
a brief note that neither demeaned nor flattered me. He had
given my profile four out of five winx. His profile showed a
bearded man in flannel leaning against a tree aflame in fall
foliage and a list of interests that was compellingly bland:
Biking. Coffee. Trivia. Public Radio.

If Lucas ever filled out a profile on ErosAble, he would
carefully curate his list to appear specific and profound: *Pi-
casso's Blue Period, development economics, Ethiopian food,
Ani DiFranco lyrics, the late novels of García Márquez.* Lucas
had read García Márquez in the original Spanish. He spoke
four languages and hated translations, said he wanted to experience authorial intent directly from the source. But Lucas

would never troll a dating website; he was too considered, too mature—a big brain in the big world, not a headless torso with a hint of hip tattoo.

I dashed off a quick note to This Cyclocross Life, asking if he wanted to meet up, not saying, *What would I have to do to get five winx from you?*

I took out my notebook of first lines. Dad's poem was written on the second-to-last page, and I let my eyes blur around it without reading. Who was that lagoon woman at the funeral, her long black scarf unwrapped, standing in the back of the chapel as I recited my father's words?

With a sudden and terrible authority, I realized who she must be. After Dad's second divorce, before he met Colette, he had gone dogsledding with an adult adventure program that brought groups to rural Minnesota for lessons in snow camping and self-reliance. Each day they would travel dozens of miles by dogsled, and at night they pitched camp in the snow. All participants had to spend one night away from the group, alone in the woods, snug in their tents. I could never quite imagine my father in the Minnesota woods, the trees draped with fresh snow, silent birds gliding from branch to sky. At home, he'd puttered around the yard, occasionally swam in the bay in summer. He wasn't an outdoorsman, but it had lingered, this time with the dogs.

There had been a woman on that trip whose water bottle broke, flooding her sleeping bag when she was miles away from the group. She thought she might freeze to death if she lay down to sleep in the pooling water, so she put on her parka and boots, brought a mat out onto the snow, and did slow yoga for seven hours until the first light of dawn, when she found her way back to the camp, where my father slept soundly surrounded by the warm breath of dogs.

It was not her capacity for discomfort or uncertainty, I think, that made my father love her but that she conserved her energy to make it last through the night. Even as a child I understood that my father pinwheeled from experience to experience in great bursts, that he was voracious, that he loved deeply and often. I imagined that he loved this woman for her restraint, her body that did yoga in the dark. In his retelling, she had no name. I'd asked to hear this story again and again, each time hoping for a new detail about the woman, a blast of acid clarity, like biting into a cold orange. I wanted to meet her, to understand her. I wanted to be her.

Maybe they had reconnected and had been meeting in secret. And then I remembered the funeral guest book and its unfamiliar name and address. I brought up the photo I'd taken of the signature: *Linda T. 14 Horseshoe Road, Lucknow.* If she was the yoga woman from my dad's time in Minnesota, she was now living in the area. It was plausible that they had been seeing each other.

I squinted down at her name. *Linda T.* Could she also be the L. M. Taylor from the will? Was this the recipient of my father's baseball? A woman who had come late to his funeral, shoulders hunched, crying into a tissue? I felt petulant and wronged as I cycled through the story again, embellishing. Had a woman he had known only briefly gotten the treasured baseball? And his own daughter, whom he had known since she was born, and had played catch with many times, had been given a gag gift. It might as well have been a whoopee cushion or a dribble glass. He'd prioritized and sentimentalized the sex he'd once had with some woman over the abiding love he'd felt for me. And I knew he did love me. But once you have a child, she and her entire generation nip at your heels and make you old. Whereas a woman in a bed makes you young. That must be it. That was the bitter story I told myself as I imagined spending the rest of my life staring into the idiotic eyes of the gingerbread-man tie rack.

The train slowed at an intersection; beyond the tracks, two men in waders climbed the riverbank, carrying fishing poles. Teenagers in swimsuits headed in the opposite direction with inner tubes. In my peripheral vision, I saw the man leap up and loom over the girl in the orange dress. "Why you have to be like that?" he said, chopping his hand through the air. The car went dark as we bolted through a tunnel and then we emerged in daylight sharp as ivory. I looked in both directions for a conductor.

"Please," the girl said in a pained voice, searching for my eyes across the aisle.

"Fucking bitch!" he snarled.

On the cracked blue seat, I hovered on the precipice of defending her, but I did nothing. The man turned and sneered in my direction, and I averted my eyes. For a moment everything was still, the air charged with the possibility of something worse.

"Fuck this shit," he declared finally, and went humping unsteadily down the aisle.

I felt the weight of her gaze on me but was afraid to look at the girl in the orange dress to see whether the expression on her face was one of gratitude or disgust. I had a good idea which it was. *I'm sorry I didn't protect you. I don't care about anything: My father is dead.* It was an excuse for everything and an excuse for nothing. By the time I'd opened my mouth to speak, the girl in the orange dress had turned away.

The first line of Carson McCullers's novel *The Member of the Wedding* was written in careful penmanship on page 37 of my notebook: *It happened that green and crazy summer when Frankie was twelve years old.* How did McCullers get away with those two unrelated adjectives to describe the season? The cruel vagueness of the word "it"?

If I could do it over again, I thought, I would keep a notebook of second lines. "First lines can be flashy," I'd told my dad once, hoping to impress him, "but second lines point to what the story is really about." "Give me an example," he'd said. "What about the second sentence of *The Member of the Wedding*," I had said, reciting it: " 'This was the summer when for a long time she had not been a member.' " And he had laughed softly, proudly.

I gathered my bag and walked onto the wobbly platform between train cars, holding the rubber cable strung from one doorway to the other. In many cultures a dead person undergoes a transition from life to the underworld; he crosses the swollen river Styx; he enters a liminal space until his soul is set free. I felt in that liminal space too.

One moment he was alive. The next, dead. I was beloved, alive; then given a strange inheritance, dead to my father. *The glow-in-the-dark gingerbread-man tie rack.* My own mother hadn't even known what it meant. I texted her to ask, and she'd replied, *No idea. So weird!!!* In the in-between space where I now stood, the sky was dark. When I glanced up, the train was pulling into Union Station and we were under the soot-black roof in D.C., waiting to disembark.

A message flashed across my screen from This Cyclocross Life. *Would love to meet up tonight.*

I met This Cyclocross Life at a hot new restaurant. I'd dropped my overnight bag at home, ducking out without seeing my housemates. I hadn't changed my clothes, but I didn't care. As I stood before him now, it was clear that he was shorter than he had appeared in his photo. He had a canvas satchel slung over his arm, and one leg of his jeans was cuffed near the knee so it wouldn't catch on his bike chain. His calf, drumstick-shaped, was thick with hair.

When the waitress came to our table, he said, "Two regulars and a coupla waters."

"Please don't order for me," I said.

He peered at me through large, stylish glasses. "It's not that I'm ordering for you. This restaurant only serves one thing."

The food came on slabs of granite. On the slabs were deep, asymmetrical bowls of noodles. Hidden inside the bowls were layers of things to uncover: scallions, pork belly, egg slices, crunchy fried mushrooms.

As we ate, he told me that it was his job to choose the music that aired between segments on NPR's *Morning Edition*. He pulled up that morning's show on his phone and we listened to the reassuring voice of Steve Inskeep report a story about Chinese sanctions. Then a tinkling, upbeat melody signaled the end of things.

"I chose that," he said.

While he talked about off-road bicycle racing, I found myself wondering whether he had to tuck his penis carefully into some spandexed corner before long bike rides.

His studio apartment was just off Logan Circle, in one of D.C.'s newest condo buildings. I'd been at my father's less than a week, but a new city seemed to have been built atop the old, as though a giant child had updated his erector set. There were construction cranes in every direction and new apartment buildings with little glass balconies the size of milk crates hanging off the sides. "The only constant in D.C. is condo," my roommate Mallory had said.

Upstairs, This Cyclocross Life grabbed two Narragansetts from a small refrigerator and fumbled with his sound system until electronic music came through the speakers. Above a brown futon hung a poster for a band called Asteroid, No. Five lanky white guys sat on a group of chairs turned backward and sideways, so the musicians were either straddling them or sitting in profile. At the bottom of the poster was the line "Ce n'est pas un groupe."

He settled on the futon, watching me. I put the cold cylinder of beer against my neck.

"I only drink 'gansett between May and September," he said. "Then I switch to pale ale until January. In the late winter I do Guinness."

"David Attenborough could narrate a documentary about your seasonal regularity," I said. He didn't laugh. I looked again at the poster. The faces of the Asteroid, No musicians were pale and lumpy. "How do you think they decided who would sit backward and who would sit sideways?"

He followed my gaze to the poster and then looked back at me. "Do you want this?" His hand fluttered uncertainly in his lap—it was this small gesture of insecurity that swayed me. I leaned over and went for his lips, but I had trouble finding them in the thicket of beard. He didn't seem to mind. In one motion, he stood up and backed me over to the bed.

This Cyclocross Life had a good body under his Full Communism T-shirt. Unlike his bicycle, his penis seemed to go at only one speed.

"You okay?" he asked, his mouth inches from mine.

"Uh-huh." I closed my eyes and tried to focus on the feeling of him inside me, but I felt nothing, no pleasure or friction, just unfamiliar weight. I'd had casual sex before, and even when it was bad, there was discomfort or pain, awkwardness or adrenaline. But now nothing. As my body was pressed into the mattress, I went cold with panic. Counted silently to myself the seconds and thought of Lucas, how he seemed to intuitively understand me when we had sex; if I wasn't present, he would feel it and stop immediately. Nothing like this man on top of me. What was I doing?

He finished and flipped onto his back, dropping the condom off the side of the bed. I turned to face him. "My father died last week," I said.

"Oh wow, I'm sorry." He pecked me on the cheek. "That's tough."

"I gave his eulogy."

"Yeah, you said."

"I did?"

"At dinner."

"Sorry." Why hadn't I remembered that? What else had I told him?

He shifted uncomfortably. "How'd he die?"

I turned my head away. I didn't want to offer him anything else.

An aneurysm

A broken heart

A catfight

An embolism

A fatal mistake

My father's face was slipping from me, but I could see Lucas's face clearly. His dark eyebrows and feathery hair. His voice that went ragged with desire.

This Cyclocross Life was talking. I propped my head up to look at him, but I couldn't make out the words. "Do you want to stick around? Or go home?" he asked again.

I swung my legs over the side of the bed. "Go home, I guess."

As I bent to pick up my things, I heard a hollow knock. The baseball had fallen out of my backpack and rolled across the floor, thumping against the leg of his futon.

I scrambled after it, but he was already reaching down to grab it. "Why do you have a baseball?"

"Give it back." I was ice-cold and prickly all over. I suddenly felt I might vomit.

"You play?"

"It was my father's," I said. "He left it for me in his will."

"Oh." He tossed the ball back to me. "I'm a Cubs fan,

which I know is dumb." He flopped back on the bed. I realized he had accepted it, as if my saying it made it true. *He left it for me in his will*.

"Bye," I called, letting myself out of the apartment.

"I'll text you," he said.

On the street, the air smelled of sulfur. Lightning flashed in staccato bursts, making the street garish. I took deep breaths until I was steadier and, turning left onto Rhode Island Avenue, picked my way over the roots of an oak tree that had burst through the pavement. The baseball beat against my hip like my own secret heart.

How wrong I had been, to think sex with a stranger would deliver me from the dead feeling and give me the control I was after. I had picked This Cyclocross Life because he was bland and unassuming—I thought he would be safe. But I couldn't seem to feel safe.

I summoned the image of Lucas's face looking at me across the pillow, reaching to touch my hair. I took out my phone to see if he had texted. Nothing. I tapped out a message. *Where are you? Just went on a date, ramen and sex*

He wouldn't respond immediately; he'd be with his wife.

The NPR app on my home screen had a little bubble in the corner signaling that it needed an update. I stood on the sidewalk, thinking of those NPR voices and the music that played between segments, all of it somehow lurking in my phone, waiting for me to press play. The NPR producer's lips on my neck. *I'm sorry, that's tough*. I pressed delete. The app shrank to nothing and then it was gone.

Four

The editorial meeting had already started when I got to the *Apogee* office on Monday. I felt wretched, displaced, my brain in a fog. I searched my pockets for the keycard that would let me in, but I couldn't find it. Monday mornings began with a public accounting of our most-clicked stories. So far, in my nine months at *Apogee,* I'd never made the most-clicked list. The reporters who did got to write about big, brassy things like elections, epidemics, and scandals, while cub reporters like me were assigned stories about education or the environment. In terms of sexiness, these subjects hovered somewhere above tort reform, just below Medicaid.

I was late because I'd slept terribly and had been trying to avoid my roommates. I didn't want to talk to anyone or answer their questions about my father or the funeral; I only wanted to hear from Lucas. My roommates tromped downstairs, made their smoothies and eggs, removed their bikes from the jumble in the hall. When I was sure they were out of the house, I risked leaving my room. I was finding that nothing anyone said felt right, including Mal, who was my favorite, and when they said nothing, that wasn't right either. But I couldn't explain why or what I needed instead.

At the door to *Apogee,* through the glass, I could see Jane Ostrawicz-Jones's hands flare up wildly, in excitement or opprobrium, I couldn't tell. She often talked with her hands. I heard a polite round of clapping, and a reporter stepped forward to receive the applause. He'd written an article last week that had received more clicks than any other on the *Apogee* site; it had to do with an Arkansas congressman's secret pig-wrestling ring. The clapping stopped, and I walked back to see if I'd dropped the keycard somewhere on my way in.

Our offices were on the second floor of the former Baby Jake's factory, where Baby Jake's snack cakes had been stuffed and packed in plastic before the factory was relocated to China. In the lobby a glass display case held the packaging for one of the original cakes from the 1950s, a strawberry-and-cream ball called a Smuffin. The building had been remodeled as loft-style office space for tech and media start-ups, aping that Silicon Valley combination of sleek design, ergonomic workspaces, and areas for occasional play. Our offices had an espresso machine, a Ping-Pong table, and life-sized portraits of Gandhi, Martin Luther King, Jr., and Steve Jobs propped against exposed-brick panels, the label *Forward Thinkers* appearing below. The most stressful thing about the office was the Leaderboard: a giant monitor that hung from the ceiling, showing *Apogee*'s top-performing posts. Every pair of eyes in the room darted back and forth from laptops to Leaderboard all day, as though our careers depended on it.

I'd met Lucas my second month on the job, when I was reporting a story for *Apogee* about political unrest in Sri Lanka. I needed an expert to tell me what was happening on the ground, so I'd phoned the think tank where he worked. I was on a tight deadline, I explained to the receptionist, and I knew it was a Friday afternoon, but was there anyone who specialized in Sri Lanka who could talk on background? The secretary waited a few moments and then coughed dryly. "I'll patch you through." She sounded like a woman who had spent the better part of her life waiting for other people to finish their sentences. After a long, staticky silence, someone else came on the line. "Lucas Ataide," he said.

"Hi, I'm a reporter with *Apogee*. It's a news website founded by—"

"I know *Apogee,*" he said. "You called because?" It was young, this voice, and not unattractive. A slight accent made me think he had been born abroad.

"I'm writing a story about the political unrest in Sri Lanka, and I was hoping to talk to you about your work on the ground in Kuala Lumpur."

There was a pause. "Kuala Lumpur is in Malaysia," he said.

"Oh God," I said. "I'm an idiot."

"Not an idiot. An overworked journalist, I imagine."

"That's generous of you. In any case, I have to go throw up under my desk," I said.

He laughed. "I'm just leaving the office, but if you ring me on my cell in an hour, I can tell you about Sri Lankan politics."

I took his number. He was politely trying to get off the phone, I could tell, and I was convinced that when I called back, the phone would go straight to voicemail.

But when I dialed him back, he picked up. Birds of various kinds seemed to be chirping directly into his mouthpiece.

"Hi. Thanks for taking my call. Are you in an aviary?"

He laughed again. "I'm in Rock Creek Park."

"So," I said. "The capital of Sri Lanka is Colombo."

The following day, the story I wrote went live. Ten minutes later, I got a text. *Not bad for an article about Kuala Lumpur.*

I was beginning to regret the *ramen and sex* text I'd sent Lucas the previous night. I kept rereading it, hoping his answer would magically appear, but with each passing minute of silence, I felt my gut twist further. I thought of my mother— I needed to give myself a Rachel Gettleman–style talking-to. My mother's talks always began with one of two phrases: "Buck up" or "Be a brave soldier."

I took a deep breath. Buck up, Eleanor. Your father is dead, but you are here. Go to work, remove your out-of-office email signature, pretend to enjoy the company of other reporters. Then at lunch call Lucas at his office, apologize for the text, make the excuse that you are grieving. He'll forgive you.

Keycardless, resigned, I went back to the door and knocked. Someone was dispatched to let me in: the boss, Steve Glanz, the twenty-five-year-old founder and CEO of *Apogee,* who had what *Inc.* magazine called "a finger on the pulse of what millennials will click." He was writing a book, *Next Web,* which the D.C. pundit class expected to be a road map for saving journalism, aligning the industry with the digital age.

The glass door swooshed open and Steve poked his head out. "Hey, Ellie. Locked out? You know the meeting starts at nine, right?"

"Yeah. Sorry."

"We missed you last week. Did you have a good vacation?"

"Yes. Thanks, Steve."

"We're over here on CF." CF was what Steve called Central Floor, an old factory term for the main workspace. The reporters sat at a long wooden table he'd dubbed the Conveyor Belt, the editors in a section called Quality Control. I followed behind him, hoping I could slip into the pack unnoticed.

"Sorry I'm late," I mumbled, though Jane had already moved on. She was an intense person with blue eyes and silver hair styled in a bowl cut. She'd had a storied career at *The Washington Post*, over the years winning a Pulitzer, two Polks, and a Peabody, but when she was unceremoniously offered a buyout along with dozens of other boomer-aged reporters, she watched her peers retire. They penned an occasional op-ed for *USA Today* and fussed over their rhododendrons, while she reinvented herself as a battle-worn adviser to upstarts in the new wave of online journalism and was hired to bring gravitas to *Apogee* and Steve. Now she was shifting from foot to foot, saying, "We're going to need to reevaluate Benson's piece. The reporting isn't all there. We'll pull it from this week's lineup."

"What's the working headline?" someone asked.

"'I Snuck onto a Military Base and Found Officers Drunk

and High,'" Steve responded. "I don't agree with you, though. The story is strong—it's clickable, it's incendiary. People are going to get fired because of it. We should.publish while the heat is on."

Jane seemed to use her entire body to shake her head. It was a common argument between them, the tension between Jane's high standards and Steve's commercial ones, but the fights managed to sound fiery and fresh each time, endlessly treading the ground between old-school reporting and online clickbait. "Benson lied about his name and his background as a reporter," Jane said. "It's a gray area. He acknowledges his obfuscation, but it's not sufficiently reported. He didn't ask for comment from the head of the military base or any of the soldiers who were drinking. It's one-sided. We have to give the base a chance to respond; otherwise it's hearsay—"

Steve cut in, "If we don't publish tomorrow, we'll be scooped. The *Times* and the *Post* were nosing around this one too. We can't afford to let a story like this wither on the vine."

"You can't levy a major accusation like this at an institution without giving them a chance to comment."

"They can comment after we publish."

"That's plain wrong, Steven. I can't—"

"Okay, Jane, you don't work at the *Post* anymore." Steve peered at us. "We'll run it today. Let's publish before noon and keep an eye on the stats. We're down five hundred thousand hits in our politics vertical, so we need this to do well. Someone should work up a story for some rage clicks. Henry, can you get on that? Guns, Clinton animosity, whatever— find a new angle. Anything else?"

I snuck a glance at Jane. She'd been undermined by a man who had been alive for fewer years than she had been practicing journalism. She was standing in front of the giant portrait of Gandhi, her arms folded across her chest. Gandhi was smiling. Jane wasn't.

"Back to work, everyone," Jane said.

I chose a seat at the Conveyor Belt with a space on either side. There was an unspoken hierarchy to the *Apogee* seating arrangements. The more-experienced reporters took the spaces nearest the windows, which were fitted with long gray shades. Newer people sat on the far end of the long table, the quality of our light determined by the senior reporters, with their coffee cups and bottles of Advil, who raised and lowered the shades. It wasn't so different from cubicles, I imagined, though there were days when I longed for pigeon-gray particleboard to hide behind, so no one could lean over and see what I was doing. Right now, for example, I checked for a text from Lucas and, finding none, googled "L. M. Taylor."

My search for the name in my father's will had returned a burial record for someone who died in Georgia in 1987, a mid-century clipping from the Ogden *Standard-Examiner,* and several academic articles about the management of dental decay. I banged "Linda T. 14 Horseshoe Road" into the keyboard. No search results. But when I put the address into Google Earth, up came a beautiful converted barn on a normal suburban street. I was zooming in and out of the driveway, combing for clues among the tidy trash bins and two-car garage, when I noticed Jane Ostrawicz-Jones waving at me from inside the glass cube of her office, both arms going like windshield wipers. I'd heard it said that she made a condition of her hire that she be given an office with a door but that Steve, who believed in the open-office concept and sat sanctimoniously in Quality Control, had spited her by giving her glass walls.

Jane's office smelled lightly of newsprint, as though she still read the physical newspaper.

"Look, Ellie, I wanted to say again how sorry I am about your father," she said.

"Thanks."

"We're glad to have you back. Have a seat. Is your head in the game?" She leaned against the edge of her desk but remained standing, so I stood too.

"I'm honestly not sure."

"Well, let's try to get you back to it. Work is a balm, I've always found, and frankly we need you. Here's the deal. We're starting a series called 'Rising Tides.' The idea is to make environmental stories more palatable to readers by writing about the scientists behind the stories. The human face of climate change. Our readers don't care about pteropods— pardon my Greek, those are sea snails—or how warming oceans are dissolving their shells. But they might care about Dr. Abel Butterbun, an oceanographer who's in a band that performs every weekend—these sweaty, generous shows—to which he brings his teenage son, Wilhelm. Butterbun is dying of cancer, and his final wish is to warn the world about how warming oceans will affect sea life. Put a Butterbun in the pteropod story and we might just teach a few readers something about climate change." Jane paused. "I want you to spearhead this series."

"Me?"

"You."

"I'm honored." I hoped my face showed something resembling enthusiasm. "Where do I find Dr. Butterbun?"

She sipped from her *Washington Post* mug. "I made him up. You'll have to find a real Butterbun, obviously." Jane cracked a smile. "I like to think of you as our resident poet."

I perked up. "You do?"

"Come back with some beautiful phrases. What was that one you had in the piece about the Georgetown sociologist?"

"I called him a pedagogical stallion."

"That's it. More of that. And don't skimp on the science either. Just try to make it interesting."

I laughed, thinking of my C+ physics tests in high school. The next semester the school had moved me out of Physics 2 and into Animal Behavior, where we had labs at the zoo, and I spent hours huddled in front of the monkey enclosure with the potheads and the football players. I didn't want skimping on science to be my specialty.

"Also, I meant to ask you, how are you fitting in at *Apogee*?" Jane asked.

"Pretty well, I think."

"You've been here, what?" Jane spoke as if she were trying to make herself heard in a large crowd.

"Nine months."

"It was a big adjustment for me, coming from the *Post*," she said. "All these young reporters partying until two or three in the morning, back in the office at nine. No one else goes home to a dog. Or a child, God forbid." Jane sifted through a pile on her desk, removed two earrings from it, and put them on. One was shaped like an ironing board; the other was a teakettle. "You don't have a dog, do you?" she asked.

I shook my head with what I hoped was the correct combination of sympathy and agreement. "Well, you have what you need for 'Rising Tides.' Keep me informed," Jane said. "I know you're the right reporter for the job." She flicked the ironing board toward me. There was something strange about a career woman wearing earrings shaped like tokens of domesticity. I socked that detail away to tell Mal later.

I was uncomfortable in the shine of Jane's attention. The problem was that I admired Jane. Respected her. And I wasn't sure that I could report on anything well now, or that I could focus, or care. I glanced out at the Conveyor Belt, searching the row of bright young faces hovering above laptops. A few of them were peeking at us, a veteran editor and her new confidante-in-cahoots.

"I like you, Ellie," Jane said, like someone who was often disappointed in matters of affection. "So don't f-up."

Five

By lunch, there was still no response from Lucas, and I was vibrating with worry.

The receptionist at the Council on Asiatic and Pacific Interests frowned as I pulled open the heavy glass door and approached her desk. "Yes? You are?"

"Eleanor Adler for Lucas Ataide."

She picked up the phone and mumbled into it. I noted her sensible glasses, the gray hair clasped thickly behind her shoulders. All those months ago, when I'd cold-called and asked about Sri Lanka, she could have transferred me to anyone at the Council on Asiatic and Pacific Interests, but she'd chosen Lucas Ataide, MBA, PhD. I should send her a Hallmark card: *To a special someone: Thank you from the bottom of my heart for making me the mistress of someone with two graduate degrees.*

While I waited, I looked for Lucas in the photo of staff hanging above her in/out box, the rows of economists studying Asia, all of them men, few of them Asian. The secretary dropped the receiver into the phone's plastic cradle. "Sixth door to your left," she said.

Down the long hallway I kept my steps short and slow. Would showing up unannounced seem passionate or desperate? I worried that my passion was always scalloped with desperation. The doors along the corridor were closed, fluorescent light pulsing around the edges, except for one, from which an economist with a very small head peered at me.

When I reached the sixth door, it sprang open. "You're here." Lucas smiled with his eyebrows raised slightly, as if they were surprised while the rest of him wasn't. His hand went reflexively to his hair, which was slightly spiky, and then to adjust his collar. These little signs of nervousness made me want to fling my arms around him, breathe him in, but he stepped back into the office without hugging me. Was he angry about my text? Or about my being here?

"What are you doing here?" he said.

Not the greeting I'd hoped for. Why had I come? I'd left *Apogee* at lunch and cycled along R Street, out for a little exercise before the rain, or so I'd told myself. I had hoped to summon the private pleasure I used to take in biking in a dress, knowing that my legs were long and bare, pumping purposefully in the sun; there had always been men watching from the sidewalks, and now I hoped their desire would make me feel real, alive again. It didn't.

Then I was locking my bike outside Lucas's building. Showing up at his office was a risk. I wouldn't have taken this risk two weeks ago, but now my father was dead. Somehow, that made me feel entitled to be here, to ask him for comfort. And there was my reckless, stupid text message.

"I just needed to see you," I said.

As Lucas turned around to close the door, I admired his height, the firmness of his body. He had the look of a man who did tae kwon do, or perhaps one who aspired to tae kwon do but didn't have the time.

"You know, I've never been here," I said. My heart bounced into my throat. What did I really know about him, his life? His desk was a mass of articles and upturned books. The blank wall opposite was stuck with dozens of yellow Post-its at odd angles, each containing scribbles, and here and there a hastily drawn graph. The times we had escaped for a few hours to a hotel, he'd brought a briefcase stuffed with papers. He was messy, like me. Involved in ideas, which I wanted to be again.

"My text was childish. I'm sorry. I feel so lost," I said.

Lucas nodded, looked away. "It's not fair for me to be jealous. But I don't see why you intentionally tried to make me feel bad."

"You hadn't texted me since the funeral. I've been doing stupid stuff since my dad died. And there are other things too . . ." I began to say, but I couldn't bring myself to mention the will, or the tie rack.

"I've been thinking about you." His voice softened. "Worrying about you. And then you texted me that you had been on a date with someone else, and I wasn't sure what to do."

"I'm sorry," I said.

"I can't imagine what you must be going through," he said quietly. I saw in his eyes that I had been forgiven.

"It's just impossible to believe he's gone," I said. "Mostly I feel numb. But my senses are messed up. It's like this beetle I saw once with a bent antenna, spinning in a pathetic little circle. Its own internal compass was lost. I feel like that beetle. I'm going in circles. I don't even know if my father loved me."

"Of course he loved you." Lucas pressed his lips to my cheek. "How could he not?"

I thought of my father's will and of the baseball, of the glow-in-the-dark gingerbread-man tie rack. But I said nothing.

"Ellie," Lucas whispered. "I'm so glad to see you." He knelt on the floor in front of me and kissed my right calf, bare above the leather of my boot. I threaded my fingers through his hair, watched the back of his neck flush. A ripple of pleasure went through me, to see that I had the same effect on him that he had on me. Maybe I existed after all. "I'm even happy to see these boots," he said.

Since we met, he had been teasing me about how I only wore one pair of shoes, low black riding boots with tarnished buckles on the sides. I wore them when I graduated from college and spring blossoms were on the trees and the grass was soggy with rain. I wore them to my first day of work at *Apogee*. I wore them to my father's funeral, with black pants and a black crepe flower that Colette tucked into my hair.

Lucas's mouth moved slowly up my leg, and I braced myself against his desk. I felt myself coming alive again as desire flooded me.

He lifted my dress and pressed his lips to my thigh, hot and puckered.

"Fuck me," I said.

Lucas removed his mouth. "Not here."

I hooked my leg around the back of his shoulders. "We can be quiet."

"I'll get a hotel room for us soon." He let my dress fall. "I got you something." At his desk he opened a drawer. "Close your eyes."

I clamped them shut. A slight weight was transferred to my hand.

"Okay, open."

"What is it?" A slender white box lay across my palm. I pried it open and found a pendant on a long silver chain, a distressed-metal coin that was pocked like the surface of the moon.

"Oh my God, it's beautiful," I said. "Just the kind of thing I like." And it was. I almost never wore jewelry, but when I did, I liked understated pieces, simple metals, things that reminded me of nature.

Lucas tucked a strand of my hair behind my ear. "I knew you'd like it. You're not like other—" He paused, and I could tell he had been about to say *women*. "You're not like other people."

I wasn't sure what he meant exactly, but I could tell it was a compliment. I fixed the pendant around my neck. We watched it fall between my breasts. He gathered me up in his arms, and I was easily gathered.

As I breathed him in, the slight dampness of his shirt where he was sweating, the powdery smell of his soap, I thought about the difference between Lucas's gift and my father's. The gingerbread-man tie rack had spent time in my father's house hidden away, suffocated by ties, before being repurposed in his will as something with "meaning." My father kept a straight face about it. Of course he did; he was dead. Why had Lucas, this man holding me now—who had known me months, not years, who hadn't been with me when I was born or as I grew, who hadn't driven me to college in a car stuffed with different-sized plastic organizers from The Container Store—why had he been able to summon the tenderness and understanding to give me a gift I would cherish, something I would have picked out for myself had I had the opportunity?

Footsteps came heavily down the hall and lingered outside the door. Lucas gestured for us to be quiet, his face scrunching with concern. I knew he worried that one of his colleagues would discover me, a young woman visiting him on a Monday afternoon, wearing a sundress instead of a suit, carrying no briefcase or sheaf of papers, no air of superiority that comes with a Harvard PhD. After a moment, the footsteps retreated.

Lucas fidgeted with a pile of papers on his desk. "I wonder if he heard something."

"Who?"

"Did anyone see you come in?"

"Just the secretary."

"No one else?"

"Someone did notice me, I guess. Three or four doors down."

"Italian?"

"No idea. He had a very small head."

"Could have been Edward. Or Gianni—he's a gossip. Ellie, you should go. Can we continue this later?"

I stood up straight and tried to compose myself. "My father just died," I said. Then some inner darkness swarmed me, and I started to cry. I had meant to explain that I was vulnerable; instead, I'd made it sound like I needed pity.

"Ellie," he murmured. He gathered me in his arms again and I pressed myself against him so that our bodies matched, part for part. "I didn't mean to be abrupt. You're in pain. I can't give you my full attention here. But I want to." Lucas kissed my forehead. "What can I do?"

I thought for a minute. I wanted to wake up in the morning and see Lucas's face on the pillow next to me. I wanted a whole weekend together—more than a weekend: I wanted him to leave his wife. But I couldn't ask for too much now, or it might drive him away. "I want a summer afternoon," I said, trying to keep my voice from quavering. " 'Summer afternoon—summer afternoon; the two most beautiful words in the English language.' " I was quoting Dad, who was quoting Henry James.

Lucas looked at me blankly. He didn't have summer afternoons. He had a wife and two assistants and was occasionally asked to draft papers for the secretary of state. We saw each other at the Union Station food court and, at night, in hotels, secret hideaway places. We met in suburbs where other people lived, the yellow light of their parlors shining onto black lawns.

"I want to go away together. Somewhere we can be together for more than a couple of hours," I said.

"I want that too. We'll make it happen." He took my hands, curled them into one fist, and pressed it to his lips. "But you have to promise me one thing."

"What's that?"

"You can't come here again. At least not until . . ." He trailed off.

My breath quickened.

He didn't finish the sentence.

Six

Colette called and asked me to take Van on Saturday while she did dead-person things—canceling credit cards, visiting the law offices of Fredrick-the-Rapacious, calling the car-insurance company, submitting piles of paperwork, picking up the ashes. I almost said no, that I had to work on my "Rising Tides" *Apogee* assignment for Jane, but that last one got me, the thought of Dad in some cardboard box being handled by a stubbly guy in a fireproof smock.

When Saturday came, I borrowed my roommate Adrian's car and drove to meet Colette and Van at the halfway point between us. Coming off the highway, I realized I was twenty minutes away from Linda T., who had written her address in the guest book at the funeral. I hatched a plan. After I picked Van up, if he fell asleep in the car—one of his superpowers was the ability to conk out in moving vehicles—I would make a detour to 14 Horseshoe Road and see if I could learn anything.

In the parking lot of a gas station, Colette, Van, and I hugged like survivors of a shipwreck. When I pulled away, I saw a tremor running through the vein on Colette's fore-head.

"I just want Van to be with family," she said. "I couldn't make him stay with a sitter, not now."

"I'm glad you called. We'll have fun," I said.

There must have been babysitters who knew Van better than I did, who saw him more frequently and could converse with him in sign language—but it was only for a few hours. Anyway, I liked Van.

Colette's fingers flew gracefully as she signed a goodbye to Van, her face as solemn as a parent's at a kindergarten drop-off.

"We'll be fine!" I called as she walked away, though once Van and I were settled in Adrian's car, I blanched. Had I ever been alone with Van outside of Dad's house? He took that moment to look up at me, peeking through the blond hair that curled into his eyes. If he spoke, I would have said, *Hey buddy,* or *Hi sport,* or some other ludicrous name for a ten-year-old boy that zinged up from the socialized folds of my brain where I also stored information about table settings, thank-you cards, and everything my mother had ever im-pressed upon me about dating. Instead, I tweaked one of his big Dad earlobes.

"I'm hungry," he signed.

"What?" I signed back.

"Food," he tried, putting his clumped-together fingers to his lips. Then he drew a circle in the air.

"You want a hamburger?"

He shook his head.

"What other food is round? Bagel? Pizza?"

Van removed his phone from his pocket and opened the Notes app.

While he typed, I sat up straight and tried to make my face seem bright and unencumbered. My mother had told me that I could achieve this by drumming my fingertips lightly over my cheekbones to bring color to my face.

Van held up the phone. He'd written, *Can we get black and white cookies?*

I exhaled, motioned for the phone. *I was supposed to get black and white cookie from that circle?* I wrote.

;) yup

BW cookies coming up. Dad loved those.

He loved old bay more

I once saw him put old bay on one!

Ewwwwww no you didnt

lol

I started the car, rolled the windows down. How did he die? asked a chorus of voices in my head.

We passed a string of strip malls and smokehouses, the sun glaring off the hoods of parked cars. Van was curled against the window, his face turned away from me. I poked him gently on the shoulder. Sure enough, he didn't stir.

Whoever that woman at the funeral had been, between her house and my father's was a stretch of bay coast so ragged and twisting that as we drove, the water dazzled one side-view mirror and then the other. I swung off the highway and found Horseshoe Road, then parked in a speckled patch of shade across the street from the converted barn I'd seen on

Google Earth, where someone named Linda T. lived. Heat steamed up out of the grass, and the brackish scent of water came rushing over the tall dark pines. Van jerked his head when I cut the engine; through half-lidded eyes he took in the unfamiliar street.

I took out my phone and tapped a text to Van. *Running into that house for a few. Stay here?*

Next to me, Van shook his head no.

"Five minutes," I said, flashing five fingers.

Who lives there? he texted back.

I hesitated. *Friends,* I wrote.

I knocked on the front door, three quick hollow raps. From deep within the house, I heard what I believed were the footfalls of my father's lover.

"Yes?" A man's voice filtered from behind the door.

"Hi, I'm looking for Linda?"

The first thing I recognized as the door swung open was the erect posture and the linen shirt of someone rich or famous. The next thing I saw was his thick white hair, pulled into a man bun at the back of his head. It had famously turned white when he was a young man, and now in his sixties, it was the color of snow. It *was* him. Standing before me was Romley Cass.

"Oh, I'm sorry." I peered at the man to make sure.

"What is this regarding?" He propped his forearm against the doorframe. The look he gave me said, *I do not tolerate Jehovah's Witnesses.* It also said, *I hope you're a fan.*

"Are you Romley Cass?"

"I am."

"Oh wow," I said. What was the poet laureate of the United States doing at the lagoon woman's house? I drew a breath, starstruck, and looked down at the wide boats of his bare feet. "I love your work. But that's not why I'm here— I actually didn't know you would be here. I came to speak to Linda. She knew my father?"

"Who is it?" someone asked, a muffled voice, and then from the gloom of the dark hall the lagoon woman emerged.

For a moment we stood in solemn, uneasy silence. Romley put his hand on her hip, a casual proprietorship in the spread of his fingers. She was as striking as she'd been when I saw her for the first time at the funeral, but at close range she was thinner, her cheekbones prominent and below them a hollow space, the way some women get skinnier as they age, their soft places scooped out. Unlike my mother, she was thin without looking as though she'd spent much of her life denying herself food.

"What—" she said.

"I'm Eleanor. Jim Adler's daughter."

Linda put her hand to her throat, glanced at Romley. Something passed between them, ancient and intimate. "Would you like to come in?" she said.

Was her question the result of some agreement that had moved silently from her to him or in defiance of it? I couldn't tell. I followed them inside, down a long bare hall to a kitchen where a sliding screen door looked out onto flowering bushes, mumbling, alive with bees. I knew Romley was an avid gardener; his collection of poetry, *Stamen Songs,* had won a National Book Award the same year my father's collection hadn't been nominated for one.

"Sit, please," Linda said.

We arranged ourselves politely in kitchen chairs. I'd hoped to speak to her alone, but Romley seemed intent on staying; he was eyeing me gravely. With his black jeans and tattooed forearm, he reminded me of an older version of the baristas at the Rattling Panther, the popular coffee shop in my D.C. neighborhood, who served each latte with a side of disdain.

I started to speak just as Linda pivoted toward the refrigerator. "Something to drink?" she said. "I have kombucha."

My oldest roommate, Nick, was into kombucha. Like half marathons, I thought of it as the purview of the recently turned thirty. But here was glamorous, middle-aged Linda, pouring out three glasses of fizzing liquid that reminded me of tree bark. "It's not flavored. We like it that way," she said.

We. Romley and Linda, tucked away in this converted barn on a muddy inlet, wearing—I glanced at their hands—matching rings that looked like twisted strands of rope. A week ago, Linda had been crying in the back row of the chapel, my father's body fitted in his coffin at the front. What had she said when she came home to Romley?

I took a sip of the sour drink. "I've never had kombucha before. It's nice." Romley sipped eagerly beside me; I heard the heavy, wet swallows of a major poet. "My father was a writer," I told him. "Do you happen to know his work?"

Romley said, "Mmmm," in a way that could have meant yes or no, but before I could say more, Linda began pelting me with questions about my life: Where did I live? What was

I up to now? Oh, wonderful, and did I enjoy D.C.? As Linda and I talked, Romley removed the elastic band that held up his man bun, shook out his thick hair, and redid the bun so that it sat higher on his head.

"And your mother?" Linda asked. At this, Romley stopped fiddling and looked at me.

"Rachel Gettleman. She's remarried. She lives in Florida," I said. My mother was probably right this minute prancing sleekly in front of the mirror in the studio Dr. Boris Gettleman had built for her in their air-conditioned basement in Tallahassee.

"I found your address in the guest book at the funeral," I said to Linda, hurtling myself into the opening in conversation. "I'd like to talk to you about my dad."

Romley pressed his eyes closed as if he was in pain.

"Rom," Linda said.

Romley's chair scraped across the floor in a short burst of sound. He stood up. "You went to his funeral," he said tightly.

"Rom." She leapt up to face him. "I had to."

"Don't."

"Look at me."

"Stop."

I watched the flame leap between them and edged my own chair back. "Sorry," I said. "Excuse me." I gestured vaguely in the direction of the rest of the house, where I assumed it would be reasonable to find a bathroom in a converted barn.

So it was true. Linda had been in a relationship with my father. What else would explain Romley's anger? I felt vindicated and insignificant; Romley had made no attempt to conceal his feelings from me—I wasn't worthy of his discretion.

My father and Colette had seemed happy, settled. In love. But what did I know? He'd gone outside the marriage. Colette could never find out about this—it would ruin her to learn the truth only after he'd died; it would open a wound that could never be treated. I didn't want her to suffer a posthumous revelation, the way I just had. In the bathroom, I washed my hands. Who had my father been? A man with secrets. A calculating man. A man who had not loved me as much as I'd thought.

I passed a table in the hall that held a statue of Buddha and a bowl of limes. Incense sticks were nested in a shallow sandalwood dish. A nearby door was ajar, revealing an old farmhouse table being used as a desk. I slipped inside. Romley's awards were laid out on a shelf above. *In the great man's study*. It could be the title of a book of poetry. Though Romley would write it better than I could.

A cut-glass bowl etched with the name of a major prize; the golden circle of the Pulitzer; three bronze plaques mounted on dark wood. Weighty, thick, made to last. I turned over a marble oval engraved with his name, a sprig of holly, the words "Stroika Poetry Prize." I made out the rubbery edge of glue on one side of the green felt base and was satisfied by the imperfection.

My father's one award, the Eugene Loafman Blatt Award Given to a Poet Over 50, had hung on the wall next to the bathroom mirror. He must have been a little ashamed of it, the "Given to a Poet Over 50" part, like a participation trophy, yet it was displayed where everyone who entered the house would inevitably find themselves. There had been a small ceremony at a nearby convention center, to which the entire family had gone, where we ate rubbery chicken and wiped our mouths with starchy cloth napkins, and at the end of the evening, while my father brought the car around, I'd watched the chairs and tables from the event being loaded up a ramp into a white rental truck. Romley's success—this wall of awards, the shelves freighted with translations, glowing newspaper reviews framed behind glass—must have been what my father had wanted. Had he also wanted Romley's wife? How had he kept this affair from all of us, especially from me? He often remarked upon how happy it made him that he and I were unusually close and open with each other.

Out in the hallway, I could hear no sounds from the direction of the kitchen. Whatever argument Linda and Romley were having was being conducted in silence. I walked loudly, so as not to startle them, and found them seated again, their heads bent toward each other like a pair of swans. When I cleared my throat, they looked up, dazed. "I'm sorry to have dropped in on you like this. I didn't realize—"

"It's all right," Linda said.

"If you want me to go, I'll go."

"That would be best," Romley said.

I paused in the doorway. "Thank you for the kombucha. You have a lovely home," I said, sounding too much like my mother. As I passed toward the outer hall, I grasped Linda's hands in my own, bending in front of her. "I made a mess here, but I honestly didn't know you were married. I didn't mean to cause you pain."

Linda's face softened. "I know you didn't."

"He died suddenly, and I was just trying to learn everything about him now that he's gone." Tears came surging to my eyes, but I batted them away. I was aware that it was hard for anyone to deny a grieving daughter, that tears went a long way. Did the fact that this was performative negate how sad I was? Wasn't all public grieving a performance?

My father had owned all of Romley Cass's books; he'd jokingly referred to them as "the works of mine enemy," but he'd never mentioned *knowing* Romley Cass or Romley's wife. I saw now, though, how strange that was—my father and Romley were both sons of Maryland and were professionally obsessed by the same things: form, syllable, meter. But my father had always seemed like he was in a different category, a regional poet, beloved by few outside the muddy mid-Atlantic, while Romley had received every honor that could be bestowed on an American writer. I'd seen a photo of him with Barack Obama at a National Humanities Medal ceremony, Obama's hand companionably on Romley's shoulder, Romley in the middle of some humorous observation, offered from within the shield of his tux, his long white hair neat and, as I recalled, pre-bun. I thought how tragic the whole thing was—my father's jokes about Romley Cass, his light, mocking tone, which must have been laced with humiliation, Romley being the poet of my father's own generation who had achieved real recognition and real fame. But this thought was a betrayal. My cheeks warmed, and I pressed the cool backs of my hands to them.

Romley got up and walked to the sink, where he put one hand on either side of the faucet. The air in the kitchen felt close and electric; my head pulsed with a vague sense of danger.

"You were crying at his funeral," I said quietly.

Linda's mouth tightened and she looked at me with a new coldness. "Is that what you think?"

"My dad never said anything. I figured it out." The watery slivers of her eyes. How she'd clutched her scarf, holding tight to the physical world. "You had a relationship."

Linda made a small noise in her throat, like a squirrel that has found a rotten nut. "I screwed up," she said. "We've worked through it, but you must forgive Romley. It's hard for him."

"So it's true," I said.

Linda went to the sink and wrapped both of her hands around one of his. "I nearly ruined our marriage. But people make mistakes," she said, affecting bravery, like a Disney princess breaking into song. "Everyone makes mistakes." Linda turned her face to mine, calmer now that Romley was again at her side. "I'm sorry. This must not be easy to hear."

I was aware that Linda was doing all the emotional labor. She was consoling him; she was consoling me. The sun retreated and the shapes in the room—the kettle, the plants, the faucet—faded to blue and gray, the life leached out of them.

There was a noise in the hallway, and out of the corner of my eye I saw Van peering into the kitchen, bewildered, his hair sleep-flattened.

"Oh no." I smeared my arm across my face. "This is my brother, Van. We were driving—sorry, he was waiting in the car."

"Hi, Van," Linda said too brightly, calibrating her voice to a new frequency.

Van came and stood very close to me. I spelled out L-I-N-D-A and R-O-M-L-E-Y with my fingers.

"Jim was your father?" Linda asked. "I'm so sorry, sweetie."

Van looked at me.

"He's my father's youngest. Lip reading is really tiring for him. We should go." I draped my arm over Van's shoulders. "My father—our father—left you this." I brought the baseball out of my bag, gripped it hard.

"What is it?" Linda took the baseball from me, her gaze blank and stunned as a cat's.

"His lucky baseball."

"But why would he—"

"It was in his will?" Romley asked.

" 'My baseball I leave to L. M. Taylor.' I figured you would know about it."

"Oh," Linda said. "Well, I'm not L. M. Taylor."

"You're not?"

"I'm Linda Tapscott." She handed the ball back to me.

I stammered out an apology and grabbed Van's hand, pulling him into the hall. My chest was tight with embarrassment and confusion. We fled across the lawn to the car, hulking in the long afternoon shadows. In a few moments we'd be out of there, clicking our seatbelts and driving to D.C., and I could try to forget about the two of them, Romley's miserable expression and Linda's fluttery excuses, but it was hopeless; I'd never get them out of my head. Every moment with Colette from now on, I would be heavy with this secret about my father, a secret that would probably ruin Colette if she knew. Meanwhile, inside their renovated barn, Romley and Linda could set about the business of repairing their bond.

His thick hair in her hands, him pressing into the cool, sharp bones of her hips.

"Wait!" Linda came up behind us. I hoped she would say something else, that whatever it was would lift the plow of pain in my gut, but when we got to the car, she only hugged Van and then me. "I'm so sorry for your loss," she said, her words falling into the air behind my shoulder.

So, then: Who was L. M. Taylor?

Seven

Back in D.C., Van and I bought enough black-and-white cookies for all my roommates. I wasn't sure which of them would be home or how many new people Van would have to meet at 1938 House. The house was a hub of social activity on weekends, which was both a plus and a minus for me, since Lucas was with his wife and there were always plenty of people around to distract me but there was never any quiet. Mal had many extracurricular study groups, and she threw a lot of parties. Practically all the young professionals of Washington were likely to turn up over the course of a night, looking for a boozy party thrown by a chic political radical with a great music collection.

The house was huge. Five of us lived there, and often a sixth crashed on the living room futon, somebody's friend in town for work or a partygoer too drunk to go home. Downstairs, the rooms flowed into one another—the living room at the front with a big bay window, a cavernous dining room in the middle, and the kitchen at the back. For parties, we shoved all the furniture into one corner and turned the whole space into a dance floor.

Upstairs were four bedrooms of various sizes, ranging from the smallest (mine) to Adrian's, which was large enough for a couch and TV and had a fire escape, where he sat to have loud fights on the phone with his on-again, off-again girlfriend, Charmaine. The third-floor attic had been turned into a bedroom without a door, where Katherine lived, though she was often away, socializing with young embassy and White House types at rooftop parties in Foggy Bottom and Georgetown.

Inside, Mal was on her knees beside the sealed-off fireplace, wearing an apron over a short skirt and scrubbing the floor like Cinderella in a porno. In two to four years, depending on how quickly Van matured, a scene like this could be fodder for his fantasies; I felt like covering his eyes. Mal whirled around and greeted Van boisterously. I stood off to the side, contemplating Mal's scrubbing, which appeared to be merely moving dirt from one pile to another.

I had met Mal my first month in D.C., when I'd been living on the sofa of a boy I'd known in college who could cook only two things. Because he offered to share his meals with me, and because I spent every night with my cheek pressed against his IKEA futon, for seven nights I ate this boy's carrot soup and dense loaves of bread. We mostly talked about college; he had been an ultimate Frisbee–playing philosophy major and now had an AmeriCorps position at the D.C. Department of Transportation. I had the sense he felt his best years were behind him.

On the eighth night, in order to avoid beta-carotene poisoning, I'd gone to a nearby coffee shop, bought lattes and sandwiches for both of us, and stood looking at the bulletin board papered with notices about community events.

A woman appeared beside me and tacked up a flyer for a clothing swap. She had an under-shave haircut on one side, which I never felt cool enough to pull off but which looked amazing on her. The other side swooped dramatically across her forehead and was dyed a grayish-purple, the ends tucked into a chunky-knit infinity scarf in a mustard color. I'd later learn that she was Korean American, that she worked at Greenpeace, and that she was a member of the D.C. chapter of Democratic Socialists of America. I liked her immediately.

"Hey," I said. "I'm Ellie. The clothing swap looks great."

"Mallory." She stuck out her hand, and I put down the tray of lattes to shake. "It'll be a lot of fun. You should join!"

"Thanks, I think I will. I'm new to D.C., so I'm doing all kinds of 'making friends' activities." I didn't usually introduce myself to strangers, or tell them I had no friends, but I was emboldened by my status as a transplant in need of community.

"How long have you been here?" she asked.

I reflected. "A week."

"You have a place to live?"

"I live on the couch of a philosophy major I knew in college."

"That's clearly temporary. Philosophers don't last in Washington." We walked together through the café door. "Do you need a room? There's an opening in my group house."

"I do, actually."

"Oh, cool. I'll schedule you an interview."

"An interview? Should I prepare anything?"

She hitched her messenger bag up farther onto her shoulder. I noticed a "Love Has No Gender" pin affixed to the shoulder strap. "It's a social-justice-themed house. We'll have you answer questions about your career," she said. "Your interests. Your social values."

"My social values? Is that code for something?"

"Like what?"

"Like you'll ask for my Girl Scout merit badges or something?"

She laughed. "Yeah. Bring your sash."

The Sunday of my group-house interview, my mother was visiting from Florida to help me "get settled." She'd rescued me from the philosopher's futon, and we were staying at a hotel in Georgetown. Before my mother married Boris Gettleman, we would have been at a bargain motel, with stale corn muffins and weak coffee in the morning. But we lived in a Boris Gettleman world now. He had paid for a place with fluffy pillows, faux marble in the shower, boutique pastries by the front desk. My mother was on the plush carpet, doing push-ups. I was sitting on the bed, eating a hibiscus donut.

"Eighty-seven," she grunted. "Eighty-eight."

I took another bite.

"Join me, Ellie. It feels so good to do this in the morning."

"No thanks, Mom. I'm still working on breakfast."

When she finished her set of one hundred, she jumped to a standing position. "I'll change, and then we can go?"

"You're not coming with me to my group-house interview."

"I think it will make you look very committed. You brought your mother as a reference!"

"It will not make me look committed. It will make me look insane."

She began vigorously toweling her hair. "Don't you want my opinion of the place? I'm very intuitive about spaces. Just ask Boris. I turned down twenty-six homes before I found the right one for us. And it's perfect."

"This is not Tallahassee, Mom. It's not a buyer's market. There is only one house, and I want to live there. You have to stay here. Or take a walk, whatever. Go to a museum. I'll be gone like an hour."

She nodded briskly, stooping to pick up the socks I'd kicked off and laying them on top of my suitcase with a pat. "Whatever you say."

"This is informal," Mallory said when I arrived. She and her roommates were sprawled across various items of furniture, flotsam of suburban nineties' childhoods and particleboard ticky-tacky moved once or twice too many times. I sat across from them on a metal folding chair.

"Although it's harder to get into 1938 House than Harvard," Nick joked. He had introduced himself as a politics nerd who worked as a "policy analyst" at the Department of Energy. "Analyst" seemed like the third-most-common job in D.C., after "consultant" and "lawyer."

"Did you go to Harvard?" I asked.

"Me? Uh, no." Nick shifted in his chair. I would later learn that college was a sore subject for him. He'd taken six years to graduate from Cornell, after an embarrassing incident involving a lacrosse player, two hundred dollars, and an impeccably written essay about the French social critic Montaigne.

"Group living isn't for everyone," Adrian chimed in. "Ob-

viously we want to find someone who is a good fit for us."
Adrian clerked for a federal judge, and he seemed the most
laid-back of the bunch. He was wearing cowboy boots. Many
displaced Texans, I had learned, wore cowboy boots in D.C.,
even with their suits and ties, even, sometimes, with shorts,
like a bat signal that alerted other Texans to their presence.

"So yeah. We can give you a quick tour, and then we just
have a few questions to see if you're a good fit," Katherine
said. She was the blond leggy one, a social secretary at the
Moroccan embassy. I hated that she'd repeated the term
"good fit." It conjured childhood trips to the mall, trying to
stuff myself into various too-small outfits while my mother
watched.

The 1938 House tour was brief. It had a grubby chic aes-
thetic. The furniture was ugly, but there were geometric prints
hanging on the walls, candles and trinkets arranged pleas-
ingly on the mantel, plants dangling in the windows. My
bedroom—I'd already started thinking hopefully of it as
my bedroom—was just off the staircase and shaped like a
triangle. On one side was a mattress that looked as if it had
been slept on by many people. Half of one wall was painted
pink. "We think the landlord once tried to paint and stopped,"
Adrian explained.

"I love it," I said.

The interview consisted of five questions. Three were
about my personal habits. The fourth question was why I had
decided to move to D.C.

"I moved to D.C. so I could use *impact* as a verb," I said.

The roommates seemed to like this answer, but I mentioned my *Apogee* job too, just in case.

The final question was, What social issues did I care about the most? I thought for a minute. The anecdote that came to me was about how I was once seated on an airplane next to an older man who reached under his seat, pulled out a life preserver, and put it on. He wore it unselfconsciously the entire trip. Other passengers snuck glances at him as if he knew something they didn't. Of specific importance was that we were flying over land from New York to Pittsburgh.

This story came to me and I repeated it. "We're all living in the shadow of terror and tragedy," I finished. "But I want people to be able to practice their art, be happy, enjoy each other, have enough money, and grow and change." That's what I said.

There was a long silence. Finally Nick broke in. "So . . . Social Security reform?"

"I guess I'm more of a generalist," I said.

"Great to meet you, Ellie," Adrian said.

"We have a few more candidates to interview, but we'll be in touch," said Mal. She winked at me, and I beamed. Even if I didn't get into this house, I was glad to have met her. I hoped we would become friends.

Now Van, Mal, and I settled at the dining table, eating our black-and-white cookies out of little wax paper bags. We set up the Monopoly board that Mal had taken from the living room shelf we called "the House Shelf." Everything on it came from previous 1938 House tenants now long gone, including a waterlogged copy of *The Catcher in the Rye* inscribed *To our rascally Sam, Love, Bubbe and Zayde.* Van liked his cookie a lot, and he liked Mal—I could tell from the little contented expression on his face.

"The really preposterous thing about this game is that we all start with the same amount of money. When has that ever happened?" Mal said, dealing out the Pepto Bismol–pink fives.

"Mallory is an anti-capitalist," I said aloud, tapping the words into a text to Van at the same time.

"I'm a socialist," Mal said.

"She says she's a socialist. I'll explain when you're older," I said, punching in a text for Van.

Van wrinkled his nose in confusion. Mal shook her head. "No way. How old are you, Van?" Van held up ten fingers. "Awesome. You're coming to my next socialist feminist reading group. You're never too young to be a comrade."

When Nick came home, we cooked pasta for dinner and had a spaghetti-throwing contest to see whose spaghetti would stay on the wall longest. Van won. "It's because of his throwing arm," I said.

"Is that pride I hear in your voice, Ellie?" Mal said, bopping my arm.

"I love this kid," Nick said, watching Van toss a strand of spaghetti in the air and catch it with his mouth.

At eight, I got a string of panicky texts from Colette, saying that she was overwhelmed and in no condition to drive. *My stepmom is having a nervous breakdown. Van's going to stay with us tonight,* I texted my roommates on our group chat. I explained to Van that I would put him to bed in my room, that there would be a party downstairs but that I would come back up periodically to check on him and make sure he was sleeping, that I'd sleep in a sleeping bag at the foot of the bed, and that in the morning he could wake me up whenever he wanted another black-and-white cookie. I sent him the message via text also, because I knew he wouldn't be able to catch everything by reading my lips. I was a little proud of myself for doing a good imitation of a big sister.

Do you want to take a bath before bed? I texted him, recalling Dad pouring water over Van's soapy head as he lay in the tub, his ears fitted with little plugs and covered with a plastic band. But that must have been when Van was only two or three.

"Shower," Van signed. I felt confident he'd said "shower" because the sign looked like water coming down from a showerhead.

"Great," I said brightly, gesturing toward the closet. "Let me get you a towel."

From downstairs came a loud crash and then a distinctly Nick-sounding "Fuck!" and Mal yelled, "Nick, watch it!" They were preparing for the party, hanging a sheet on which they would project some obscure experimental film while people were dancing. I'd been to enough 1938 House parties to know that all those young D.C. people would turn our house into a scene of vibrant chaos. I decided I wouldn't drink and that I would go upstairs early to watch over Van. I wouldn't be able to sleep with the music pounding below, but I wanted to take good care of him, to be responsible.

Behind my eyes, I saw my father's body heave in the morning light. What was the sound of his body falling? In my mind he went down like a Summer Christmas tree, needles swishing the floor.

In my room, Van pulled the covers up until only his blond head stuck out from the sheet. He smelled of my passion-fruit shampoo and Nick's sharp body wash for men. The day was over. It had been the longest time the two of us had ever spent alone together. "Good night," I signed. That one I knew. I'd been signing it to him since he was a toddler.

I wanted my father; I had his son. I wanted to write poetry; I had a reporting job. I wanted Lucas; I had a group-house party. These feelings were dark and shivery in me, like cold night water. At the door, I paused to switch off the overhead bulb. The room went black. I lifted my hand to tell Van I loved him, but there wasn't enough light.

Eight

Van and I drove back to Colette's the next morning. The three of us spent the day in the living room, reading and watching movies. It was beautiful outside, but the house contained us and our grief. After dinner, Van played Angry Birds on his phone and I sat beside him on his bed, leaning against the wall and turning the tie rack over in my hands. It occurred to me there could be something hidden inside it—maybe the tie rack was part of an elaborate mystery; maybe my father had been a secret agent, secretly. A secret secret agent. There might be a scroll of paper inside, or a microfilm. A message for me. What did a microfilm even look like? And why was it sometimes called microfiche? I started going down that rabbit hole as I hacked at the tie rack with a spare pen.

Van tapped my arm, took the tie rack away from me, and used his thumbnail to pry open the catch at the back. He held the halves together for a moment before separating them, and I drew in a breath. But inside was just a hollow, empty space. I felt something that seemed less like disappointment and more like heartbreak. I didn't want to let it show, to seem like a crazy person who would search anywhere, everywhere, for an answer to a question about her father, the question of why I wasn't important to him, a mystery that would be of no interest to anyone else on earth. Instead, I just shrugged, then closed the two halves back up again, like a surgeon who has taken a peek inside a patient and realized that nothing can be done.

Van tapped out a text message to me. *Who were those two people at that house we stopped at?* he wrote. *They weren't really your friends*

When I didn't answer right away, Van grasped my upper arm.

I texted back. *They knew Dad. I thought he left them the baseball but I was wrong*

Not for them?

No. Don't tell your mom ok?

Colette appeared in the doorway. "There you are," she said. She plopped down on Van's other side, and he mashed his face into her collarbone. They entwined easily while I sat separately, the sole issue of my father's failed first marriage.

"Your father had such nice hair." Colette tucked Van's hair behind his ears. "Short here and with a little length here." I could hear the sadness stoppering her throat. With a cough, she cleared it away. "But he was so handsome. Those green eyes."

From downstairs came the sound of a woman selling earrings on television, cutting shrill and clean in the summer dark. "These are real opals, folks!"

Colette signed a phrase that involved a toothbrushing motion. Van screwed up his face and crawled over her toward the bathroom. She leaned back against the wall and shut her eyes.

"I am so tired, Ellie," she said. "I read somewhere that grief is like one of those devices that pull the sap out of a tree to make maple syrup. And your energy is the sap."

"Where did you read that?"

She thought for a moment. "Maybe I made it up," she said. "I can't even remember anymore, that's how tired I am. But it's how I feel."

When Van returned, he was holding scissors. He'd cut his bangs so short that what was left stood up in little blond nubs. "Colette." I nudged her. "Look."

"Oh!" Colette gasped. "Oh wow. Oh gosh. That's okay!" she said. Her voice was bright, but as she signed to Van she sank slowly on the bed until she was curled up. Van's smile dissolved.

I hugged him, my way of trying to tell him it was all right, and took the scissors downstairs, hiding them in one of the drawers of Dad's desk underneath a bottle of screen cleaner and an empty tin of Altoids. In a little while I would drive back to D.C., fall asleep in my own bed, far away from here. Tomorrow I would go to work. I would try to write a story that cracked open and shimmered, illuminating some dark and unknown place. I would force myself to get on with my life. To matter to myself, if not to my dad. I wanted a weekend with Lucas. I wanted my career to skyrocket. I wanted to be out by the moon.

———

Colette and I sat cross-legged on the sofa, drinking wine. She was wearing an oversized T-shirt, my father's flannel bathrobe, and, for some reason, purple lipstick. It was nine o'clock on Sunday night.

"I've got to get going. I have work tomorrow." I put my glass down.

"Stay with us. It's late already. You could drive home early in the morning?"

I rubbed my neck, considering. "Yeah. Okay."

She removed the wine bottle from where it was resting in the crook of her arm to pour more. "I don't usually drink like this. Everything is just so insane. That haircut." She shook her head. "How does Van seem to you?"

"I'm not sure. I didn't really know him well enough before . . ." I trailed off.

Colette gave me a weak smile.

"He's smart," I continued. "Really smart and nice. He'll get through this."

Colette didn't look convinced. After all, what did being smart or nice have to do with managing grief? I thought of all of us with little holes drilled in us, our energy gushing out, rendering us empty and dumb. I was the intellectual one, the writer, confident that my father had expected me to take up his mantle. Colette was . . . wifty. My half-sisters, Sadie and Anna, were at the self-involved stage of teenagerhood. Van was a child. I would keep my father's baseball, and through my reporting I would try to make his name resound.

But the baseball wasn't mine; I had been given a novelty tie rack. I had a job because I'd flattered the male CEO; I had a lover because I was young and feisty. What did being smart and nice have to do with anything?

"Ellie, I have to ask you something." Colette put her hand on top of mine. "Did you take Jim's baseball?"

"Did Van tell you that?"

"No, I noticed it was gone. I have to get it to that guy, L. M. Taylor."

Angry heat rose to my face. "How do you know it's a guy?"

"Doesn't L. M. Taylor sound like a man's name? Why would your dad leave his baseball to some woman?"

Poor Colette, I thought. Of course he would have left his baseball to a woman. The surprise to me was that L. M. Taylor might be a man.

"I was just looking at the cutest photo of Jim in his baseball uniform in his old yearbook," she said. "He was buff!"

"Did Dad ever mention knowing the poet Romley Cass?"

Colette looked at me and my stomach sank. Then she shook her head. "I don't think so. But we have some of his books lying around."

We were quiet for a minute, sipping from our glasses. Out the window, the garage light shone in a perfect circle on the grass. "I want to tell you what I learned today," Colette said finally. "I talked to a shaman I found online through a friend. The shaman said your father can contact us through portals. I know it sounds crazy, but hear me out. This woman wrote a book about her experiences channeling the dead, called *The Shaman Inside You*, and in it she talks all about how spirits make contact through flickering lights and phones. Messages. I have to show this to you." She reached into the pocket of Dad's bathrobe and pulled out her cell phone. "Look."

At first I didn't understand what I was seeing. Then I realized it was a series of automated messages telling her to update her Facebook password. The messages had long strings of numbers in them, as though displaying errors in the computer code.

Colette's eyes welled with tears. "It's your father," she said hoarsely.

"Dad wouldn't contact us through Facebook."

"He's using what's available to him."

"He was an intellectual and an artist. He thought Facebook was stupid."

She waved away my statement with her wineglass hand. "I want to figure out what he's trying to tell me."

"He's dead," I said. "He's not trying to tell you anything."

Colette stood up. When she drew the robe around her, her breasts rose and tightened. She was still a young woman, I thought; she could remarry. She could have another husband. But I would never have another father. Out of this new sense of victimhood, my anger dissipated. "Colette, wait. I'm sorry."

She kissed my cheek on her way out. "Everyone is tired, not just me. Tomorrow I'll order you a copy of that book. I'm going to see that shaman woman soon. Maybe you'll come with me."

On the couch downstairs, I tried to sleep. I thought about how teacups shattered but did not reassemble, eggs could be scrambled but not unscrambled. People died but did not undie. Entropy—the disorder in a system—always increased.

I'd learned this in Mr. Vinokurov's eleventh-grade physics class, which I had nearly failed for being unable to design a contraption out of wooden dowels and a stocking that could prevent a raw egg from cracking when dropped from the ceiling. I'd remembered the bit about entropy, though. It seemed so indulgent and perfect, the idea that the world created ever more disorder.

I heaved off the sheets and got up for a drink of water. The night-light in the bathroom was throwing dinosaur-shaped shadows over the sink. Colette had blotted on a stiff piece of paper towel that had missed the wastebasket—there were purple lips on the floor.

"Dad, I miss you," I said, speaking in the direction of the night-light, but it didn't flicker. "I loved you blindly. And now I have this insulting gift."

I took his high school yearbook, *The Castle Hill Moat*, with me on my way back to the couch and lingered over the page with my father's baseball team. I was sure I'd seen this years earlier, but now I started poring over all the names, searching for an L. M. Taylor. In the back row, far from my father, third from the left, there *was* a Larry Taylor, a shortstop. He wasn't tall like my dad, but he was uncommonly handsome, with a strong jaw and long dark hair, typical of its time, and a sensitive-looking face. Could this Larry Taylor be the L. M. Taylor from the will? It was such a common-sounding name, but baseball was the common ingredient.

It was probably demented to search this way, but I did it anyway. I ran an image search under "Larry M. Taylor," and dozens of men came up. Men at Ford dealerships, school superintendents, men who had died tragically in a fire. There was one, a manager at Metro Central Bank in Crosskeys, Maryland, whose face looked like the face of the shortstop in that long-ago photo. He was still beautiful—age hadn't changed that. It was him. I slapped the laptop screen down as if I'd been burned.

In the swimming lavender darkness, from the lumpy sofa, my fingers felt for the zipper on my purse, found their way to the baseball. I tossed it into the air and waited for it to return and smack the skin of my living hand.

When I opened the laptop again, a few quick searches produced an email address. It was the middle of the night. I wrote:

To: L. M. Taylor
From: Eleanor Adler
Subject: bequest

Dear L. M. Taylor,
You don't know me, but I'm the daughter of James Adler, the poet. I understand that you may have been friends with him when you were young. He died recently, and he left you something in his will, an object that was important to him. I see that you work in Crosskeys. I'm in D.C. Could I meet you for a cup of coffee? I'd love to give it to you in person.
Sincerely,
Eleanor

I pressed send and lay back on the pillow. Every so often the ceiling above my head buzzed; Colette had left her cell phone on the floor. I imagined the messages she was receiving, thinking they were from my father, the strings of numbers lighting up the bedroom where he once breathed and slept and read a biography of Bruce Springsteen and made love and blew his nose and whispered good night and listened to the thump of his own heart beating.

Nine

The thing about married men is they are never available when you need them.

When my father was still alive, in November, I met Lucas for the first time. From the start, it felt deeper than it had with other men, and deeper than sex. The day that my Sri Lanka article was published, he'd texted me to say he liked it. Then I noticed a strange comment on the *Apogee* website. One thing you quickly learn as a journalist, especially a female journalist, is not to read the comments on your articles. Rarely is it productive to see the bottom feeders of the internet issue their provocations.

I'd written an article that day about Senate Democrats struggling to renew the Violence Against Women Act, which funded domestic-violence prevention and support programs. Conservatives were largely opposed. I'd gotten a tip that a group of Republican senators were working on a ridiculous amendment to the bill, designed to create a stranglehold over progress so the legislation would stall; apparently they were taking meetings with men's rights activists. I was a tiny bit proud of the connection I'd made, a link that no one else seemed to be writing about. Jane didn't usually put me on political stories, so I felt I'd been tested and done well. Maybe that was why I broke my own rule and scrolled down to see the comments: *Liar, whore, Satan-lover, you deserve to be raped, I shud rape ur fat ass.* Toward the bottom there was something different: *Appreciate the multifaceted reporting on this critical bill. This reporter called out people who deserve to be called out. Well done.* It was posted by someone identified as ColomboFan. The back of my neck shivered. It was him!

It was a Wednesday evening, and I was supposed to play poker with a bunch of male science reporters at the National Press Club. Someone had added me to a Facebook group for science and environmental journalists, and the poker night gave me an opportunity to network without having to make small talk. Flying high from what I assumed was a comment from Lucas, I played a few hands, drank two beers. I was seated next to one guy from the *New York Times* science section, in town for a conference, and another from *Biology* magazine, both of whom eyed me with the kind of generic interest most young heterosexual men evinced when there was only one woman in the room. That was the case with the handful of men I'd dated in college; all of them wanted a girlfriend, none of them wanted *me*.

Still, I checked out the dude from *Biology*. He had a membership to the National Press Club, an institution that was as shambolic and venerable as journalism itself. He would pay the members-only price for the chicken club sandwich. But I couldn't stop thinking about Lucas Ataide, comparing the sparks I'd felt between us on the phone with what was currently in front of me: a pile of American flag–colored poker chips and a reporter whose idea of a fun evening was getting one more flush than Reuters.

After a few hours, I called it quits, leaving the male reporters to their long night of saying the things they really wanted to say but couldn't when a woman was around. Outside, I unlocked my bike from the heavy metal grate surrounding the Press Club's sculpted green bushes. During the day, two million people swarmed to D.C. from the suburbs, filling the Metro seats and sliding their cars along the Beltway for seven and a half hours of tepid governance. But at night downtown felt like mine alone. I'd always loved staying up late—the night and its dreaminess suited me. All the stately marble buildings nearby—the White House, the Wilson Building, the Department of Commerce—were lit up in gold spotlights, showing off for an audience of no one. It was one kind of distinctly American boasting. Show, not substance.

I mangled a bobby pin into my hair and put on my bike helmet. Riding at night through empty streets was magical, cajoling me to boldness. I felt a thrum between my legs, thinking of ColomboFan. I'd spent some time googling him, looking at his professional photos, his close-lipped, slightly mischievous expression. I had googled every combination of "Lucas Ataide" and "wife" and "girlfriend," I could think of. "Boyfriend." There was nothing. His Twitter account was purely work related—links to papers he'd written, articles he wanted to share. Still, I'd scrolled through hundreds of tweets, looking for selfies or mentions of family, but there weren't even any artful pictures of shadows or coffee mugs or windswept fields. Who didn't post personal things to social media? I already felt this was sexy, superior. I glided north to K Street, turning at McPherson Square, where Occupy tents were huddled. Mal and Adrian had been going to protests all fall. Mal said that Occupy brought collective rage into the streets.

It was quickly becoming clear to me that in D.C. there was the mostly white professional class who moved to the city from elsewhere, shopped at Whole Foods, and sent their kids to private school, on their way up and out to the suburbs, and then there were the Black families who were longtime residents, deeply connected to the history of the city, often in poorer neighborhoods where children were enrolled in some of the worst schools in the nation. Segregation between the two populations was near complete. Young people like my housemates and me, transplants from elsewhere, who'd come to D.C. for the jobs and opportunities, were riding an elevator into that professional class. Mal said this was why we had an obligation to step up, to protest and to organize. I had been meaning to go with her to Occupy, but I'd just started at *Apogee,* and my hours were overwhelming. Plus, if I was being honest, I felt uncool compared to the protesters—their perfectly ripped black jeans, bold eyeliner, sticklike bodies, cardboard signs. I was already too establishment for them, I thought, drawing a paycheck from a journalist start-up, lusting after a man who worked at a think tank. Mal would have scoffed at this and found some way to make me feel included. But feeling like an outsider, I was realizing, was my specialty.

All of this faded as I pedaled, crafting the perfect text message to Lucas Ataide in my mind. I was riding through the hub of D.C.'s elite, a street packed with office buildings, take-out salad places crammed into every storefront. On K and 17th, I stopped beneath a concrete building with tinted black windows. I knew from my internet stalking that the Council on Asiatic and Pacific Interests, CAPI, was on the fourth floor. I got off my bike and agitated my phone, scrolling until I found his text. *Not bad for an article about Kuala Lumpur,* he'd written four days before. I'd texted a brief thank-you, hoping the conversation would continue. It hadn't, but then today there was the post from ColomboFan. Now I typed another message. Why not, I told myself. He could always ignore it, delete the message, refuse to see the subtext. *Coming home from poker at the national press club and passing CAPI made me wonder if you're still there, correctly identifying Asian capitals*

I wouldn't get a response. Still, I felt relieved. At least now I'd done something; I'd know if the flirtation I sensed on the phone was real. I stood for a moment on the sidewalk, watching a water bug crawl up from between the bricks. D.C. was like that. You were always one step away from a cockroach. I glanced down at my phone and felt a rush of shock as three blinking dots appeared in the text chain—Lucas was typing a response. I watched the dots disappear and then reappear. Then disappear again. I realized I was holding my breath.

My phone bleated.

I actually AM still at work. Poker, huh?

Do you want to take a walk? I wrote back, in a blaze of excitement. It had been real. It was real. As I took off my bike helmet, I examined the steak restaurant across the street, the green awning with white letters announcing to D.C. think-tank types that this was where they could come after work, loosen their ties over oysters and tenderloin. Was this where Lucas Ataide relaxed? I hoped not. He seemed too sophisticated to frequent such an obvious and bland place. In a car window I glanced at my reflection, ran my fingers through my hair. I looked flushed from exertion and a little orange in the streetlight. I almost turned sideways but decided against it, since turning sideways in mirrors, no matter how often I did it, had never resulted in my stomach looking flat. What if Lucas found me fat or unattractive? What if I saw dissatisfaction in his eyes when he looked at me for the first time? It was like my mother always said: "If you'd just lose some weight, you could enjoy your young body." What she meant was that if I lost weight, men could enjoy my young body. I never questioned why she would think about someone else's ability to sexualize me.

Revolving doors swooshed somewhere over my left shoulder. I turned around slowly, but there was no way to seem nonchalant—it was nine o'clock on a Tuesday night and I had texted Lucas from outside his office building.

"Oh, hey." I laughed nervously. "I guess you exist outside the phone."

He laughed too. "How are you?"

We shook hands over my handlebars. He had academic hands—warm and soft. He wore a slim gold band on his ring finger. I tried not to stare. The combination of arousal and disappointment writhed in me.

"To be clear, it's for the glory, not the money," I said.

He seemed slightly startled.

"Poker," I said.

He laughed again. His deep-set brown eyes looked kind, quizzical, calmly assessing. So far, I thought his assessment was positive. He did not seem put off by my forwardness. He did not seem disappointed by the fact that I was the kind of person in the department-store dressing room who always required the saleswoman to find her a bigger size. Though he hadn't checked me out either—his eyes hadn't left my face.

We kept my bike between us as we walked. The ticking of the spokes forced a rhythm to our steps. He was born in São Paulo, he told me, but had grown up all over because his father was a diplomat. Lucas had come to the States for college. Harvard. Then a PhD program. Also Harvard. Then an MBA. He said where, but I immediately forgot, trying to keep all the facts in my mind, bright little orbs in the Lucas solar system. He'd been in D.C. for nine years.

I did the math in my head.

"I'm thirty-nine," he said. "And you?" I kept my head down, not wanting to meet his eye. Would I be too young for him?

"I'm twelve," I said.

"You look great for a twelve-year-old."

"I get that a lot. No, I'm twenty-four."

He didn't react. "So, you're new to the city? What are your impressions?" He seemed genuinely curious.

I thought for a moment. "Do you remember in college, when it was cool to get good grades without trying? The less you appeared to be working, the better? In D.C., it's cool to brag about how late you stayed at the office. Moving here, I got whiplash from the difference in social posturing."

"In that case, I've achieved cool status. Finally, after all these years of trying," Lucas said. "I had fashion sneakers in high school and everything."

"Calling them fashion sneakers clearly means you were a dork." It felt natural, teasing him.

"Ouch. At the ripe age of twelve, you've turned into a mean girl."

I liked amusing him. He laughed easily. I went into my newly developed taxonomy of ID badges. D.C. was the kind of town where interns wore their badges on the outside of their jackets on the Metro, I told him. The more senior you were, the more your badge migrated beneath layers, until finally you were so powerful that other people carried it for you. He seemed to like that, so I did a little riff on how at parties in D.C. everyone was always like, "Hey, have you read the new CBO study on federal highway spending?" and then when they got a little bit drunk, they were like, "Hey, have you read the new CBO study on federal highway spending?"

Why was I trying so hard? In the back of my mind was his ring. My father had had many women and wives. What was I doing taking a late-night walk with a married man? But he didn't seem to want to go anywhere, and I was electrified by him, by his interest in me.

We walked on the path around the Washington Monument, which rose in a smudge above the stately flagpoles. We looped past the Korean War Veterans Memorial, where spotlights were shining up on giant soldiers, frozen in their slickers in the tall grass. Visitors were cordoned off with low wires because the larger-than-life men could not be touched.

"I'm actually glad to live here," I said. Our eyes met and

lingered on each other until he looked away. It was true that I was proud of the life I'd started to make, getting on my bicycle in the morning, dismounting lightly at a glowing little start-up, then returning home to my ad hoc salon of housemates, whose drive and purpose and hopefulness about the world, I hoped, might spur me on too.

"It's a good city," he said. "I feel very lucky. I have my dream job."

"When did you know it was your dream to be an economist?"

"My family lived in Sri Lanka when I was young," Lucas said. "I had a babysitter, Abishani, whom I really loved. She was like an older sister. After we moved to Belgium when I was eleven, my parents hired someone to take care of me after school, a college student. I don't think she was around long. I don't even remember her name. At the end of her first week, I saw my mother count out her wages onto our dining table, and I realized it was five times what she had paid Abishani to do the same job. I was a little math nerd, so I did the calculation between Belgian francs and rupees. My mother explained that now we lived in Europe, where people earned more. I was incensed. It was unfair and arbitrary. Growing up between worlds the way I did, I saw how the accident of your birthplace determined whether you lived a good life or an impoverished one. Whether you were stable or on the edge. Whether you had access to healthcare or not. It was a natural leap for me, to study economic development in college and then to make a career out of studying poverty and how to lift people out of it."

I was quiet for a moment, taking it in. I liked that his

thoughts were about the world, not just about himself or D.C. I liked that he had been moved by injustice and that he'd cared about an important woman in his life. "Did you stay in touch with Abishani?"

"For a while. We lost touch a few years after we moved to Belgium."

"I'm sorry."

He shook his head. "I don't usually talk about her. It feels good."

I saw him look around, as though taking in our surroundings for the first time. We were headed toward the tidal basin on a path flanked by cherry trees. It felt right, for the present moment, to bring us out of the emotions of the past.

We reached the river. I leaned my bike against a tree and we sat down on a bench, with several feet between us. Whatever was happening, I didn't want it to end. I was pretty sure I was grinning like an idiot. All I wanted was to keep talking to him, to know him, to see what would happen. I felt as though the river could overflow, the Lincoln Memorial could crumble to the ground, the Pentagon could burst into flames—none of it would matter, as long as we continued this conversation. This was what love songs were about, I realized. This blindness, this feeling of tripping into another realm. I hadn't understood it before.

He looked like he was trying to articulate something but was struggling to get it out. We sat for a few moments in silence. Across the wide darkness, the Potomac River rolled over, sending barges and fish and grit southeast into the Chesapeake Bay.

"This reminds me of a Louise Glück poem I love," I said

carefully. " 'Go ahead: say what you're thinking. The garden is not the real world.' "

"Louise Glück is one of my favorites," he said. "I read her in college when I first got to the States." When he looked at me, his eyes were blazing with confusion and desire. I saw the struggle in them. "I—" he said. He looked away from my eyes, at my mouth. "I'm married."

"I know. You wear a ring."

"You didn't know that when you asked me to take a walk," he said, excusing me.

"Yes," I said. "But you did."

"I've been married for nine years."

I realized that his telling me he was married was an admission that something was happening for him too, that this wasn't just a walk. I didn't know what to say, now that he'd laid bare the power difference between us. He was older. Sophisticated, worldly. Off-limits. All the life he had lived and the things he knew! He probably had *The New York Times* delivered and not just on Sundays. He'd be the perfect date at a dinner party—stimulating, thoughtful, easy to talk to. He was nothing like the boys I'd dated in high school and college, who approached sex and dating the way they approached a flight of beer: a sampler, theirs for the sipping, with little flirtation, almost no foreplay. With Lucas, listening and talking was a joyful discovery. It was in harmony with the desire, the wanting.

"I should go," Lucas said. He glanced in both directions. I followed his eyes. There was no one, not even a lone jogger chugging beside the river.

He looked like he couldn't remember how to seduce a

woman. His nerdiness, the way he glanced at me and quickly away, as though he was embarrassed for me to see how much he wanted me, drew me to him even more.

We sat facing forward, toward the dark water, on opposite sides of the hard bench. I counted ten long breaths, waiting for him to get up. Then another ten. My throat tensed with hope. Still, he didn't move. I understood then that he didn't want to go and that I had to be the one to act, to initiate.

In a swift move that surprised even me, I got up from the bench and straddled him. I cupped his face in my hands and kissed him hard. For a moment his lips were still, as if he was in shock and clinging to the idea that this was a platonic walk. Then his head tipped back and his lips parted. I held his face in my hands, smelling his cologne, fingering the dampness of sweat at his hairline. I didn't know where I'd gotten this nerve. "Oh God," he said.

He lifted my dress and brushed a hand against my stomach, and I felt his touch jolt through me. I sucked my belly in, overcome with self-consciousness.

"Am I too heavy?" I asked, shifting my weight to my knees.

"Of course not." His voice was breathless.

But I felt myself cooling, thinking about him touching the roll of flab on my stomach. This was a question I asked almost automatically with anyone new. There would come a point, usually right before my clothes came off, when I asked to be reassured. It was a sad question, a shameful one, a question that skinned me bare, but I couldn't help myself. Based on how the men answered, I would put them in categories: shallow, tolerant, or turned on. I brushed the thought away.

"You're beautiful," he said, fingering my hair.

So this is what it felt like to desire and to feel truly desired: It was the thrill without the fear. I pulled his face toward me and kissed him again. When I drew back to look at him, it was as though I was looking at myself: His eyes were greedy and passionate and scared shitless.

I felt his hardness through his pants and reached down and grasped his belt, undoing it, and unzipped his pants so that we were separated only by our underwear. Then I rocked back and forth on top of him, moving my pelvis bit by bit, slightly more each time, looking into his eyes, which were so close I could feel his long lashes against my cheek. I had to go slowly so that I wouldn't finish. But then I thought of him inside me, on top of me in bed—in our bed, tangled in soft sheets, the rain going against the window—and I tugged his lower lip between my teeth. "I'm going to come," I said softly. He moaned and shifted under me until I felt his cock pulse through his underwear and then I came hard, listening to the sounds he made. He collapsed forward against my chest and began kissing me frantically, my lips, my nose, my cheeks, my neck, my hair. "I didn't even know that was possible," he whispered. I didn't know which part of it he was referring to.

Soon, he gave me his hand and I braced myself against him, climbing carefully to my feet. I went over to my bike, making each motion slow and careful, aware that his eyes were on me. I heard the creak of his zipper, the click of his belt. When I turned around, he looked like he was trying to formulate something else to say, but anything he said would diminish what we had just done together. "Good night," I said, wanting to prolong the dream.

"Get home safe," he said. He sounded dazed. I cycled home, dizzy with joy.

That was seven months ago. Since then, there had been many late-night walks on empty streets. Stolen afternoons in hotel rooms. Then my father's death, my stupid text, showing up at Lucas's office, asking him for a night together. Wanting more, and more, and more.

Ten

Lucas texted to say that he'd booked us a room at an inn for Saturday night. We'd never spent an entire night together. My body was humming with excitement; I couldn't seem to stop smiling.

It was Wednesday. I needed to get a "Rising Tides" story going right away, because I planned to take the whole weekend off. I figured I'd need time to get ready, to sleep enough that I was alert for Lucas. I didn't want to be worrying about work while I was away. Jane had given me an admirable challenge—to get a little sex, money, power, and personality into my reporting on the environment, to make people care about the destruction of the known world. I wanted to live up to the challenge.

I looked quickly through the daily environmental-news bulletin for reporters, which had arrived on my phone at 6:45 A.M., even before I lifted my head off the pillow. I searched for a promising scientist, a good subject. The earth had been diagnosed with end-stage cancer, and every morning I learned that diagnosis anew. At the end of this avalanche of disheartening statistics and thinly veiled recriminations, some volunteer administrator who had clearly been spending too much time with an adolescent granddaughter enclosed a GIF of a cartoon penguin leaping with joy. The penguin, meant to end things on a lighter note, was the worst part. "Soon this will be the only penguin you'll ever see," it seemed to say. "Your grandkids will know only computerized penguins; and if in fact the planet still exists for your grandkids to process a computerized penguin, it is highly likely the planet will be so overcome that your grandkids will no longer know joy."

I dressed for work.

That evening, I was at the office late, after most of the other reporters had left. It had been staff lunch day, another Silicon Valley–style contribution to our harried-reporter lifestyle, which did not mean that we had a leisurely social lunch together—it meant that we ate free Chipotle bowls in front of our laptops, chewing in tandem. At eight-thirty, I went to pick through the leftover burrito fillings in the kitchen, loading up a plate with scrapings of carnitas and sour cream. Back at my desk, I checked for a text from Lucas and refreshed my email, hoping for something from L. M. Taylor.

The "Rising Tides" feature was a long-term project on top of my normal workload; already that day I'd written my quota of six posts (volcano eruption, ice caps liquefying, whales beset, river dehydrating, heatstroke killing, sanctuary razed). I was knee-deep in an article about pesticide over-exposure changing the color of howler monkeys' coats, when a message popped up in Gchat from Jane.

JANE OSTRAWICZ-JONES Still at the office?

ELEANOR ADLER I'm doing research for Rising Tides!

I pressed enter and immediately regretted the exclam. Exclamation points had become little signposts announcing, *I mean well!* and had become so normalized that in their absence I felt a deep sense of foreboding. But every now and then you found yourself up against someone who refused to give in to exclamation points, who typed what they meant with zero reassurances, making the rest of us look like overzealous clowns. Jane was one of these people.

Jane is typing . . . Gchat explained. I bit my thumbnail. She typed for an endless amount of time, probably coming up with a firm but fair way to chide me for how long I was taking with the assignment. I decided to cut her off at the pass, before I could perceive disappointment seeping from behind her encouragement.

ELEANOR ADLER I will have a pitch for you shortly

Jane's typing stopped. Then began. Then stopped again.

JANE OSTRAWICZ-JONES How are you feeling about your dad?

I glanced up at the dark corner where Jane had her glass office. A few different monitors winked their green eyes at me. I was touched that she'd asked. No one else seemed to.

But what if her check-in wasn't purely heartfelt? Did Jane think I couldn't keep up, couldn't function over my grief?

ELEANOR ADLER It's sad and hard but work is distracting, so that's good.

JANE OSTRAWICZ-JONES Must be hard to resume normal life.

ELEANOR ADLER yeah. i'm lucky to be busy! Thank you again for rising tides . . .

JANE OSTRAWICZ-JONES It wasn't a pity assignment.

ELEANOR ADLER I know. But i'm into it.

JANE OSTRAWICZ-JONES Glad to hear. Well, I'm off. Must take my nightly constitutional around Logan Circle.

ELEANOR ADLER You circle the statue of that dead white guy?

JANE OSTRAWICZ-JONES The Civil War guy? Yes. Though I can't say I know anything much about him. Never read the plaque.

ELEANOR ADLER Those who don't learn about statues are doomed to make the same statues.

JANE OSTRAWICZ-JONES That made me cackle.
Don't stay later than I would.

ELEANOR ADLER last week you were here when I left
at 11pm . . .

JANE OSTRAWICZ-JONES Well, as soon as I got home
that night I took a clonazepam.

I felt a shift, an opening toward friendship with this revelation of a slightly offbeat but intimate detail. Was this how it
was in the modern American workplace—your boss could
inch toward becoming your friend, one prescription anxiety
medication at a time?

ELEANOR ADLER I take mine too, when I can't
sleep.

JANE OSTRAWICZ-JONES Clonazepam?

ELEANOR ADLER lorazepam. I have a bottle for
emergencies.

JANE OSTRAWICZ-JONES We're like two southern
ladies: Clonaze and Loraze Pam.

ELEANOR ADLER Haha!

JANE OSTRAWICZ-JONES See you tomorrow.

Jane's away message came on. I shoveled mouthfuls of pork from my plate. I felt fluttery and excited, loose-limbed, energetic. Suddenly ravenous. Jane *likes* me, I thought. This older, fearsome, accomplished journalist likes me. A smile exploded across my face. *Exploded:* good headline verb. I wanted to tell someone. Lucas. I picked up my phone to text him, and that's when I saw the email:

From: L. M. Taylor
To: Eleanor Adler
Re: bequest

Dear Eleanor,
It was a surprise to get your email. I'm sorry to hear about your father. I do live in Maryland, but at this time I don't have availability to meet. Please pass along my condolences to your family. All my best,
Larry

Eleven

I spent the hours before Lucas picked me up on Saturday trying on clothes. The outtakes formed a high pile on my floor. Currently on top was a black pencil skirt that was too D.C., and a red tank dress, which was not D.C. enough. Mal wandered into my room while I was wearing a floor-length peasant skirt and informed me that I looked like a grandma dressing for her cardiologist in South Beach.

She lay on the bed and commanded me to try on several other outfits. When I put on a gray blazer, she said, "Are you going to a Smithsonian ribbon-cutting at the Edith and Jonathan Wisner Hall of Petrified Wood?" We finally agreed on jeans and a tank top, and I stuffed a few other options in my overnight bag. I took a long, steamy shower, feeling a flutter at my neck when I thought of falling asleep beside Lucas and waking to his face.

Lucas and I arrived at the Glory on the 'Morrow Inn in the late afternoon. It abutted a Civil War battlefield. Our room had an antique bed, a bathroom with a clawfoot tub. As soon as we set our bags down, Lucas kissed me. I wasn't expecting it; I had been looking out the window at the history-obsessed

men ambling across the hillside, surveying the period can-
nons. His lips caught the corner of my mouth. I turned my
head to meet him, surprised by the intensity of his kiss, heat
spreading across my belly and between my legs. We undressed
and tumbled onto the bed. The sex we had was urgent, vigor-
ous. We both came quickly, first me on top, then him. "God,
I missed you," he said, his nose in my hair. I realized with
excitement that we still had eighteen hours together.

Lucas went to the bathroom to change for our hike, and I
thought through the little stories and observations I had
stored up to tell him—like the party I'd gone to with my
roommate Nick on Thursday night, full of Hill staffers and
lawyers speaking in worshipful legalese, their ambition more
naked than that of my friends in journalism and the nonprofit world and therefore somewhat of a relief.

When Lucas was with his wife, he and I went days without
talking. During that time I narrated my life to myself in the
past tense, articulating the tableaux, describing the non-
player characters. I was accustomed to storing up material;
I'd done it for my father. During my childhood, the quotidian
had been the purview of my mother; she and I were together
all the time, our daily routines entwined. Visiting my dad
was a break in the routine, automatically special, and whatever we did together achieved the exalted status of ritual. I'd
have stories ready for him, each one articulated to make him
laugh or to make him think. I'd prepare jokes ahead of time,
practice them in my mind. Though the jokes he laughed at
the hardest were always the ones I came up with spontane-
ously.

Lucas emerged from the bathroom wearing dorky sneakers and khaki shorts, his ankles slightly pinched from the elastic of his socks. "Let's hike!" he said, and he sounded so eager that I laughed. It was new, to have enough time together that we didn't have be touching every moment.

We set out on a trail, talking a little but mostly enjoying the day, being out, listening to the birds in the trees. "I forgot how great it is to be in nature," Lucas said, just as a man in a Union Army uniform emerged from a fork in the trail.

"This way to the reconstructed stone bridge over Bull Run," the man said. "Confederates used it until 1862, when the Union rear guard destroyed it." He saluted us before continuing the opposite way along the path.

"You have to admit, this is a weird hotel choice." I squeezed his hand.

Lucas laughed. "At least I didn't book the room with the bedrolls."

"Next time let's try the rival Civil War inn, 'Carry Me Back to Old Virginny,'" I said. "I hear their restaurant serves excellent hardtack."

"Nothing says romance like hardtack."

Eventually the shaded trail emptied into a sunlit field, and we came to a two-story stone house. There were curtains in the window, an herb garden in front. I entertained a fantasy that Lucas and I lived here, typing on our separate laptops across a farmhouse table, coming outside to water the tarragon and mint. I'd recently declared to Mal that I never wanted to live outside a city again, yet as I stood beside Lucas, I felt I would live anywhere if he asked me to. Maybe we would have picnics on the lawn and in the winter build fires in the stone hearth—

"This was a field hospital during the war," Lucas said, reading the plaque. "The site of hundreds of primitive amputations. Oh wow, look at this photo."

He pointed to an enlarged image of the wooden floorboards upstairs, where two infantrymen had chiseled their names. One, a twenty-one-year-old, had recovered, left the field hospital, and lived a long life after the war; the other, seventeen, had succumbed to his injuries. He'd managed to carve just half his name. I stood for a long time in front of that half-finished name, wondering what secrets he'd taken with him.

The air around us seemed to cool, as though a draft from the old house had escaped into the sunny field. My bitterness and incredulity about L. M. Taylor—Larry—surfaced, and I felt my shoulders tense. When I'd received his email saying he didn't want to meet me, it was as if I'd gotten an electric shock. The email was cold, impersonal, brief. What kind of person would reject a man's dying wishes? Why had this man been important to my father?

Lucas put his hand on the small of my back, and I jumped.

"Are you okay?" Lucas asked.

"Let's walk some more," I said.

Later, at the hotel bar, Lucas said he'd heard the inn was famous for its negronis. A bartender in suspenders and a tricorn hat set down two cocktails, a basket of breadsticks, and a pitcher of water. Slivers of ice moved purposefully across the top of the water like ducks. The negroni was sharp and aromatic, and I sipped steadily from my glass. Soon I was a little woozy. Lucas began talking about a new paper he was coauthoring that looked at transformative assets. I liked how the skin around his eyes crinkled up when he talked about ideas that excited him. I liked that he felt he could talk with me about serious things.

"The wealth gap is widening," Lucas was saying. "The estate tax was supposed to level the playing field, but it hasn't worked that way. The wealthy are still passing on transformative assets."

"Are transformative assets houses and cars, that sort of thing?" I asked.

"Exactly. Stock options. The kind of growth engines that rich families disproportionately leave to their children."

Leave *to* their children, I thought. Leave their children. What a difference a preposition makes.

"Mal believes in a hundred percent inheritance tax," I said. "Wouldn't that level the playing field?"

Lucas shook his head with enthusiasm. He loved a good argument. "A hundred percent tax would stifle innovation." He listed Northern European countries in his economist voice, making cases for various incentive structures. I poured myself water from the jug. Unearned inheritance, I thought. A crate of Van Morrison records. A tie rack. A baseball.

"The current inheritance tax in the U.S. has been corrupted by loopholes," Lucas said. "There are ample opportunities for people to circumvent it. It doesn't have much meaning."

"Well, I guess it must have *some* meaning." I set my glass down too hard, and the liquid sloshed against the edge. "At least those billionaire children knew their parents loved them." I was reminded of the line from *King Lear, How sharper than a serpent's tooth it is to have a thankless child,* which was read aloud by my high school English teacher in a tone of voice that suggested she knew what Lear was talking about.

Lucas put his hand on my knee. I linked my own hand on top, and when my fingers touched the hard curve of his wedding band, my stomach jolted. "Hey," he said. "You seem distracted."

"I'm fine."

Lucas scanned my face. "Is something on your mind?"

"It's just the old 'dead dad' thing." I forced a little laugh and my cheeks heated up. That was another thing I was learning—I had to read how much people could handle; I had to tuck in my sadness when too much of it showed. I picked the orange peel from my glass and sucked the bitter alcohol from its flesh.

Leave to your child.

Leave your child.

"You don't have to do that," Lucas said. "Shut off."

I looked up at him, startled. How had he known?

"Oh," I said. I was frightened that my interior world was apparent to him, both frightened and exhilarated that he'd read me.

"You're going through a storm, and I want to know about it." He took my hand. "I know it's not the same, but my childhood best friend died in a car accident when we were twelve. I know what it's like to suddenly lose someone I loved. It was a long time ago, and I'm not trying to compare a friend to a father," he said. "The point is, I'm here if you want to talk."

I could see the compassion in his face. Still, I wanted to protect my time with him for fun and pleasure and to safeguard his image of me as a girl who was lovable, loved by men, including her father. How would he react if I told him the whole miserable story? But he was looking at me with gentleness and interest and understanding. I didn't want to demur when he asked me about my pain or to squander an opportunity for us to get closer.

"There was a thing with my dad's will," I said. I snapped a breadstick in half, then put it down without eating it. "I don't know exactly what to think. It's not about money. My dad left each of his kids an object. And everyone else got something super meaningful to them that was about their relationship with him. And I got . . . It's funny actually—"

I laughed spitefully. Lucas stroked my knee, though I couldn't really feel it. I told him about my father's will, about the tie rack. How no one in my family could figure out why he'd left it to me, not Colette or my sisters or anyone. How I'd called my mother to tell her and she too was bewildered. I explained the baseball and Linda, and Romley Cass, and how I'd gotten Larry's email and now the trail of clues was cold.

I hadn't meant to reveal so much. When I stopped talking, I scrutinized Lucas's expression. He was listening intently, his mouth open slightly with concern. On my phone, I scrolled to a photo of the tie rack. "I mean, look at this thing," I said, placing it on the bar between us. "It feels like I was disinherited. And the one person who could maybe explain why I didn't get the baseball told me he didn't want to see me."

There was a long moment of silence in which I tried to work out if he was shocked or horrified or perhaps trying to come up with something to say that would change the subject. Instead, he said, "What was your dad like?"

No one had asked me that question. I realized how much I wanted to talk about him, but how could I explain him in a few sentences? To talk about him in the past tense was to admit that Lucas would never meet him, that my father had been finite, when of course the opposite was true—he was boundless, or at least my sadness made it feel that way. Choosing a few words to describe him meant that I'd have to summarize the character of someone I had loved more than anyone.

"He made life feel exciting," I said. "I know that's corny, but it's true. He was a book person, a words person. He told the best stories. He was charming, but he cared about what other people thought. Maybe too much. I spent a lot of time trying to be the person in the family who was closest to him and understood him the best." From my phone, the gingerbread-man tie rack smiled its beady-eyed smile, and I felt a violent pulsing at my temples. "I guess I wasn't his favorite after all—who gives their favorite a tie rack? Why would he have led me to believe that I was his favorite? Like, what was he playing at? And then he took that away from me and I'm just the tie-rack daughter? But what kind of person is angry at their dead father?"

Lucas looked down at his glass, seeming to consider his

words. "I don't know why your dad did what he did. But you're allowed to be angry and confused—how could you not be? You've been dealt a double blow, losing him and then losing your sense of where you stood in his eyes. It's a lot to contend with. I don't want you to hide your feelings. Especially not with me."

I had felt jumbled and sick inside, afraid that Lucas would be repulsed by what I'd told him. But he hadn't reacted by changing the subject or trying to solve a problem. He'd said he wanted *more*. The intimacy between us seemed to be vibrating the air. I took his face in my hands, like I'd done the very first time we kissed, and pulled him toward me until our lips were touching. He put his fingers in my hair, and my tongue found his tongue, and soon all my thoughts fell away and there was only the sensation of his nose against my cheek, his lips on my neck, his hand on my thigh—

"Um, sorry," said a voice beside us.

I drew back, dazed.

"I'm sorry to do this," said the waitress, twisting her hands together, "but I'm going to have to ask you guys to leave? You're making some other guests uncomfortable."

In the inn's ancient, creaking bed, under a thick white comforter, we had sex, and then Lucas slept while I lay awake, my body refusing to calm. I longed for it to be morning so that we could talk gently, sleepily, our faces close together on the same pillow. Near dawn, the light changed in the room, and there was a soft glow from the window, early birdsong. Lucas stirred and sighed deeply, pressing against me in sleep, his heat warm and slightly moist, like fresh bread. When I shifted against him his erection bloomed, and suddenly he was groaning, and then he was on top of me, inside me, and we were breathing together and he was moving in and out of me slowly, as though we had all the time in the world. And then it was morning, and the sun was high in the window, and Lucas was leaning over me, smelling of aftershave. He whispered that he had gotten us croissants and coffee and asked if I wanted to eat in bed.

I spent the ride to D.C. with my sunglasses on, leaning back in the seat. Lucas kept his non-driving hand in my lap the whole time, even while executing a U-turn when he missed an exit in Centreville. My body felt sluggish, immovable. We pulled up in front of 1938 House, and Lucas said he'd walk me to the door. The thought of him depositing me there and driving home to his wife made my stomach squeeze to a painful fist. The moss growing on the uneven front steps, the living room curtain opened partway, lazily—these mundane sights signaled the sadness and confusion that waited for me inside, once I crossed the threshold of my normal life.

I got up on the first step, so we were at the same height. "I don't want this weekend to end."

He wrapped his arms around my waist and looked straight into my eyes. "It was wonderful, Ellie. We'll do it again soon." He kissed the tip of my nose.

Behind us, the front door opened, and Katherine came

down the steps, a bright-pink yoga mat rolled under her arm. "Excuse me," she said as she brushed past us. She glanced at Lucas just as he swiveled his head to look at her.

"Oh, hi—" she started to say. But then her face twisted into confusion. Lucas let go of my waist. He had gone white.

Katherine gave an awkward wave and slipped away down the street, her yoga mat bobbing with each step.

Lucas kissed my forehead, a quick, dry peck. "I have to go. I'll call you."

Upstairs in my room, my breathing felt ragged. Lucas and Katherine knew each other. Had they dated? Had he slept with her? I typed out a text to Lucas: *Did you date Katherine?* I deleted it without sending it. My eyes refused to focus. Maybe Katherine was Lucas's real type—thin, blond, heavy eyeliner—and I was just an outlier. I needed to know when Katherine would be home. How long were yoga classes? Katherine was so sculpted, hers probably lasted hours. I lay back and tried to will my head to stop thudding. Whatever had happened between them, I needed to know, no matter how it walloped me.

An hour later, the front door squeaked open and Katherine's footsteps pattered into the kitchen. I flew after her. "Hey, I have a question," I said.

She opened the refrigerator door so I couldn't see her face. "Okay," she said, peering at the shelf of half-empty mustard bottles.

"How do you know Lucas?"

"I don't think I do."

"You clearly do." I moved to the other side of the fridge door, until we were both standing in its cold kingdom.

Katherine screwed up her mouth, reached for a bag of kale. "I really don't want to get involved."

"Were you ever with him? You have to tell me. Katherine, please." I heard my voice tremble.

"God, no, Ellie. I barely know him."

Mal appeared at my side. "What's going on?"

"Katherine knows Lucas," I said. "But she's not telling me anything."

From this close to her face, I could see Katherine's pores. "I've met him before, okay? At an embassy event. With his *wife*," she said.

Mal put an arm around my shoulder. My knees went weak. "I know he's married," I said.

Katherine raised an eyebrow. "Why is he with you if he's married?"

"You don't know anything about our relationship."

"Whatever. It's weird that you're with him. He's, like, old. And his wife is a famous economist. She was honored by the embassy for her work on microfinance loans. We gave her an award in April. There was a big gala—salmon with hollandaise, chocolate lava cake, the works. I sat next to them at dinner. I talked to her for like an hour."

"He's not old," I said.

"He has that droopy cheek skin of someone in their forties."

"He's thirty-nine!"

I knew all this wasn't the real point. The refrigerator

gaped. No one moved to shut it. Cold air resolved in front of my face in wisps of mist.

"I *liked* her, Ellie. His wife," Katherine said.

"Should we take a beat here?" Mal said. "Maybe sit down and talk about this?"

"Mal, can you stop being everyone's therapist for one second," Katherine said.

"I'm not leaving until Katherine apologizes to me," I told Mal.

"Apologize to you for what? Talking about microfinance with your boyfriend's wife?" Katherine tossed the kale back into the refrigerator.

"You're judging me! And you're supposed to be my friend!"

"Oh, now I'm judging you? Five seconds ago it was Lucas I was judging. You don't even know what you're saying. I'm actually trying to protect you. Believe me, this isn't going to end well for you. He's being dishonest and you're being naïve."

"Katherine, lay off. Her dad died," Mal said.

"That's exactly what I'm saying. She doesn't need another loss right now."

I slammed the refrigerator door and bolted out of the room.

Twelve

I wasn't sure what I was expecting when I googled "Larry M. Taylor" and "Crosskeys, Maryland." Some people used social media as their personal ouroboros of anxiety and distraction; I searched for the mystery man to whom my father gifted a baseball. Across the city, Lucas was at home with his wife, who Katherine thought was cool. If only Katherine hadn't seen us on the stoop at that exact moment, with her kale body and her hornet's nest judgment. I never wanted to see her again.

My first search result was a page for the Maryland Birders' Association. A thumbnail photo showed a man in profile, holding up a pair of binoculars. I zoomed in to see if this was the same Larry, the handsome face, the strong jaw, but instead of getting larger, the photo pixelated. "Larry Marcus Taylor has been an Osprey Watch volunteer for twenty-four years. He tracks threats to the osprey population nesting in and around the Chesapeake Bay, including exposure to pesticides, algal blooms, and other impacts of climate change." At the bottom of the page was a different contact email: larry@marylandbirders.org.

Maybe I could work on my environmental reporting and find Larry at the same time. I opened my dump email, the account I used to sign up for discounts so I wouldn't get spam in my real inbox. Every young person I knew had an account like this. No one from my parents' generation did. When I'd tried to set one up for my father the previous year, he'd asked for the address iwillneverusethis@gmail.com.

The email I sent to larry@marylandbirders.org was brief. I wrote that I was a freelance reporter working on environmental stories and currently reporting an article about the plight of osprey in the Chesapeake Bay. I was hoping to accompany him on one of his bird-watching expeditions for the Osprey Watch project. I didn't mention *Apogee* or anything that could identify me. I signed the email Alice Levy, using my grandmother's maiden name. Who was Alice Levy? Not Lucas's lover, his guilty pleasure. Not my father's daughter. No resident of 1938 House with its windowsill dust and globs of toothpaste in the sink. Just an environmental reporter searching for a story.

It's what would make me a good journalist, I thought—an uncompromising nose for the truth. If Larry was going to refuse to meet me, I would find another way.

That was how I found myself traveling east. Jane had signed off on my osprey-reporting trip. Larry had responded that he would be happy to show me around, his email appreciative that a reporter wanted to write about the Chesapeake Bay osprey. I was pretty sure he was L. M. Taylor, because in both of his emails—the one to me and the one to Alice Levy—he'd used Baskerville, which seemed retro, eighties, the kind of font my mother would use unironically.

I'd researched statistics about the Chesapeake Bay, how as the largest estuary in the country it was a harbinger of the effects of climate change on the nation's waterways. The bay was in terrible shape. Environmental scientists at the University of Maryland had given it a grade of D+ the previous year. When I'd mentioned this to Mal the night before, over our sheet pan of "weeknight nachos," she'd said, "If the Chesapeake Bay were a white kid, it still would have gotten into college."

An effort to save the Chesapeake Bay had been ongoing since I was a child spending weekends at Dad and Barbara's. There were years when the water was broccoli-green, choked with algae; years of angry environmentalists on the radio talking about the twin devastations of industrial agriculture and rampant construction that flooded the tender soil with excess phosphorus runoff. I remember being told by my dad and my friends' parents that we couldn't swim because of enterococci bacteria in the water. Language that confused and inflamed us, since the water was just as squishy and muddy as it always was, rippling in the sun, and couldn't we see with our own eyes that there was nothing wrong with it, nothing wrong at all? The trouble was no one could see this stuff. Runoff. It was so dull-sounding. Invisible chemicals leaching into the groundwater, poisoning the wildlife, causing thousands of fish to die at once, bobbing to the surface like smelly bits of confetti.

There was an image in my head that I conjured while

driving—the two of us, Dad and me, on the dock at the marina, a pile of rocks between us. The horizon was pink and blue, evening colors, and boats strained at their pilings. Someone at the marina had the radio on, commercials and pop songs offered up to the air. In my memory my father was wearing a child in a sling and couldn't bend over, so I picked up the stones we'd collected for both of us. I didn't remember which child it was who slept against his heart. We skipped our stones into the water, breaking the bay's twilight skin, trying to force the fish back down where they belonged.

Google Maps suggested that I had arrived. I'd bought Adrian a little plastic blue crab with articulated claws as a thank-you present for letting me use his car, and he'd liked it so much he hung it from his rearview mirror. Now I studied larry@marylandbirders.org through the blue crab's impressive claw span.

Larry came down the porch steps alone, pausing in front of a bed of flowers hemmed in by large gray stones. His dark hair was cut short, no longer loose and freewheeling as it had been in the yearbook photo. Glasses stuck out of the breast pocket of a polo shirt. Around his wrist was a bright-yellow Livestrong band, which I hadn't seen on anyone since circa 2009.

I swung open the car door, the heat blew in, and then I was standing face-to-face with the man to whom my father had left his most important possession. He had a beautifully articulated jaw, the features of a minor movie star, but his head was angled down, suggesting shyness or perhaps an old-fashioned courtesy. With most men, I could tell from their eyes whether I was a woman to them or a daughter. But Larry's face was unreadable to me. I was startled into silence. Larry held out his hand. "Larry Taylor. You're . . . the writer?"

"Uh, yeah. Hi, I'm Alice." I liked that he'd said *writer* and not *journalist*.

Larry tucked his hands under his armpits, looked down at his clean white sneakers. "Alice, how does this work?"

I was careful to talk only about birding and climate change, how with my article I hoped to raise awareness. *Raising awareness* was a tired term—it seemed to be a favorite in D.C.—but it was well-meaning and undefinable. It seemed to put Larry a little at ease.

Squinting at the sky, he said, "Looks like it might storm. But we'll see some birds before the rain. Hop in." He motioned to his truck.

There was a bottle of water in my bag, and to give myself something to do, I took it out and chugged it down. As Larry navigated the back roads, water sloshed in my stomach and hot gravel struck the undercarriage in sharp bursts. I drew a few unsteady breaths. "Have you lived here long?" I asked him.

"About seven years on this street."

"It's not so far from Washington, but it couldn't be more different around here," I said, but that remark did not lead to further conversation—Larry merely inclined his head in what might have been agreement or opposition. In D.C., reporters were used to talking to people who'd spent their lives talking to reporters. Larry was not one of these people.

The sky had darkened, clarified. We turned on to another road and I smelled the bay, sweeping over the scrubby trees.

"Did you grow up around here?" I tried again.

"Not far. Different county. Did you bring waders, Alice?"

"No. But I brought my inappropriate city footwear and soft hands."

He smiled charitably as we parked in front of a many-winged house made of glass. A rich person's house, elegant and modern.

"So this is your summer home?" I was trying to tease him lightly, establish a rapport.

"Not on my salary. It belongs to the head of the Chesa-peake Bay Task Force. He lets me come check the osprey plat-forms in the back. And the osprey cam."

Osprey cam, I scrawled in my notebook, wondering if Larry knew that sounded like a seabird sex tape.

He pulled rubber waders over his sneakers, and we went around the side of the house to the back lawn. Through a glass wall I caught sight of a gleaming grand piano and a white leather sofa. The lawn connected with the river over a field that turned to marsh grass near the water's edge. On the other side of the narrow river inlet was a small island. There were seven osprey nests spread out over this island, built on wooden platforms that sat atop tall, skinny poles. "We build those nesting platforms so the osprey chicks are protected from rats," he explained.

"Because a rat can't shinny up those poles?"

"Correct."

"I bet a D.C. rat could."

"We've seen raccoons try. But the osprey are fairly pro-tected way up there at the top."

"Osprey skyscrapers," I remarked, and he chuckled under

his breath. So far Larry was quiet and considered, with none of my father's charisma. I didn't understand how they would have been friends, let alone how he would have left this man his baseball.

The water was muddy and cool in the shade of the high marsh grass. Larry put on a dorky khaki hat secured with a strap under his chin; I saw why when the wind picked up and blew my own cap into the water. He waded gallantly into the shallows to retrieve it just as an osprey lifted off a nearby platform.

"There's one!" I cried. The bird rose smoothly, sifting the air with great wings the color of leather on a horse's saddle.

"That's Luna," he said.

Luna was an enormous bird. Her wings were crooked like bent knees as she soared against the sky. She had a hooked beak and a fluffy white underbelly. From high in the air she issued two screeches.

"She's warning us to stay away from her chicks." He pointed downriver. "She was born right over there twenty-four years ago and comes back every year to mate."

"She's my age," I said. I thought immediately how Lucas would love this.

"These birds normally make it to fourteen, maybe fifteen if they're lucky."

"Is she special?" I remembered Lucas saying, *You're not like other people.* I heard my father say, *You bring out the best in me, Ellie.*

Larry explained that the Chesapeake Bay Task Force broadcast a live feed of Luna's nest from a hidden camera.

You could watch Luna groom her mate, feed her chicks, and repair her nest, all in real time. You could see live fish wriggle as they were pecked open, the sharp flashes of bones picked clean, and listen to the high cheeps of her chicks. You could tune in to the osprey nest from your mother's basement or your cubicle. From Washington, D.C. From Sri Lanka. Larry, the volunteer osprey-cam manager, turned it on when Luna arrived with her mate in spring and kept the camera running through when her chicks fledged—left the nest for good—in August. Only when the birds began their long fall migration to South America did the feed go dark.

Luna had no knowledge of any of this. She was an osprey stuck in *The Truman Show.*

Larry snapped his binoculars to his eyes. "She's heading out to do some fishing. See how she's scanning the river? Her chicks are four weeks old, and when they're that young, most female osprey stay in the nest while the males get food."

We watched Luna make wide arcs over the river, looking for the shadows of schooling fish beneath the water.

"But Luna's unusual in that she does more of the hunting than her mate. He does the nest maintenance, and she brings fish for the family."

"A feminist osprey."

Larry glanced at me. "I wouldn't go that far. Nature is dividing its behaviors according to ability. Here she comes." He pressed his binoculars back to his eyes, and I did the same with his extra pair.

Luna was coming up from the river, holding a silvery fish in her gnarled talons. The fish's tail was deeply forked, and it shivered and thrashed, its black eyes open, as it took its final forced swim through the gray air. Luna landed on the edge of the platform, folded her wings, and dropped the fish into the nest.

My notebook was filling up with lots of colorful osprey factoids, but as Jane said, if I wanted readers to learn about the environment, I had to bury facts in a riveting story about an unforgettable person: "the human face of climate change." How was I going to write a profile of this man? He was not forthcoming. Or he was shy. I knew it was wrong to conflate the two. Someone had written a whole book about introverts, about how they seemed to vibrate at a lower frequency than extroverts. There was the example of introverts recharging alone, but sometimes it seemed to me to be disguised pride or wanting to hold the best of themselves in reserve until they felt safe—when I thought about it, like Lucas or me. I didn't know which it was with Larry. Had high school Larry been the cautious, considered introvert to my father's defiant, self-confident extrovert? I had been that cautious, considered introvert to my father too.

Larry suggested we cross the channel to the island to get a closer look at Luna's nest. He dragged a small rowboat into the water and paddled us the short distance across. On the opposite bank, he swung out of the boat with ease and moved briskly over the marsh. When he saw that I lagged, stepping unevenly in my city boots, he paused until I caught up, looking out at the chop on the river, one hand on his hip. I knew I was lying to this kind man. He was thoughtful and measured,

so why had his email about my father been clipped and dis-
missive? What had made him refuse to see me? What was he
thinking? Automatically I thought of one of my father's favorite passages from Eliot's *The Waste Land: What are you
thinking of? What thinking? What? I never know what you
are thinking. Think.*

Larry unfolded a rusty ladder and pressed it against the
platform where Luna's nest perched high above. He climbed
up quickly, and at the top he wiped the lens and checked the
camera, which was protected from the elements by a plastic
sheath. Two kayakers moved steadily along the far side of the
river. Clouds puckered and light rain pecked holes into the
sand. Overhead, Luna and her mate were circling the nest,
screeching warning calls.

"The chicks aren't cheeping anymore," Larry called down.
"They're listening to their parents. There's the remains of a
meal here. Looks recent. A menhaden."

"Men hating?"

"Menhaden," he said from above. "It's a type of forage
fish. Packed with omega-3s. Osprey love it."

He pulled something out of the nest and tossed it to the
ground a few feet from where I stood. It landed in a patch of
sand, a jumble of blood-slick bones. Its meat and eyes had
been plucked out and only the gristle and fin remained.

The sky was soon white. The river paled and the kayakers
were swallowed in mist. Everything lost its contrast, one
thing disappearing into another.

"How long have you been involved with the Maryland
Birders' Association?" I called, hoping this might reveal an
interesting story or anecdote. I noted with some amusement

that the organization's acronym was MBA. I shifted my arm, pimply from the cold rain. Nature was indifferent; people weren't.

"It's been almost twenty-five years now," he yelled down. "I've been president for seven."

"And you're a volunteer? So I imagine you have a day job?"

"I work in banking," Larry said when he reached the ground, which of course I already knew but had to pretend was new information: It was Ellie who knew, not Alice.

"Which bank?"

"I consult for a few."

If Jane was beside me on this muddy bank, she'd know exactly how to get Larry to open up. She was an expert interviewer, somehow putting people at ease by asking curious, nonjudgmental questions that got them to reveal things that surprised everyone, even themselves.

I switched tacks, pressing Larry for a reason the osprey were disappearing, a concrete causal link. "What's going on with them?" I asked.

But he said there wasn't only one thing that was causing the osprey population to decline. The Chesapeake Bay and its tributaries were a complex system, he told me. Pollution from construction and agriculture had overfertilized the bay and the rivers that fed it, causing blooms of algae and fish kills. Larry said that it was taking Luna longer to find fish. "She uses up energy when she circles the river. Sometimes she has to fly many, many miles to feed her chicks."

According to Larry, the island should have been festooned with young osprey testing their wings by this point in the summer. But many of the nest platforms were empty of their sentinels, their fishers and queens. I scanned the vacant sky and then the horizon, the vague shapes of buildings and houses across the water. Overfishing and rising water temperatures were tightening a slow noose around the osprey population, he said. Some years were better than others for pollution and fish availability, but the overall trend in the Chesapeake Bay was toward what Larry called a "climate-change-related catastrophe." That was good, and quotable. I made a note on rain-splattered paper. Bad for the earth, good for the story.

When the mist cleared, Larry went to check on a nesting pair on the other side of the island, a male bird he seemed fond of called "Wegman." I didn't know why Luna got a pretty name and Wegman got a name reminiscent of a grocery chain, but I didn't say anything. I sank down in the sharp grass. To watch Luna fish was a beautiful thing. She'd glide down as though on a slide in the air, flap her great wings just above the surface of the water, swivel her talons in front of her body, startle the fish between them. As she lifted out of the water, the caught fish was iridescent, gleaming. She used her talons—thick and curved like commas—to position the fish until its head faced forward rather than sideways, an aerodynamic arrangement to conserve her energy as she soared into the sky.

As I observed her, everything felt far away—Lucas, his wife, my roommates, Colette, my sisters, Van. My father. I'd spent weeks wishing my grief could be lifted off me. Now I thought that maybe my grief was showing me the ordinary pleasure of nature, the beauty of watching an osprey dive into the water and surface with a fish. My relationships with other people felt fraught and strained; observing Luna was pure. I watched her for a long time, until there was a sort of melting in my stomach, and I saw that though my father was gone, this bird was alive, this bird beat its wings on through time.

Through my borrowed binoculars, I saw her lift her wings and fly once around her nest in a low circle. She veered east, rising higher. My breath caught at the sight of her. She floated through the air like a toy plane, all sharp line and tilt. And then there was a convergence of elements so sudden and seamless, it felt as though it had been choreographed. I heard the drone of a lawnmower from across the water, and I scanned the far side of the river but saw nothing except a thick stand of trees and a drafty-looking gray house. When I looked back, Luna had curved again in the air, as though returning to her nest. There was a shift in the quality of light, a gray cloud batted up against the horizon; through it, the sun shone fiercely in streaks of orange and gold. A goose honked from somewhere close by, a single, plangent note that hung low over the river. As if in response to all these elements, Luna wavered, pausing flightless in the air. For a single vertiginous moment, she was performing a magic trick for me, showing off her ability to hover in one spot without flapping her wings. I laughed, delighted. I felt she was communing with me, showing off, but my laughter morphed into a gasp as I saw that Luna was falling.

Osprey don't just fall from the sky, but that's what Luna did—folded her wings and plummeted, letting the wind take her, beak over tail, into the black river. Where she fell, the water pocked and leveled, and then she was gone. I waited breathlessly for her to resurface. One second stretched to two. When I finally did run back across the island in my black boots, ignoring the scratch of beach grass against my bare legs, I didn't know how much time had passed.

"Larry," I screamed.

"Alice?" he called. "What's wrong?"

I winced to hear him use the name I'd invented. As I ran toward him, I told him in a mess of words what had happened to Luna.

"We have to get her." He lunged toward the rowboat. "Where'd she go?"

He slapped an oar into the water, drawing a brown stream along the paddle and then releasing it. I sat on a stack of musty life preservers and held on as the boat lurched into the inlet. It was a short ride across to a landing where part of the bank had eroded and a young tree, felled in a storm, stuck out perpendicularly from a sandy promontory. "Here," I said.

"Don't let the boat drift." Larry leapt over the side in a single motion.

Something inside me compacted neatly, like a heel pressing a lit cigarette. This feeling resolved into the image of my father on the floor, hair at his temples mussed at odd angles, like when he ran his fingers through it after exertion. I hadn't seen his body, so the little grotesqueries were my own: the blue-gray tint of his skin, the lips chapped, and inside them a blood-red tongue. By the time I'd gotten to the house, paramedics had already taken him away. Colette and I had stood in the bedroom near the spot where he'd fallen. I asked about going to the morgue to see his body. The sun shifted and lit up the carpet; Colette moved into the shade. She said no, I probably didn't want to see him. "He'll be cold," she said. "But I'll go with you if you need to go."

I didn't go. This was before the funeral, before I learned about the will, when my grief was pure and simple. Now I longed to return to that time, when my father's love for me was sure.

There were three quick knocks on the side of the boat, as though a giant fish were thrashing its tail against the side. "Larry?" I cried into the muddy water.

He came up spluttering, holding in one hand what looked like a soggy brown ball. When he dropped it over the side of the boat, it released a fishy whiff of air.

"Are you okay?"

Larry heaved himself into the boat, and my words were lost in the rush of water that poured from his shoulders. He rubbed his fingers in his ears.

"Oh, Luna," he said, gazing down at her. I wondered if he was crying. But within a few moments he had returned to brusque efficiency, wrapping Luna in a towel and treating her body like a body. It was only then that I understood: He wasn't going to save her; he was going to *recover* her. Even now he was telling me about the biologists at the University of Maryland who could look in her stomach to see what she'd eaten and whether that had been fatal. They would autopsy her to assess her fitness. She could provide clues about the ecology and health of the bay. "In death, she can be useful," he said.

I leaned down to feel the stiff ridge of her wing, folded and unmoving. Larry's calm detachment cracked open my grief. At my feet was a dead animal, her life snuffed suddenly out. And for what? Why had my father died? The boat rocked, a spray of river water coated my neck, tears slid from my eyes. I pressed my cheek into her feathers, as though it were my father's body I was embracing, my tears mixing with the oily sheen on her feathers.

When I sat up, Larry was staring at me. "I have something to tell you," I said.

At his house, Larry pulled into the driveway and cut the engine. I'd told him everything, and we'd driven back in complete silence, anger radiating off him like steam. Through the cracked windows came the smell of exhaust mixed with the pale, fresh rain. Two teenagers were walking down Larry's street, wet hair stringy against their faces. Luna, behind us, was a lumpy shape underneath the towel. If her wings were spread, she would be too wide for the back seat. Curled as she was, we'd made her small. Long minutes passed, while Larry's silent discomfort spread across the space.

"Why were you dishonest?" he said finally. The wind picked up and one of the teenagers turned her back; the wind billowed her wet dress and then blew it back against her skin.

"I wasn't totally. It's true that I'm a reporter. I *am* working on a story about osprey."

Larry flinched.

"But, yeah, I'm working on it because of you. I didn't tell you who I really was. That was wrong. I'm sorry." I fished the baseball out of my purse. "This is what my dad left you in his will."

Larry reached for the ball. Our fingers brushed, and when he took the ball away from me, he was silent for a long time, looking down at it.

"I'm sorry—" I began again. Larry shook his head, but I went on anyway: "When you didn't want to see me, I felt crazy. This baseball was like a talisman to my dad. He never wrote a poem without it. I thought he would leave it to me. I need to know why he left it to you instead."

Larry straightened, deposited the ball into the cup holder next to him. He swung himself out of the car and came around the side to open my door. Wordlessly, he stepped back and waited until I got out. "My husband is waiting for me." His movie-star jaw was clenched.

I stood in the driveway, disoriented, unsure of the direction of the sting, as though I were swimming through a sea of jellyfish.

The garage door rumbled to life. I watched as Larry got back in the car and drove inside, and then from an inner door another man emerged, also wearing a polo shirt, and walked toward him, angling sideways to fit between a lawnmower and a snowblower. I got only a glimpse before the garage door closed.

What was going on? Had my father been gay? It seemed impossible. The wives. The affair with Linda. It was becoming clear that I knew nothing—maybe my father had been married to three women and had a relationship with a man he'd known in high school. Rain pinged off the pavement, leaving a film of grit on my bare legs. What had I done? I had carried out my father's wishes. I gave the baseball away. Back in Adrian's car, I drove too fast, swerving on the wet streets, steeling myself against the pain, the disappointment, the loss of Luna, Lucas and his brilliant wife, Larry with his binoculars on a string.

Thirteen

I went with Colette to the shaman. I thought, why not? I wasn't getting anywhere on my own with understanding my father or figuring out who Larry had been to him. Also, I was worried about Colette. She had been handling all the logistics surrounding his death, a constant reminder of what she'd lost.

Despite the heat in the un-air-conditioned room at Potomac Elementary, the shaman, whose name was Wendy, wore a gray pantsuit and pearl earrings, which gave her the appearance of a functionary at the Federal Trade Commission.

"Welcome to our circle." She addressed the seven of us sitting before her in kid-sized chairs. I raised my hand and asked for Wendy's full name. My plan was to google her, see who she really was. Maybe she was a medium-in-training. Maybe I'd find court filings showing a decidedly unspiritual dispute with her ex-husband. But the shaman didn't take the bait.

"We go by first names here," she said kindly, squinting at my name tag and appearing to register that I had written,

Hello, my name is the Dark One. I thought about crossing out everything I'd written and just leaving *the*. But a smart-ass act is hard to keep up when you are the only one doing it or appreciating it. "First names are how spirits announce themselves when they join our circle," she said. "Sometimes they only use initials."

"Then how will we know if we have the right spirit?" I asked.

Colette squirmed in the chair next to mine. She had begged me to come with her to "the 60-Minute Shaman" and was clearly regretting it.

Wendy said something placating about how she identified ghosts, but I barely listened. I'd asked a question to establish my superiority and then hadn't dignified her response by listening to it. I hated myself. Luna had died. I was fatherless. Baseball-less. Lucas's texts seemed distant. I might as well stop engaging in what my mother called my "smart aleck behavior" and try to help Colette get something out of this.

"Let's begin," Wendy the shaman said.

At Dad's funeral, mourners had bent their heads down in prayer; here, faces were tilted toward the fluorescent lights pulsing on the ceiling. There was a lonely-looking widower, a grandmother in a seashell-colored Ocean City sweatshirt, and an overweight young man holding his hands in front of his stomach. Death did not discriminate, and neither, apparently, did the ability to connect with the dead through a thirty-nine-dollar-an-hour intermediary.

As Wendy's hands batted a rhythm against the legs of her pantsuit, I thought of a game my father had invented called

"Opposites." The only aim was absurdity. *What's the opposite of a lamp?* he'd ask. *Zebra,* I'd say.

The opposite of a violin?

Chocolate milk.

We played it on long car rides, just the two of us. He would initiate and we would switch back and forth, asking and answering. As I got older and went off to college, there weren't as many car trips together, but I'd sometimes get a text before a final exam. *Opposite of a paper shredder?*

"I'm getting a sign from a spirit with an N name. N-A or N-O. This spirit has joined our circle." Wendy gazed into the middle distance, where a shiny blue backpack hung inside a cubby.

What's the opposite of third grade?

Shamanism.

There was a brief silence, while everyone pieced together the initials of various dead people they had known.

The grandmother gasped. "My sister Nancy? Nancy O'Leary?"

"She's talking . . ." Wendy's eyes went unnaturally wide and unblinking, as though the spirit were controlling her tear production. "Nancy is telling me that she wants to apologize to you. She's saying that she never meant to hurt you. She's pointing to the ground—she hurt you on the floor, or the carpet. She's very sorry. She's asking if you understand what she means."

The grandmother tapped her fingers against her cheek. "She may've roughed me up when we were children. She was my older sister. But not for sixty-five years!"

"Perhaps the way she pushed you down is more of a meta-phor. She's gesturing like she really wants you to understand something."

The grandmother sank back in her chair, stumped. "Well, now, let me think on it."

Wendy tried again. "She wants to tell you that she'll come to you as a fox and as— oh, that's unusual. She says she'll come to you when you eat ice cream."

The grandmother gave a loud, delighted laugh. "She ate ice cream every day of her life! That's her, all right."

Wendy, smug, opened her arms again with a flourish. "I'm getting a signal from a J name. Let's see, it's J-O."

"My wife, Joan?" the widower asked. "Joanie?"

"It's a male spirit."

Colette pitched forward. "Could it be J-A? James?"

Wendy the shaman nodded. "He's pointing to his head. He had headaches before he died? Something with his brain."

"He did." Colette nodded. "He had headaches!"

"That's not how he died, though," I said.

"No, of course not, it was his . . ." The shaman put her hand out as if testing the air. "It was his heart, wasn't it." I was beginning to see how this shaman operated. She avoided questions, spoke with a commanding certainty even when she was wrong.

"It was his heart!" Colette's eyes flitted wildly over my face. "It's him, Ellie. He's with us."

"James will come to you in various forms from now on. When you see butterflies or forget-me-nots, that will be him telling you he's present."

Colette reached over and gripped my hand. Tears were making fresh tracks down her cheeks. "So he's okay, where he is?"

"More than okay. He wants you to know that he's at peace. He has no regrets."

"Oh!" Colette clapped a hand over her mouth. "I'm so happy. Oh, Jim, honey. You're here with us."

"No regrets?" I pressed.

"He has wonderful memories of his family. He doesn't want you to suffer."

"He doesn't want me to *suffer*?"

The shaman looked in my direction. Her eyes were cloudy, unfocused. "Your father is standing behind you," she said.

I whirled around. On the opposite wall, student assignments about the Atlantic Ocean ruffled in the breeze from a fan.

"If he's really here, I want to talk to him," I said.

"He's a presence, not a person. More like an essence."

"Dad, who is Larry Taylor to you?" I directed this question toward an essay entitled "Tides Are Controlled by the Moon."

The shaman cleared her throat in a way that suggested this was not going to go well for me.

"Why did you leave Larry your baseball?" I asked. "Why did I get the, um"—I lowered my voice—"tie rack?"

For the first time, I wondered if it had something to do with Lucas. *Not that Lucas character,* my father had said in the car on Summer Thanksgiving. Could a man who had himself been married three times and had an affair with Linda be this harsh in his judgment about his eldest daughter dating an older, married man? *I don't want you to get hurt,* he'd said. Why had I even told him?

When my father was alive, I'd never whined at him. I'd been careful to reflect only how he treated me, a peer worthy of his confidences. Now I let loose. He wasn't really there, so I could say anything. "What were you thinking? It isn't fair," I said. Aside from ordinary grief, there was the twisted pain of feeling insulted, punished. "If I did something wrong, why didn't you talk to me about it? Why was there this posthumous betrayal?" I asked. How hurtful it was, at the reading of the will, when Colette had flipped the page over and told me about the tie rack. I felt like all the blood had drained out of my face and whooshed down to my feet.

I imagined my father hovering against the bulletin board, in front of the student handwriting marooned there on lined paper.

"Do you love me?" I listened to myself say the words, the quiet desperation in my voice. I heard them without understanding their meaning. A tender cord was pumping in my throat. It was enough now, I saw that. Hunching over in my seat, I avoided the eyes on the baffled faces of the believers. A spurned relative complains about an under-inheritance. It was an old story. Biblical.

What is the opposite of love?

A glow-in-the-dark gingerbread-man tie rack.

A hand landed on my shoulder. Close up, Wendy looked older. The makeup on her face had been caked on unevenly; yellow streaks were melting on her chin. Lines fanned her eyes. When she spoke again, she whispered, "Ask your mother. Your mother will help you answer your questions."

"She's not my mother." I pointed to Colette, who was staring at me with an uneasy, troubled expression. I knew I had embarrassed her. And myself. And maybe frightened us both.

"Also, he wants you to know"—Wendy cocked her head, listening—"that he loves you." She said this as though it was the most obvious love in the world, the love of a father for his child.

Colette and I had dropped Van off at the National Mall before we went to get shamaned. Van had wanted to do the tourist thing while he was here in D.C., and Mal had offered to take him. The mall was packed with summer visitors holding little American flags on sticks. Rivers of people streamed around us in sensible shoes. It had been many minutes since either Colette or I had spoken, and as we walked I felt the silence build walls around us, until I couldn't figure out how to apologize for what had happened or whether I should.

The pebbly path we traversed was wide and grand, the color of Katherine's blond hair. I thought again of the bitterness I was harboring toward her, for exposing Lucas, the reality of his wife and marriage. Because of her, I didn't know where I stood with him. We'd gone away overnight for the first time, we were halfway up Gumdrop Mountain, and Katherine had cast us back to the Peppermint Forest. She had made me question whether we could ever summit Gumdrop Mountain at all.

"Ellie, I didn't know how upset you were about the tie rack," Colette was saying now. "He did love you, you know. It was obvious that he did. Very much."

This was the most intimate Colette and I had ever been with each other; I was grateful to her, even if I didn't quite believe her. "I'm sorry," I said. "I feel embarrassed about what happened with the shaman. It's just that Dad would have known the tie rack would make me feel terrible. He knew me so well. He'd understand exactly what it would do to me. He'd know I'd want the baseball."

"Are you angry?" Colette asked.

"No." Yes.

"You sure?"

"No."

We looked out over the plain of marble, searching for Van and Mal. "You're allowed to be angry," she said after a moment. "But it's not me you're angry at. Or Wendy. It's your father."

Colette could surprise me. She had some substance beneath those herbal remedies. I suppose I'd known this, but I'd been so focused on my father when he was alive that I hadn't spent much time thinking about her. We drew up beside the reflecting pool, where a shadow image of the Washington Monument fizzed in the water. "This is a weird question," I said, "and I don't want you to take it the wrong way, but is there any chance Dad was gay?" I must have spoken loudly, because a woman in a GW T-shirt glanced at us as she jogged past.

"Of course not. Why? Is the tie rack a gay symbol?"

I laughed. "No. But Larry Taylor is gay. L. M. Taylor from the will."

Colette's smile had a hint of pleasure in it, as though she was recalling a private moment between them. "Trust me.

I'm positive your father wasn't gay. Though it's weird your dad never mentioned this guy. But I wouldn't worry so much about it, Ellie. Oh, there they are," she said, waving happily.

When I followed her gaze, I saw my father. The breath I inhaled was so sharp it hurt. I catapulted forward. It was *Van*. Van, walking toward us with a slight hitch in his left leg, confident and reflective, his arms swinging powerfully at his sides. Van was doing my father's walk.

"Is he doing it on purpose?" I asked Colette.

"Doing what?"

"Imitating Dad."

I watched my half-brother interpret our father in a wordless language. So he had inherited some of our father's magnetism. I wondered what else of my father's Van had received.

What were you thinking? I'd asked my father's ghost in the elementary school classroom. I'd wanted to ask Larry the same thing. *What are you thinking?* I'd wondered when Lucas kissed me greedily on the bench by the tidal basin in November, a few yards from where I was currently sitting. With a start I realized it wasn't *What are you thinking?* It was *What are you thinking about me?* Men didn't have to explain themselves the way women did. Women were always having to bring men out, to get them to talk, to explain, to emote. Always wondering where they stood and figuring out how to get the answer.

Mal and Van joined us on the grass. From her backpack, Colette produced a sleeve of Fig Newtons and handed it to Van, who unwrapped it, stuffed a few in his mouth, and passed the package around. He gazed out at the reflecting pool with his bright, watchful eyes. Mal took a sip from the iced coffee I'd brought her. I put my hand on her shin, which was stretched out next to me.

Van tapped my shoulder and signed something, his mouth still full of crumbles. "Ellie, how tall would Lincoln be if he stood up?" Colette translated.

I turned to look up at Lincoln in his great marble catacomb. "I don't know. What do you think? Maybe three stories?" I gazed at Lincoln's stern expression, the judgment in his brow. What was he thinking?

"At least five stories," Van signed.

"This kid's going to be an architect." Mal ruffled Van's hair.

Colette translated Mal's prediction, and Van smiled. "Or maybe I'll be in construction and I'll earn a buttload of money and Mom will never have to work again," he signed.

It took Colette a moment to translate. "A buttload?" she said, looking at Van. He grinned. "Don't say buttload," she said.

"A buttload! Right on, little dude," Mal said at the same time. She smiled sheepishly.

Colette rolled her eyes, but I could tell she didn't really care. She was glad Van was enjoying himself. We were lucky to have Mal with us as our family facilitator and all-around good sport. She was a buffer against mourning. We wouldn't talk about Dad when she was around; we were forced to be present in the sunshine, the sweet breeze off the Potomac.

"It would be a cool idea for a movie, actually. *Lincoln Awakens.* If Lincoln stood up, what would he do?" I asked.

Colette signed my question. I was starting to recognize the sign for Lincoln—an L shaped with forefinger and thumb at the side of the forehead.

"He'd go to the new ham-and-sherry bar on R Street," Mal said.

"He'd stomp over to the nearest computer and surf the interwebs," I added.

Van's hands made large swoops and then fell to his lap. "No, he'd help Obama pass a better version of Obamacare," Colette translated.

I giggled despite myself. "That's a nice thought." I reached over and found Van's hand, squeezed it. After a moment he squeezed mine back. Twice. I was newly conscious of how little I could communicate with him without Colette as an intermediary. I had been focused on my father when he was alive, and I hadn't taken the time to get to know Van or to learn his language. Our communication had been purely functional: What do you want to eat? Should we play? Where are the keys? Everything between us as basic as air.

When Colette and Van went to poke around the gift shop, Mal and I took over the Fig Newtons. Mal always looked so cool, I thought. Today she wore a high-waisted blue-checkered dress like Dorothy in *The Wizard of Oz*, though she had doctored hers with her punk elements: a jean vest, black nail polish, thick black eyeliner.

"I saw my father," I told her through the cookies that had coated my mouth in a gluey paste.

"At the shaman workshop?"

"Just now. I thought it was him, but it was Van."

Mal smiled. "He's a good kid, Ellie."

"I know," I said. But I didn't really. Not well enough. I understood that now.

"We never checked in about what happened with Katherine. Are you ever going to make up with her?" she asked.

"I guess, eventually. But I don't want to talk about Katherine," I said. "Hey, can you do something for me?"

"What?"

"I need you to google her. His wife."

"Is that a good idea?"

"No. But if you won't do it, I will. And that would be worse." In the months since Lucas and I had been together, his wife had been a faint and ghostly shape. It had worked best that way. A few times I'd tried to figure out who he was married to, but the internet gave me nothing—no wedding website or shared photo album. But now I knew too much. The details Katherine had given me about the event at the embassy had contoured her. I had put Lucas's wife together piece by piece. High cheekbones in an oval face. Glossy dark hair that fell in waves. European elegance. Her blouses were silk, pleasing colors, maroon, marine blue. She left lipstick traces on teacups. She ate only vegetables and seafood, not because she was watching her weight—she was naturally slim!—but because she cared about the carbon cost of beef. She was soft-spoken, but her opinions were carefully considered. The questions that concerned her were the profound rather than the mundane.

Mal pulled out her phone, thumbed the screen. I watched her face for a reaction.

"Are you on the Moroccan embassy events page?" I asked anxiously. "It was an event in April."

"Okay, it looks like there was a panel honoring economists from the Middle East. Maybe that's it." Mal lifted her bangs away from her face. "Her name is Mina," Mal said.

Mina.

It was a soft name, like marbles rolling around the mouth. A name that came from the back of the throat, a deep place. Ellie was a teeth name.

"Is there a photo?"

Mal hesitated. "Yeah."

"Is she thin?"

"That's your insecurity talking, boo."

"Show me." My voice caught and I reached for her phone. "Wait, actually, don't." I withdrew my hand.

Mal clicked her iPhone off with a snap. "Getting involved with a married man is not exactly a recipe for success. You're going to get hurt. Plus, he's much older."

"Only fifteen years!"

"Fifteen years ago you were nine." She screwed up her mouth and looked around the memorial as if someone among the crowd of tourists could verify my age.

"I've never felt this way about anyone."

"Though your sample size remains small, no?"

"I've dated other people!" I said defensively.

I told myself that Mal didn't understand what it was like to lose a parent. When I had told her what happened, her eyes went wide with shock and she'd said, "Oh, Ellie, I'm so sorry," and I'd cried in her arms, but then when I came home to 1938 House after the funeral, she was acting uncomfortable around me, and shortly after that she was back to normal, as though the world hadn't unmade itself in the split seconds it took for my father's heart to constrict and then fail altogether. How could I expect her to understand that Lucas was the one person around whom I didn't feel pain, only hopefulness? Now that I knew his wife's name, though, it felt different. She was real.

"From what you've told me, Lucas seems nice, and he's hot in that sensitive academic kind of way." Mal sniffed a big, wet, uncomplicated sniff. "But you'll meet other men, lots of them, who are less, you know, married."

"I'm in love with him. I've never been in love before," I said.

"You aren't on equal footing with him. You need to fall in love with someone single. I don't believe there's only one person for any of us." She chewed on the straw of her iced coffee.

"I know he loves me. I don't know why he isn't just choosing me. Maybe I still seem too young to him? I need to give him more time, I guess. He doesn't know me that well yet."

"Ellie, do you want my honest opinion?" Mal put her coffee down and touched my arm. "It's kind of harsh."

"Okay."

"Why are you spending all this time thinking how you should be different, when he's the one cheating on his wife? There's nothing wrong with you, and if he makes you feel like there is—well, that's what I'm worried about. I'm sick of seeing men do shitty things to women and then only the women feel bad about it. It makes no sense, and it happens constantly. And men don't stop that shit just because they're older. I bet you can come up with like a million examples of what I'm talking about. Just think about it for two seconds."

I thought of the looming man and the girl on the train when I was coming back to D.C.; instead of being angry at him, I had excoriated myself for my lack of action. Instead of being mad at my father about the tie rack, I wondered what I had done wrong. And I didn't feel any anger toward Lucas, none at all, only love and hope and despair—

"He has too much power over you," Mal said. "You have to be honest with yourself about what you want. What you *really* want. Protecting men's feelings is like the least feminist thing you can do."

"I thought you were a socialist, not a feminist," I said.

"Lol," she said. "You're hilarious." She paused. "Oh, they're back."

Mal greeted Van fondly, and I watched him light up in her presence.

What is the opposite of Ellie? I'd asked my father once.

A waffle iron, he said.

Maybe we had it wrong about opposites. Two things, however absurd, couldn't be opposites if the mind linked them. True opposites would not even glance off each other in the night. *This is my daughter,* I imagined him introducing me to a colleague of his at Chesapeake College. *She's a waffle iron.*

A swirl of butterflies flew overhead, getting the hell out of town, and Colette threw her head back, her mouth a cavern of longing. The butterflies flapped, spun, danced away. Maybe they were headed to Florida, to clubbed yellow forests and rivers of bilge, armored beasts in the reeds. They'd be welcomed by my mother and Dr. Gettleman. What would the butterflies do when they arrived? Unpack. Take a quick rinse before dinner.

Van scampered up the marble steps toward Lincoln, his hair full of the sun's gold. No longer walking like our father.

Fourteen

It wasn't difficult to get my father's lawyer, Fredrick-the-Rapacious, on the phone. I had to find out if my father had been trying to punish me with the will, and so I peppered the lawyer with questions. He did not seem to understand that I was on a mission. He answered my questions as if he were simultaneously reading his email.

He confirmed the gifts—my father had intended for me to get the tie rack. The baseball was to go to L. M. Taylor.

"And when did he draw it up? The will?"

"Looks like February eleventh, 2006."

"No revisions since then?"

"Zero."

Six years earlier I had been months away from leaving for college. I hadn't known Lucas. I hadn't known anything. So the tie rack wasn't a reaction to his disapproval about Lucas; if it was a punishment, it was in response to something that happened a long time ago and nothing I had done in the intervening years had repaired it.

"Did he mention me at all?" I asked.

Fredrick-the-Rapacious began chewing what sounded like a sandwich. "As I recall it was a quick meeting. He came with his wishes already drawn up"—he swallowed heavily—"and I filed the paperwork."

Then he volunteered that I could sue my father's "estate," and he threw in a few complicated Latinate legal phrases, including something called *quantum meruit*.

"Thank you, but I won't be suing my family." I scrawled *quantum meruit* in my notebook.

"I couldn't represent you, because your father's estate is my current client." Through the phone I heard the squeal of a foil bag being opened.

"This isn't about money. I just wanted to ask if you knew anything about how he came up with his wishes."

"I caution my clients not to use their wills as weapons. But it happens sometimes that beneficiaries are unhappy, even if the deceased had the best of intentions."

"Is that what you think in this case? That my dad used his will as a weapon?"

"I'm speaking generally."

"But how was he when you saw him? Did he seem upset?"

"Not that I recall. But this was many years ago."

"Okay. If anything else occurs to you, please let me know."

"Sorry for your loss," he said, chewing again. "Your dad was a nice guy."

"Fredrick? Do most people leave wills with specific objects? Like specifying which objects should go to which people?"

"Some do, some don't. If they don't, it can cause a lot of

fighting. And then there are the people who die without wills. That's no picnic, lemme tell you. Opens you up to all kinds of flimflam."

What is quantum meruit? I asked the internet when we got off the phone. And the internet replied: *As much as one deserves.*

Jane Ostrawicz-Jones was on the phone in her glass office. Without pausing her conversation, she tucked the receiver against her shoulder, pointed at me, and flapped her arms like a bird. I flashed her a thumbs-up.

Monday morning. Outside, it drizzled. Inside, I punched a sentence about osprey into my laptop. Steve was at his workstation in Quality Control, looking smug. He had the air of a twenty-five-year-old who'd been told that he was going to save the industry he'd been working in for just four years—and that was if you counted the competently-reported-but-uncompensated articles published under his byline for the *Yale Daily News.*

Fox News was playing on the TV screen closest to where I sat—every man appeared assembled out of hair mousse, every woman seemed cloned from Megyn Kelly. It would have been a good line, but I wasn't allowed to write hot-take hit pieces about Fox—that was reserved for Steve Glanz and his ilk. The other reporters and I were arranged at the Conveyor Belt, and though we sat on reclaimed wood and ate company-sponsored organic popcorn, we were expected to generate six posts a day, a frantic, unrelenting pace. We typed, we snacked, we leaned back in our chairs. We thought we had a future in journalism.

I glanced over at Steve. From the look of satisfaction on his face, he must have been penning *Next Web,* his book and magnum opus. Meanwhile, I was writing about a seabird. Every time I thought about Luna, I remembered the look on Larry's face when I told him the truth about why I was there, and a sick feeling flooded my throat. Still, I cared about Luna. I wanted it to be a good piece.

I typed in the link to the osprey cam, and soon the nest filled my screen in real time. From eighteen feet below, as I stood with Larry on the spit of marshy island, the nest had looked like a mess of twigs and dry straw. Now, peering into it, I saw it had been constructed out of ingenious found materials. There was a brittle corn husk being used as batting. A shredded black garbage bag fluttered in the breeze, mirroring the motion of the green river below. I made out the soft paper skin of an ice cream sandwich wrapper pressed into one corner.

Two chicks were huddled together as a breeze ruffled their feathers. The nest was dry; there was no fish skin or slick of blood, nothing to indicate a recent meal. They trembled, their bodies thinner than adult osprey, their feathers mottled rather than pure brown, but with the same distinctive white underbellies and thick black talons.

What had Luna left her chicks?

One ice cream sandwich wrapper.

One black garbage bag.

Underneath the video stream was a message posted at 7:52 A.M.

LARRY TAYLOR We regret to inform our viewers that
Luna died on Friday. We are lucky to have observed her
and the many broods she raised here on our river.
Although we are deeply saddened, we at the Chesapeake
Bay Task Force will continue our important mission to
monitor and protect the osprey population here in the
bay.

Twenty-one responses had already been posted on Larry's
original thread.

BIRDERBOY1949 This is terrible news. My condolences.

MAGPIE447 Wow, I didn't realize I could be this upset
about an osprey!

MR. JOSEPH DAVID AIMES I followed this camera
since it began. My wife of 53 years and I took pride that
Luna had decided to settle here on "our" river. We drove
to see her some weekends until my wife was diagnosed
with cancer. We'll be saying prayers for her and all her
osprey "family."

ED BAKER Was she sick? Watched her this week and she
seemed fine . . .

CHARLIE HUTCHINSON Ed, it is well known that
osprey in the Chesapeake have been in bad shape
because of overfishing of menhaden and other forage
fish. Luna's death is surely related?

Toward the bottom, the tone of the comments changed, all variations on a single theme: Osprey-cam viewers were reporting that they hadn't seen Luna's mate.

GEMINI BIRD LADY Father abandonment much? Men are the worst.

CHESAPEAKE DAVE Not all men are bad!!!

MAGPIE447 He's an animal, not a person. There's no chance these chicks would survive, so he's right to go find another mate. He must propagate the species.

MARY ALICE HOFFSTRA Is there any chance he'll come back

MAGPIE447 I haven't seen him at all today!

GEMINI BIRD LADY Fucking a-hole osprey!

LARRY TAYLOR We have ascertained that Luna's mate has flown due west. In 2010 we tagged him with a satellite band, so we know that his current location is in Edge Creek, where he is likely trying to find a new mate, as there are several unpaired female osprey habitating there.

I kept scrolling. The reactions became dire.

GEMINI BIRD LADY Oh no! What about her chicks?

LUVS ETHEL MERMAN Someone please help those poor little chicks!!!!!@ You can still hear them singing for their parents. But their cheeping is getting fainter.

MARY ALICE HOFFSTRA It's not right. I will be writing to the Chesapeake Bay Task Force in the morning. Getting a petition going now.

SUZIE349 They are dying and NO ONE IS DOING ANYTHING??!

LUVS ETHEL MERMAN There must be a way to help them. I'm naming them Alan so at least they'll be christened as God's creatures before they die.

GEMINI BIRD LADY You want to name both of them Alan?

LUVS ETHEL MERMAN Alan and Abby

ED BAKER I'll be signing petition. Thank you Mary Alice for what you did.

When I looked up from my keyboard, I was at *Apogee* again. The office muttered with keyboards. The world moved. Appearing on my screen, by the dozen, were comments being typed in real time. I was astonished at how many people knew about the osprey cam and cared deeply enough to comment in a public forum. I clicked on a few of their profiles;

they looked like residents of my father's town, middle-aged, middle-class, white. Backyard birders, maybe. Powerboat owners.

Rain announced itself on the window, under which young professionals of Washington tweeted their fleeting thoughts. Across the bay, on camera, Luna's chicks were being lashed by the same rain.

BARB.WEBSTER Those chicks don't deserve to die!!

Somewhere north of my heart, south of my neck, my skin prickled. *Quantum meruit:* as much as one deserves.

How much does one deserve?

Fifteen

Lucas glanced down the street as he let me into his house. "Neighbors," he said. He brushed his fingertips against my temple, and the backs of my knees tingled.

"You always find new spots," I said.

"New spots?"

"That I didn't know could be erotic."

He moved to kiss me, but I held back. I was standing in the foyer of his home; Lucas had called to say that he had the house to himself for July Fourth weekend. Would I come over? I hoped he was sending me a message that he wanted our relationship to be deeper and more intimate. He wanted me to see how he lived.

"I'd like a tour," I said. I kicked off my boots, abandoning them by the door, where anyone coming in would see that someone was here. He had a real, adult house—no clutter of roommates or inherited grime, no water stains flourishing on the ceiling. Things were artfully designed: the brown leather sofa with a brightly colored throw; the stainless-steel frying pans on pegs above the sink. A palm frond arched from its pot like the arm of a ballet dancer.

As I followed him through the rooms, I kept imagining Mina. Here she was opening her mail at the table in the hall, her purse draped over her arm; there she stood at the bathroom sink, squeezing toothpaste from the tube. Had she chosen the brass candlesticks on the counter, or had she and Lucas shopped for them together? Everything that was his was also hers; this was the house where they had created a life.

I followed him uneasily up the dark steps. No light came from the second floor, and as we climbed higher, I had to feel my way in the darkness, pressing against the smooth polished banister. At the top of the stairs, Lucas creaked open a door, clicked a switch, and a panel of brilliant light fell over us.

He sat down on the bed and positioned me so that I was standing between his legs. "I think about you all the time," he said. Over his head I saw the side of the bed where Mina must sleep, the nightstand with a thin silver bracelet on it, a small framed photograph. The question was there, breathing with its own soft lungs. Would he ever leave her?

Lucas laid me back on the pillows, looking at me like he was memorizing my knees, the way they parted, the knobs of my bones. Is that love? I wondered. A centipede crawled along the molding near the window. If I turned my head a few inches, put my nose to the pillow, would I smell her, or had he washed her off the sheets? After I left, would he wash me off? Lucas kissed my ear, the bend of my neck, but the sensations were not registering as they usually did in my core.

"I didn't even ask if you wanted anything. Water? Wine?" he asked.

I nodded, unsure.

"Stay put. I'll be right back."

Under the big window was a green dresser laid with a brush and two combs and a small enamel tray, which held a pair of pearl earrings and two bottles of perfume. I thought of getting up to look at his wife's things, but my body was heavy with confusion. A car passed in the street below, blasting the national anthem, an operatic voice reaching for the highest notes.

Lucas returned with a bottle of wine and two glasses clutched in an X. They clinked together, chiming a note that had many other notes inside it. After he poured, I took one of the glasses and sipped from it, waiting for the tannins to sing in the back of my throat. The bed, soft, not my bed. The man, firm, not my man. The wine, the dresser with the brush and combs. He moved toward me again, and I could see the desire flashing across his face, but I didn't want to have sex anymore.

"Do you need anything?" he asked.

"No," I said. "Just to be here." But that wasn't exactly true. I suddenly wanted to be with him anywhere but here. Lucas put one hand on my stomach. Was this how he and Mina lay together? Companionable, easy with each other's bodies? With other men I had always sucked in my stomach as their eyes swept over my body like searchlights, but I wasn't doing that now. I would let him see me for real. Usually, Lucas looked at me as if I were a plum and he wanted to bite me all over until the juice dripped, sticky, sweet. But now I saw that he'd been distracted by his phone. He had it in his hand and was checking Twitter, looking concerned.

"Aren't you writing an article about osprey?" he asked,

his thumb flicking tweets up and away. "There's a hashtag trending, *Save Alan and Abby*. About osprey. You heard of this?"

It took me a moment to register what he was saying, but when I did my insides dropped like a pin pinging to a wood floor. Luna's chicks—the same birds I was writing about for *Apogee*—were all over Twitter.

Don't let these orphaned osprey chicks die! Sign this petition: bit.ly/savealan&abby

We're up to 3,498 signatures! #savealan&abby

Obsessed with these little chicklets #can'tstopwon'tstop #savealan&abby

Do osprey eat fish? I'll deliver. #fishtakeout #savealan&abby

The chicks were going viral. Many people were retweeting a recent post:

Larry Taylor here, president of the Maryland Birders' Association. There is nothing we can do to save the chicks. They would never learn how to fish without their parents to teach them. As sad as it is, we must let nature take its course.

The responses were coming in faster than I could read them:

Take the camera down and let them die in peace
#savealan #chicklover #survivorstories #savethebirds

Anyone wanna take a trip there tomorrow for a protest?
I'm in Ellendale but willing 2 drive #savealan&abby
#birdcaravan

You call yourself a conservation organization?!
CONSERVE THE CHICKS

I breed parakeets! I can adopt these osprey! #birdmama
#savealan&abby

I brought up the osprey cam on my phone. The livestream
was grainy and pixelated, but the camera angle was familiar,
the air pink and cottony around the nest. I held the phone for
Lucas to see. We peered at the chicks, mushed together, a
blob on my screen. *Alan and Abby.*

"It's nuts. People want the Maryland Birders' Association
to rescue these wild birds," I said. "You can't teach an osprey
to fish, apparently; only a parent bird can do that. So these
chicks wouldn't survive no matter what, but the internet is
losing its mind. This one woman is offering to adopt them
because she has parakeets as house pets and thinks she can
raise wild seabirds."

"Scroll down?" Lucas pointed to the message from Larry.
"It's not great, though, what he said."

"Why? He explained why he can't intervene."

"Not that. He shouldn't be engaging. It'll fan the flames

of the protests, and then his sane voice will get drowned out. A Twitter battle can't be won with facts."

"What is all this Twittering for, if not to take a stand? Especially when there is a clear right or wrong?"

"I love your optimism." He kissed me.

There was that word, *love,* but it was paired with praise for something a child might express, a daughter's naïveté. I defended myself, perhaps too strongly. Being in his house— his wife's bedroom—was making me testy. "Scientists make value judgments," I said. "Like what is their research for? Is it to preserve the osprey? Is it to preserve the osprey for the human enjoyment of them? Maybe if parakeet lady was allowed to save this osprey chick, she'd have a new appreciation for conservation work and donate gobs of money and change people's minds. Maybe one-on-one advocacy is the only way to get anything done. It just seems like environmentally we don't have that kind of time, so why not take a stand on Twitter, even if it means a backlash?"

Lucas put his palm flat on my collarbone. "You're so passionate." He kissed my ear. "You're clever." He kissed my temple. "You're sexy." He kissed my nose.

If I'm all those things, be with me, I thought. Choose me.

I reached for a book from the nightstand and chucked it in the direction of the centipede. It hit the ceiling and fell to the ground. The centipede reversed course away from the windows.

"Do you want me to kill that for you?"

"No." I laid my head on his chest. Lucas's heart two-stepped beneath my ear. Not mine. Not mine. Not mine.

We lay there a long while, until I felt his breathing deepen. For days after my father died, I feared sleep, worrying that in my first waking moments, with the sun streaming through the curtains and the dazzle of children playing in the street, I would forget he was dead and the sudden memory of it would be a plow overturning all the quiet earth that had stilled and grown cool in the night. What if Lucas fell asleep and when he woke, in that first jolt of awareness, he said Mina's name?

"Lucas, wake up. Lucas." I kissed him on the crisp apple of his throat.

He opened his eyes. I could see myself in his pupils. "I'm not sleeping."

"You've met my roommate Katherine before," I said. "At an embassy event. They honored your wife."

His head jerked slightly. In his pupils my reflection got smaller, then I was gone. "They did," he said.

For a moment he looked old to me, or at least older than I thought of him in my mind or my fantasies. That frightened me, and I sat up and leaned against the headboard, instinctively putting distance between us. "When we first met, I tried to figure out who she was, but I couldn't find anything online. Then, because of Katherine, I found out her name and looked her up. Now I can't get her out of my head."

There was a long silence.

"When we're out in the world, I can sort of pretend that we're really together. But being here"—I gestured toward the dresser, the pearls, the combs—"it's hard to ignore that your wife exists."

"I understand," Lucas said.

"Does she know about me?" I focused my gaze on the trees outside the window.

Out of the corner of my eye, I saw him squeeze his eyes shut, shake his head. I'd already known the answer. We hadn't talked about her since the night we first met, our walk by the tidal basin, when he told me he had been married for nine years.

"Do you think you'll ever tell her about me?" My heart was pounding so hard I didn't think I could look at him.

"It's not a good time, Ellie. What she and I have is complicated. You knew I was married when we started this."

I sat back, stung. Of course I had known. What had I wanted him to say? "What does that mean?" I said.

"I don't know. Can't we just enjoy this? Be in the moment?"

"I can't enjoy the moment. This is her house. She's all around us. This situation isn't fair to either of us."

"Or to my wife," Lucas said.

"That's who I meant. It's not fair to her or me."

He exhaled heavily. "No, it's not fair."

"What's she like?"

"Why are you asking that?"

"Is she anything like me?"

"I'm not going to compare you. You're different."

I was ashamed of asking questions with such naked need and hurt that he hadn't reassured me. He must have sensed this, because he reached for my hand.

"I didn't expect to have such strong feelings for you," he said. "When we first started, I didn't know it would happen this way."

I lay down next to him. "Does it bother you that I'm young?" I asked.

He turned to face me. Our noses were inches apart.

"No." He spoke quietly, barely moving his mouth.

"Not at all?"

"I don't think so. My friend said that you might be too young to know what you want."

"You talked to your friend about me?" This was a good sign, I thought. "I don't feel too young."

We moved toward each other. I was light-headed, hushed. He'd mentioned me to a friend. I wanted to close whatever distance I'd put between us, to hide the insecurities I had revealed. But when he kissed me, I thought about the way my lips were connecting with his; when I moved my lips in a trail down his neck, I wondered how many times I had done that already. Did his wife do the same thing? If he was ever going to leave Mina, would I have to outdo her, to fulfill his dreams and fantasies that she could not? I felt competitive with Mina, there in her bed.

Why had he brought me here, where I couldn't help but compare myself to his wife? Was it equally strange for him, to have me here where Mina usually lay? Didn't he feel guilty, keeping all this from her, especially now that it was happening in her house?

Lucas was still kissing me, completely unaware of any of this. I pushed him away.

"Hey," he said, clearly confused. "What's wrong?"

"I don't want to do this."

"Do what? Have sex?"

"Do this." I gestured vaguely. I was seized with the desire

to hurt him, and I knew that he'd interpret what I said as a signal that this was over.

Lucas sat up. "What are you saying?"

"I'm saying I can't be here." I got up from the bed. "I need to figure some stuff out."

"Wait, Ellie." His face dropped, he stood up. "Please don't go. Can we talk about this? I'm sorry." He ran a hand through his hair. "I thought you wanted to be physical. I thought you wanted to lose yourself in it."

I twisted a strand of hair around my finger, hating that I felt better now that I was the one in control. "That's the problem. I don't want to lose myself. I can't be myself here. I feel like an actress playing the role of your mistress." I spat the word *mistress,* like a child uttering a curse. "You're going to have to choose," I said, with more confidence than I felt.

Lucas nodded, his eyes wide. He started to say something and then stopped. My mind skittered with unwanted images. Luna high in the gray air. Crabs burrowing in seagrass, discarding their hard shells. My father's copy of the Springsteen biography, fallen to the floor. Larry's lip twisting in anger. What was I doing? If I forced him to choose right now, he would choose Mina, wouldn't he?

"You're so beautiful," he whispered. "Every part of you."

That could be the opening gambit of a breakup, or it could be the first sentence of the rest of my life. The thought of losing him right then made my throat squeeze. I struggled to swallow. Was this over?

"Wait," I said, panicking. "I'm not asking you to choose this minute."

"Are you—"

"I just mean in general. We need to talk about this, to figure it out. We can't go on like this forever." I had confused
myself by making an ultimatum and then retracting it; I felt
powerful and powerless and undone, and the best I could do
was take myself away. "Sorry," I said. "Give me a minute."

I crept down the stairs. In the kitchen it was cold and still;
a clock ticked the seconds passing. From the refrigerator I
removed a bottle of black-cherry seltzer water and chugged it
straight from the neck. I surveyed the foods that Lucas and
Mina had purchased. There were fancy things with Whole
Foods labels: chicken pâté, smoked mackerel, organic yo-
gurts, three different types of olives in plastic tubs. I took the
olives out of the fridge, set them on the counter.

When I bumped the refrigerator door closed with my hip,
I noticed the magnetic poetry set scrambled across the front.
My fingers moved the words into position, leaping ahead of
my conscious mind, until they spelled out the beginning of
my father's poem.

but if time could kneel

Let Mina find it, I thought. I was on the bow of a ship, a
storm whipping around me, the sky dark with my purpose.
But this feeling was short-lived, flushed with adrenaline. It
was gone by the time I finished sampling the three varieties of
olives. If Mina was going to find out about me, I wanted it to
be because Lucas decided to tell her. Because he chose me. I
scrambled up the magnetic words again, so she wouldn't see.

In the bathroom, I pumped expensive-looking lotion into
my hand and spread it over my legs. It smelled of something

subtle, edible, fig and plum. Sweet and acidic both. In the mirror I looked very young, my cheeks flushed, my hair mussed. I opened the cabinet across from the tub, saw a shelf full of clean folded towels. On top of the stack was a pastel-blue teddy bear. It looked plush, new. Why did they have a bear?

I heard Lucas in the kitchen running the faucet, waiting for me. When I came out, my stomach had soured from the olives. "I have to go home," I told him. This time, I led the way and he followed.

At the door, we kissed. I love you I love you I love you, my mind told him. He was all around me and through me, and I was myself again, my own throbbing need.

At home that night, when I finally fell asleep, I dreamed of my father. We were walking in a leafy green park in spring. I was yelling at him, saying things I'd never said during his life. "Why did you leave me?" I shouted as we passed a playground full of children. "Why did you have so many other kids? Why did you abandon me! Look at me!" Suddenly my father's arm fell off his body. We stared at it in surprise. My body quivered, but I concealed my disgust from him. "You don't need that," I said, trying to reassure him. A few paces later, his leg came off, and he began to hop. "You'll be okay," I said. "I didn't mean to yell at you." A minor organ fell with a splat, shining up at us from the pavement. Step by step he disintegrated, pieces of him coming off onto the path. Still, I walked beside him, until there was nothing left to walk beside.

Sixteen

The next day, my dream and my time in Lucas's home were infecting everything as I biked to my office through the syrupy streets, the air smelling of wilting trees. Young people were picnicking in patchy grass at LeDroit Park, laughing and toasting with plastic cups. Families were out on their stoops, reclining in lawn chairs, reaching into coolers of beer and soft drinks on ice. Toddlers splashed in inflatable wading pools set up on the sidewalk. There was merriment, a prevailing sense of safety and wonder. It was clear that none of these people had just seen their father's spleen fall out of his body. Or walked out of the house the person they were in love with shared with his wife. I cycled tentatively, wary of speeding cars, the uncertainty of my relationship with Lucas burning in my stomach.

At *Apogee,* it was just me. Because I was a newish hire, I was supposed to "cover" the holiday weekend, spend the afternoon at the office in case anything newsworthy happened, while everyone else was outside barbecuing and eating pie. I was relieved to have a reason to be alone at work; I wanted to chase this osprey story, the Larry story. I wanted to have something else to think about, to matter on my own merits. By the time I'd pulled my laptop out of my locker and sat down, my head was clear, and I was ready to work. Jane Ostrawicz-Jones had sent me three emails. *Look at Twitter,* she wrote in the first.

Twitter!!! the second one said.

OSPREY!!!!!!!!!!!!! was the third.

If Jane had stooped to using exclamation points, I was in trouble. I'd gone to bat for this osprey story, and now I had to perform under a spotlight. And I had to prove to Larry that I was worthy of his attention after I'd lied, deluded him, forced my father's baseball into his hands.

On Twitter, I searched #savealan&abby and saw that Larry had engaged with the protesters again, just as Lucas had warned against.

LARRY TAYLOR We're touched that many people are thinking of the Choptank River osprey and chicks. However, we have a responsibility to understand the natural world, and part of that is witnessing even the sad or savage. We won't be taking down the camera.

In response to the protesters' overidentification with the birds, Larry had removed the name he had given Luna more than twenty years before. In death he had taken away their relationship. *The Choptank River osprey and chicks:* I thought of Larry wrapping Luna in a towel, depositing her on the back seat. Ropy strands of seaweed appeared before my eyes, as though I were swimming through briny water.

The #savealan&abby petition was gathering momentum,

with signatures from Illinois and California, Canada and the UK. Memes had been generated from screenshots of the chicks with their pink mouths open, Muppet-like, waiting for phantom morsels of fish. Someone had called the Maryland Birders' Association an "amateurish bunch of sellouts." Larry was accused of being cruel and heartless.

A few days ago I had been writing an obscure story about how pollution and overfishing were causing a decline in the numbers of fish that osprey liked to eat. That version of the story was *yawn*. It had required many layers of explanation. What kinds of fish made up their diet, why did osprey have to search harder for those fish, and how did that decrease their chicks' survival rates and increase their vulnerability? And then there was the basic question of convincing people why they should care about osprey. Why did it matter to have a biologically diverse earth? What if the forage fish died off, and the osprey died off, and a great cascade of extinction spread like a virus, like outrage on social media?

That story, even if focused on a personality—Larry— would probably not have been a big story, read only by those for whom a bird's nest in a quiet corner of the Chesapeake Bay was a fascination, but now I was writing a story about a subject that was trending on Twitter. I realized that if I wanted to, I could blow it up into a *thing,* capitalize on all this attention, and hit the Leaderboard for the very first time.

From deep inside the kitchen came the shriek of an espresso machine, followed by a weak cough that I recognized immediately as Steve's. I wasn't alone after all. I braced myself for the appearance of my boss. Technically, my boss's boss. In every industry there were people on their way up and people on their way down; like some kind of corporate Rota Fortunae, they counterbalanced one another. At *Apogee*, though, everyone was on their way up except for Jane, and as a result there wasn't much to offset the soaring ascent of all those hotheads, Steve the king of them all. Steve hit the board all the time. And a few weeks ago, there was that viral post about the Arkansas congressman hog wrestling. Maybe, just maybe, these orphaned osprey were *my* Arkansas congressman's deviant passion for pigs.

But I didn't want to sensationalize. Jane had specifically asked me to come up with a new way to communicate science to readers. She'd wanted an interesting personality, and I had found her one, except his name was Larry M. Taylor, and he spent his free time in rubber boots, peering through a pair of binoculars, keeping close watch over a seabird.

I started writing. I described the way the river looked as Luna plunged toward it in death—translucent, thin as tracing paper. It wouldn't have taken long for the sea lice to find her as she lay on her side in the channel. The crustaceans would click their way toward her on eight legs, nibble at her eyes. Feathers heavy in the murk.

Luna would have stayed there, I wrote, at the bottom of a channel in the Choptank River, were it not for the president of the Maryland Birders' Association. A man who recovered Luna's body to understand more about the suffering of the Chesapeake Bay osprey. His goal was to keep osprey breeding and nesting in good habitat with abundant fish to eat. Yet he was being villainized on Twitter for a situation he hadn't caused and was simply trying to prevent in the future. The Twitter protest, #savealan&abby, was a story about two orphaned chicks that detracted from the larger story about climate change and overfishing, water pollution and the destabilization of the natural world. It was the more important story by far. It was the one we'd be telling for generations.

I banged out paragraphs, inserting facts about the osprey disappearance, quoting some of the online reaction, focusing on the science. There were plenty of reports to cite. I gave Larry a long comment, using my notes of our conversation. I loved his phrase *witnessing even the sad or savage*. I threw that in the piece. It may have been the boring version of the story of Luna's death, but it was the fact-based, scientifically sound, foolproof way to reach the climate-change people and possibly zero other readers—i.e., the kind of reporting Jane loved. I hoped that it would be like a laser beam of apology directed at Larry. He would read it and, I hoped, be impressed. While Twitter lost its mind, *Apogee* could stand up for truth—and for Larry. Maybe it would even make him soften toward me enough that I could someday learn what happened between him and my father.

"You working on the osprey piece?" Steve said from behind me. Without getting up, he scooted his ergonomic desk chair across the room from Quality Control to the Conveyor Belt until he was seated beside my workstation, his head just below the sloping brass lamp.

"There's kind of a Twitter situation," I said, "so Jane wants to get this up ASAP."

"I saw it. Great stuff. Let's capitalize on it. Emphasize the suffering of those baby birds. That'll get us baseline clicks and we can build from there. Photos, tweets, the works."

"The works," I repeated.

"Keep me posted."

"Got it."

Steve scooted back to his man cave. *Apogee* reporters were two types of young men: the Brooks Brothers types, who could tell you how the junior congressman from Indiana voted on the third rider in the last farm bill, and the carabiners, guys who wore skinny jeans with carabiners of keys dangling out of their back pockets, who when they weren't riding or repairing their bicycles were making frequent, reverential references to John Hersey's *Hiroshima*.

Steve Glanz was a Brooks Brother. He wore loafers, and I'd once heard him talk about his "tailor," as if that service was native to a twenty-something who occasionally went home to his parents' house to do laundry.

An hour later, I uploaded the draft of my article to the "Save for Review" folder, which triggered an automatic email to Jane and Steve that it was ready to be edited. I went into the kitchen to make coffee. Steve poked his head in a few minutes later. "Ellie, this isn't what we talked about."

"What?"

"Your osprey piece."

"It's the direction Jane gave me for 'Rising Tides.' It's mostly a profile of Larry Taylor and his work with the osprey cam. The series is supposed to be teaching readers about climate change."

"But we talked about using the human-interest angle. You

know, the osprey chicks and how their parents abandoned them?"

"Well, they didn't really abandon them. The mother died. The father has a biological imperative to find a new mate."

"Exactly. A cheating osprey. That'll be gangbusters for Web traffic."

"It's not what Jane asked for—"

"Leave Jane to me," Steve said. "By the way, have you read the John McPhee book about shad?"

"Nope." I didn't know what a shad was, but I wasn't going to ask Steve and suffer through his explanation.

"Take a look. It's real long-form journalism. Probably the greatest fish book ever written. He has a style that reminds me of yours, actually."

I tried to look pleased. He was comparing me to a giant in journalism. But I knew I was nothing like John McPhee, which meant Steve was trying to flirt with me. He continued to sit beside me, smiling with anticipation. Oh God. Talking to him was like getting tapped repeatedly on the shoulder by an octopus with one wet tentacle.

"I noticed you were on ErosAble," he said. "Word around the office was that you were seeing someone."

"Uh-huh." I couldn't believe I was having this conversation, that my boss's boss was crossing this line with me. There was nowhere to hide from Steve; I didn't want to offend him, and I didn't have an office to escape into, and even if I did, it would be made of glass.

"Hey, if you ever want to talk about it at all, let me know," he said.

"I'm not really sure that's office-appropriate."

He watched me thoughtfully. "What we're trying to do here is really revolutionize the whole concept of 'office.'"

"Right."

"Well, I should get going. I'm headed to a party at Maureen Dowd's." Steve tried to say this with nonchalance, but it was clear that I had to make noises that suggested how impressed I was.

"Ahhhmn!" I arranged my face into an expression of delight.

"Don't pull an all-nighter. Bad for the skin," he said. The glass doors swooshed open and the hallway swallowed him up.

I looked up Jane's home phone number. She answered on the first ring, and I explained the situation. "Leave Steve to me," she said.

Back at 1938 House, Nick and Adrian were playing poker. Adrian clerked for a federal judge who played cards after hours in her chambers. Her weekly Friday-night poker game was the best chance for junior staff to get to know her. Adrian had been through twenty-two years of schooling, summa cum laude from Bowdoin, law degree from some Ivy League, I couldn't remember which one, but he knew nothing about cards. Nick, on the other hand, had no such résumé but had spent his formative years playing Texas Hold'em in his childhood bedroom while his mother leafed through JCPenney catalogs in the next room.

It looked like he and Adrian had been at it for hours, amassing empty IPAs, tossing bottle caps into the cardboard sleeves of six-packs.

"Hard at work, you two?" I said.

"Sort of. We have beer if you want." Nick slid a poker chip from his pile.

"I'm okay, thanks."

"You bluffed, but you one hundred percent should have folded," Nick explained, the two of them with their shirt-sleeves rolled back and their black leather office shoes on, even though it was a weekend, hunched over the poker chips with the somber dignity of two people determining our nation's political future. Which, to some extent, they were.

Sometimes it seemed as if people in their mid-twenties did all the work in D.C. A twenty-five-year-old junior policy wonk would write the position paper that the twenty-five-year-old Hill staffer would read in order to write a policy speech for a congressman that would be covered by a twenty-five-year-old cable-news producer pushing it out into the world in a chyron for a twenty-five-year-old junior reporter to cover in the echo chamber that was D.C. congressional news. Real expertise was often an illusion. And a costly one. Many of Washington's young professionals seemed inflated with self-importance and burdened by ignorance, coming home each night to their group houses. After a few years, they'd burn out and head to graduate school, or into finance or law, skittering across the country and back to the cities and states they came from, feeling clean and pure in the mountain air, mowing the lawns of their suburban ranch homes—their days of moral turpitude behind them.

Some did remain, like Lucas, into their thirties and forties. Like Mina, his wife. Like Jane. Building entire careers around

the singularity of the federal government, or the fourth estate, or the consulting class that catered to both. Would I be
one of the ones who stayed?

Mal was holding court in the living room. From behind
the closed door I heard the oratory of someone in her Marx-
ist study group. I did not have the fortitude at the moment to
engage with a bunch of people who called one another "comrade."

My phone pinged—Jane telling me my article had been
posted on the *Apogee* site. From the look of things, she had
prevailed over Steve; my spirited but factual defense of Larry
Taylor was intact, though she must have compromised on the
headline, which definitely had a whiff of Steve about it: THINK
BIRDS ARE MONOGAMOUS FAMILY MEN? THINK AGAIN. I pulled
up a new email and sent the link with a note to Larry.

> *Dear Larry,*
> *I didn't write this awful headline, but the article is*
> *about why we shouldn't allow a sentimental approach*
> *to a particular wild animal to distract us from the*
> *importance of conservation in the face of climate*
> *change.*
> *Best,*
> *Eleanor Adler*

I read it over and then added another paragraph:

> *I'm sorry about what happened. I deeply regret my*
> *actions and how they must have hurt you. If I can ever*

*do anything to make it up to you, I would welcome
that opportunity.*

I pressed send.

Stories could have such unsatisfying and unlikely out-
comes. More and more, I felt we willingly built entire worlds
on very little information. Like sandcastles, if you poked
them anywhere, the whole structure would revert to its com-
ponents. It was our nature to do that, to fill in the details and
become convinced they were true and not our own fantasies
and imaginations bumping up against someone else's reality.
I thought of all the stories I'd concocted: My father and
Linda. My father and Larry. Larry and me. Lucas and Katherine. Lucas and me.

"You guys want to go to the Rattling Panther? There's live
music tonight." Nick collected the poker chips in a sweep of
his hand.

"I'm beat," I said. "Going to head to bed early." I wanted
to be alone, in the dark cave of my bedroom. Upstairs, I rooted
under the bed for my pajamas. My mother had helped me put
the futon on risers to make space underneath for a plastic bin
of what she called "leisurewear." I imagined myself in Lucas's
house, the handsome chests of drawers and dustless surfaces.
All the above-bed storage! I could have run my hands over the
wood for no purpose other than to feel the grain.

I got into bed and turned off the light. I was jealous—
that's what it was. I checked Twitter to see if the Maryland
Birders' Association had posted a link to my article. *Great
journalism. We are proud to represent the Chesapeake Bay
osprey in the media,* Larry had written before the shortened

link. I retweeted his tweet, feeling enormous relief; maybe Larry wouldn't forgive me, but at least I had done some small, redeeming thing.

Sometime later I woke up, disoriented, to loud thumping through the wall. "Adrian," a woman shrieked, and a headboard banged three times. Charmaine must have come over.

I knew what all my roommates sounded like when they had sex, except for Nick, whose room was on the other side of the bathroom and who never brought anyone home. Nick had been engaged for a few years and was devastated when she left him for a woman; he'd moved out of their shared one-bedroom into 1938 House, where he'd been ever since. The worst was when Katherine had someone over. Katherine, who had no door on her attic bedroom, must have learned to make sex noises from Meg Ryan in *When Harry Met Sally*. It was like every partner she'd ever been with touched her deep in her core. I once heard her scream the word *orgasm*! The next morning I ran into her and Arvind in the kitchen, making smoothies.

Fireworks split the sky. I opened my curtains to watch them. Someone in my neighborhood was still celebrating the Fourth of July. In the intermittent seams of colored light, I ran my hands over my breasts, touching the places Lucas had touched. On my dresser was the necklace he'd given me. He loves my optimism, I thought. He doesn't want to lose me. The fireworks broke, scattering bursts of yellow and pink across my skin. "I'm coming," said the woman through the wall. The headboard banged: one, two, three, four. I imagined Lucas touching himself, groaning, thinking of the sex we had. "Oh, Ellie," he moaned, and then his words were in my mouth, and I was him, lying in my wife's bed and thinking of my young lover, her body a wet gash into which I'd spill my seed.

The next day, I was still tired. I took a long nap in the afternoon, waking past three. Steve called as I was poking around the fridge, trying to figure out what my stomach wanted. I greeted him chirpily to cover up my sleep voice. I hated when the very first words out of my mouth after waking up were to my superiors.

"Hey, so you've seen the protests?" Steve asked.

"What protests?" I pictured a revival of Occupy D.C., imagined myself at McPherson Square surrounded by radical young people, notebook in hand, reporting on a real movement.

"The osprey protests," Steve said.

"Oh." A flicker of unease passed through me.

"You have to get out there and write this up. This story is getting bigger by the minute."

"Actual, real live people are protesting over two osprey chicks?"

"There's videos of them carrying signs on Twitter. And they have some kind of chant? I'll text you the link. There's apparently a whole busload of people coming in from the Midwest."

"Okay. Yes. I'll go right away." I wondered about Larry, what he was thinking about all of this, though I was pretty sure I knew. He had earnestly tried to explain himself online, and now I imagined he was going to earnestly explain himself to a bunch of bright-cheeked zealots who had just taken an eleven-hour bus ride from the Midwest with Magic Markers and oaktag. There was no way that could go well. I needed to stop him from engaging, if he hadn't already.

"Listen, this isn't a climate change thing anymore," Steve said. "This is a big piece now. Front-page stuff. It's a great chance for you."

I got off the phone and pulled up the video. A small group, seven or eight people, had recorded themselves circling the marsh around Luna's nest. They held posters glued to plywood sticks. JUSTICE FOR ABBY AND ALAN! one read. Another had a photo of Larry Taylor's binoculared face on it, with a big red diagonal slash through it. Had poor Larry fanned their flames by responding to them with such patient firmness?

I turned up the volume on the video and heard them chant. "One, two, three, four, we won't take this anymore! Five, six, seven, eight, change the baby ospreys' fate!" A woman in a bright-yellow shirt was reaching into a bag and pulling out handfuls of birdseed, tossing it into the air like confetti.

A few minutes later I was in Adrian's car, this time with promises not just to pay for gas but to get *Apogee* to throw him some dollars to make up for all the miles I'd been putting on it. I didn't have Larry's number, but I would stop by his house first and, with any luck, intercept him before he made things worse.

I was close to the turnoff from the highway when my phone rang: I was relieved to hear that it was Larry.

"I'm so glad you called," I shouted into the speakerphone. "I'm actually on my way to Luna's nest right now."

"That's what I'm calling about. Please," he said desperately. "Please don't write another article. Don't write another word. I need this to go away."

Seventeen

Larry agreed to meet at a Mexican place off Route 50. Neutral ground, I figured. Not his town, not mine either. When I arrived he was already seated at a booth in the window, his backpack beside him on the bench. He seemed older than he had the first time we'd met. Lines around his mouth and forehead looked drawn in pen.

"Thanks for meeting me," I said. As I slid into the booth, he glanced nervously around the restaurant, as though ensuring no one he knew was there. Two men in bikers' leather sat in the far corner, drinking beers, pale logs of burrito in front of them. They were paying no attention to us. A waiter came by and deposited a basket of chips and a ramekin of salsa on our table; I loaded a chip and crunched it down, not out of hunger but because I needed something to do with my hands.

"I had to turn off the osprey cam," Larry said.

"I'm sorry," I said. I hoped he heard my empathy; I knew it must have pained him to do so. In his first post, he'd said that we had a responsibility to witness the natural world, even when it was sad or savage.

"I've never been in this situation," Larry said. "I tried to live my life keeping my head down. Even at my wedding, we had five people. And apparently the chair of the Chesapeake Bay Trust is just furious. Those people—they're all over the land. He's upset, but I am too. The whole point of this place—" He broke off. "Well, I don't even know the whole point of it, but it was a place where Luna liked to be. It was a sanctuary for the osprey, for nature undisturbed, and now the idea of it turning into an amusement park for misguided eco-warriors is just . . . well, Eleanor, is there a way you can help me stop it?"

I thought for a moment. "I have to write a piece, but it will be very fair," I said. "In fact, I'll make it really dry. It will attract no attention. It will be as dry as these chips." He didn't even smile, so I just went on. "These things pass in days," I said, mostly meaning it. "Nobody stays interested. One of the byproducts of the internet is that everyone's attention span is flea-like."

A baby-faced server, pants belted high on his waist, appeared beside our table. "Hello, my name is Alex, are you ready?" he asked, pen poised.

"I'll have a Coke and two chicken tacos," I said, glancing quickly at the menu. *Burrito Mondays: $1 shots with purchase of burrito!!!!* it read. *Taco Tuesday! 2 for 1!* Poor Tuesday, always forced by alliteration to be paired with tacos.

"I'll try the cactus salad. Thank you." Larry handed him our menus. Alex nodded gravely and continued to stand by our table while he separated the perforated page from the order pad.

When he moved away, I went on. "I can write the most brilliant piece about this and it will be painted over in two days by a protest against . . . I don't know, clarified butter. Or tube socks."

But Larry looked unhappy and shaken. "I want the marsh quiet again for the birds," he said.

"It will be."

"I know we don't know each other," Larry said, sitting perfectly still with his fingers laced together, "but I'm asking you not to write about it anymore."

His composure seemed to mask a deep well of vulnerability and tenderness. I could see it in his eyes, how he couldn't quite bring himself to look at me. And so I found myself nodding, agreeing not to write the piece I had promised Steve I would. The front-page piece. I felt bound to Larry, and it was easy to let Steve fade in my mind. I wanted to learn everything I could about this man who had known my father and known him with a vehemence I didn't yet understand. Steve would be angry, but I would figure out a way to explain. I knew Steve only cared about the piece because of himself, his ego, the brief flutter of clicks it would generate for *Apogee*. It wouldn't teach readers anything; it would be giving a platform to people who were anti-science, anti-evidence, who protested by pillorying a well-meaning environmentalist and by throwing birdseed in the air, as if wild seabirds were interchangeable with the suburban sparrow. Everything that Jane argued *Apogee* shouldn't be. Everything I knew my father would be against too.

Our plates were set down with extra napkins tucked beneath them. I stared at my dish, the tacos sagging in their shells. "Thanks for seeing me and giving me another chance," I said.

"It wasn't me. You should thank Drew, my husband. He thought I should meet with you. That it might bring me some closure, after everything." Larry cupped both hands around his water glass. "It's all been weighing on me, since I got your first email."

I waited for Larry to say more. This was a journalist's strategy, not to rush to fill a silence. If you let silence bloom, the other person might tell an unvarnished truth, not the version of it they'd prepared in their heads.

"Also"—Larry looked at me—"you're not your father."

It was true, I wasn't my father. But it hurt to hear him say it. It sounded as if Larry didn't think my father was a good person. "How did you know him?" I asked finally.

"We went to high school together. We were on the baseball team."

"I found a picture of the two of you, in *The Castle Hill Moat*. You were a shortstop, right? And my dad was first base." Baseball friends. My dad had left his baseball to an old pal. *Old pal*. The words felt wrong. I knew there was more to it.

"Right."

He didn't elaborate, so I said, "The school jocks?"

"No." Larry shook his head firmly. "We were artistic kids. We loved baseball, but we were artists first. Jim encouraged my photography when no one else did."

"He always loved photography."

"Jim was the only other person in class who cared about art. He could talk about the latest foreign films. He read everything. That really impressed me. After baseball practice one day, I was showing him some of my photographs. We were sophomores, so we weren't allowed to use the school darkroom. The photography course was an elective for seniors only. The principal had basically said that anyone using the darkroom without permission would be suspended, but Jim convinced me that I should develop my film there, that it was my right as an artist. One day he stood outside while I went in through the curtain. The chemicals were all laid out in bins, and there was a string lined with wooden clothespins where you could hang photos. All those pins waiting—that was thrilling to me. So I rolled up my sleeves and got to work.

"Then in a while a teacher passed by. I recognized his voice. Mr. Trillin, our English teacher. We both adored him, especially your father. He worshipped him. Trillin asked what he was doing there outside the darkroom. I froze, thinking, shit, Jim is going to give me up—but he didn't. Jim distracted him with some story about the Orioles first baseman. First he was doing the sound the ball makes when it cracks against the bat. Then he switched to the Orioles stadium announcer. Trillin thought it was so funny; he was really cracking up. Jim made it seem perfectly natural that he was just standing outside the darkroom. When it got quiet again, I poked my head around the curtain and saw Jim sitting on the floor with his back against the wall, reading a book. He didn't want to disturb me."

Larry stopped to take a long sip of water. For the first time since my father's death, I felt he was alive again. This was a real story, one that I didn't know and couldn't embellish and could only listen to. A story outside my own memory. Not like everything I had made up in my head to explain my father's actions toward me. I tried to float inside the image of

Dad sitting by the darkroom, guarding his friend. A cinder-block wall painted white. My father's backpack next to him, unzipped. His face a study in concentration. Alert for footsteps. I was greedy for more.

"In the darkroom that day," Larry said, "I remember thinking that was a very unusual thing to do. Jim believed in my work, and that meant a lot to me." Larry went on twisting his palms around his glass of water as though his mind had forgotten what his hands were doing. "Later, he asked to see the photos I developed. He really studied them. It was a series I shot of my parents dancing at my cousin's wedding. The ceremony was at the county fairgrounds. They were on an empty carousel in their wedding clothes, slow-dancing beside a painted horse. In the first frames, they're laughing and looking at each other, but then my father says something that makes her sad. In the final shot, they're kind of gazing into the distance. My mother isn't smiling anymore. She looks just to the left of the camera. Her eyes are fierce. Jim said, 'She's thinking of what to say that will wound him.' He suggested I call that final photo 'The Retort.' I loved that title. I loved that he thought it should reflect my mother's experience, her viewpoint. My father was a difficult man."

Larry picked up his fork. I watched slim green pieces of cactus disappear into his mouth. I sipped from my Coke, picked up a taco, and let the grease from the meat run in rivulets between my fingers. Finally, Larry set down his fork.

"Toward the end of our senior year, for whatever reason, the school closed the darkroom. Budget cuts or underenrollment, I can't remember. They stopped offering photography classes. Jim came up to me one afternoon in the locker room before baseball practice. He had the idea that we could build our own darkroom. Neither of us had the kind of money we'd need to do that. But Jim had just read Nietzsche. He said that we should steal the supplies on the basis of property rights—that those who will make greater use of things are entitled to them. This was an eighteen-year-old's interpretation of Nietzsche. I said, 'Are you kidding me? We could never get away with that.' Jim said something like, 'Extraordinary people are allowed to transgress. It's expected of them. We should aspire to break moral codes to achieve great things.'

"I refused, of course. He didn't understand what the consequences would be for me if I got caught doing something like that. My father was a—" Larry stopped, coughed. "He'd been in the military, and he was angry with everything and everyone. But he took it out on me most of all. I was quiet. Artistic. I was gay, but I wasn't out. What could I have said to Jim? That gay people aren't allowed to be reckless, because the consequences are worse for us? The truth is I was in love with your father, but I couldn't admit it to myself, and God knows I would never admit it to him. And I'm not quite sure why I'm admitting it to you."

Larry looked out the plate-glass window and blushed slightly, as though his shyness had caught up to him. I wanted to say something reassuring, but I didn't know what that would be. I never moved my eyes from Larry's face.

"One weekend we were hanging out in his basement," he

went on. "It was the afternoon and we were drinking beer. We could drink beer at his house, because he had no father to tell us not to. Sad but useful. I couldn't have Jim over—my father was too controlling and cruel. I didn't want anyone around him. At Jim's house, the TV was on, and we were just sitting on the couch and shooting the shit, and Jim started talking about how he was going to get the darkroom chemicals. A cousin of his worked part-time at the hardware store, and he'd explained that the inventory wasn't matched against the money in the register until Fridays. So if we snuck in on Saturday night, no one would notice anything was missing until the following Friday. Again I refused. I tried to talk Jim out of it. I said he was just drunk. At some point we'd had so many beers, there were crumpled cans all over the floor, and he fell asleep. When he woke up, he saw that I was staring at him, and I'm sure he knew what I felt about him. We never discussed it, but he knew, and I knew that he knew."

Larry paused. Then he said, "Again Jim started babbling about stealing the chemicals, but this time he wouldn't look at me. It was just a few bottles of chemicals, a few trays, he said. Nothing they would go crazy over. This cousin of his often took little things, a box of nails here and there, and no one noticed. He was almost pleading with me, in that charming way he had, making it sound fun and exciting, the start of our lives as true artists. We were both sitting up, foot to foot, and he said, 'We need to do this for our art.' Then his mother called us to dinner, and he got up off the couch and left the room. He must have known on some level I would always do what he wanted. I was in his thrall."

Thrall. That was the word for the air around my father that contained him and drew people in: men, women, children, probably random small animals. Me. I'd never thought of it before, but it was perfect. What a strange word, one of those words that didn't even sound real if you overthought it: *thrall*.

Larry stopped speaking and emptied his water glass. I watched him drink until the ice rattled inside the deep cup. "Jim was someone I admired and looked up to. That night we had dinner with his mother, like we'd done dozens of times. She made some kind of tuna casserole with lima beans. She was the worst cook—"

I laughed softly. Dad had often referred to his mother's horrible cooking and her paranoid hoarding of food. He'd said it lovingly, with compassion. He'd told me that after his mother's funeral, long before I was born, when he was cleaning out her house, he found a hundred cans of lima beans in the basement.

"Jim was praising her casserole," Larry said. "At any other dinner he would have winked at me, included me in the secret of her terrible cooking. But this time, all his attention was on his mother. I was just there, poking my fork around those lima beans and rubbery noodles slathered in mayonnaise. His poor mother was too grief-stricken to notice the weirdness between us. Jim's father had died that winter. Jim didn't look at me once that entire dinner. I felt he was testing me, showing me what life would be like if we weren't friends. He had all the power, and at the time I felt I couldn't lose him. But really it was that I couldn't lose the way he made me feel.

When you were the center of his attention, you felt like a million bucks, better than anyone else had ever made you feel. But when he was cold, well . . ."

Larry took a handkerchief from his pocket and dabbed at his forehead.

"So I agreed. I told him I would do it," Larry said. "We must have made our plan. I don't remember that part. We went there on Saturday after the store had closed for the night, and we slipped in through a back window. Jim's cousin must have told him how to get in. The rest was easy. We found the jugs quickly, and we could have left, but Jim couldn't do anything in an ordinary way, so he began poking around the shelves. He saw a stack of baseballs and took one out of its packaging."

The baseball, I thought. The baseball, finally making its appearance in this unlikely scene.

"He tossed it to me and I caught it," Larry said. "He threw his arm around my shoulders, like old times. He backed up into the aisle so we could throw it back and forth. In the dark, that baseball was so white it glowed. We were there a few minutes later when the lights of a police car lit up the back wall. Jim said, 'Shit,' as he caught the ball. We froze. I was closer to the front of the store, near the counter. Jim was hidden in the aisle when the cops came in. Their flashlights were in my eyes, and I remember the relief when the beams shifted down to the jugs at my feet. They asked for my name and spun me around so they could cuff me, and I tried to catch a glimpse of Jim, but I couldn't see where he was. I wanted to call out for him, but it was only when the cops pinned me, and my cheek was resting on the counter, that I saw him. He was walking down the aisle to the back door. He never said a word. Never turned around to see if I was okay. Those two policemen didn't see him. That pompous, slow walk Jim had. I'll never forget the sight. His back was to me, and he walked with that limp on his left side. He was still holding the base-ball."

Hearing this, I burned coolly, like I was sitting in an ice bath with a fever. My father's walk, with the hitch in his leg, the walk I'd known my entire life, the walk Van had imitated at the Lincoln Memorial. "What happened?" I asked, my mouth dry.

"They put me in a holding cell with a bunch of drunks. It was humiliating. My father came down to the station later that night, wearing a long trench coat and a hat, like he was trying to hide himself. I don't know what he did or said, but the police let me go with a warning. And then my father didn't talk to me again, basically ever. Not only was I gay, which he knew on some level, but I was a thief. He was dis-gusted. He couldn't punish me for being gay, because I'd never admitted it. But he sure as hell could punish me for being a thief. And for embarrassing him."

I put my hands on my knees and found that they were trembling.

Larry's face was drawn, and sweat was collecting at his temples. "He never forgave me. Barely spoke three sentences to me before he died."

He reached into his backpack and brought out my father's baseball. "Jim was my friend, and he sold me out. The con-sequences for him would have been minor. A distracted, grieving mother who doted on him—what would she have cared about his teenage mistake? I've gone over it and over it in my mind. He knew what I felt for him and knew it wouldn't end up anywhere good, because he didn't return the feelings. So I guess he took this as an opportunity to get rid of me. In the end, he was careless with my heart. And then a million years go by and he leaves me a baseball in his will?"

Tears were coming to my eyes. My stomach clenched and heaved.

"Never heard from him. Nothing," Larry went on. "Right before graduation I was driving to pick up something for my mother, and I took a detour down his street. He was out in the yard, raking leaves. When he saw me, he let the rake fall. I thought he was going to come over, but he just bent and picked it back up. He had a chance. He didn't take it."

I took in what my father had done. I wished I could not only refuse to write the osprey story; I wanted to go to the protests and club the protesters to death. This man, whom my father had treated so badly, just wanted to live his life. He couldn't have his best friend treat him decently. He couldn't even have a quiet place for the osprey. And I had been close to adding to the chatter about that in order to please Steve Glanz with clickbait.

I drew a deep breath. "But you're married? You have a good life?"

"Drew and I—we have a terrific marriage. Ups and downs, like anyone. But that's not the point. Your father was my best friend."

"He never apologized?"

Larry shook his head.

"He never wrote you? Never called?"

"The last time I talked to him was 1978, in that old hardware store."

That old hardware store. I reached into my purse and brought out my notebook of first lines, where I'd transcribed "The Catch" to read at my father's funeral. *Tossing the ball from end to end / in dusty store aisles.*

My hands shaking, I pushed the notebook across the table. "I always assumed the store in his poem was this general store in our town. And I thought the poem was about me. But it wasn't." Some mixture of dread and relief was blooming hot in my stomach. "My father's best poem, 'The Catch,' is about *you.*"

Larry removed his glasses from his breast pocket, looping them around his ears one side at a time.

THE CATCH

but,

if time could kneel, as a catcher
shifts to his knees when the pitch is wild

For the summer we played in ruffled green grass,
or indoors if the sky shivered with rain,

Tossing the ball from end to end
in dusty store aisles.

Would the solid walls still echo with the hollow
slaps of our hands to leather mitts,

Or would I leave you there
your arms outstretched

as if to receive me.

"This has been published?" Larry's voice was low and tight.

"Yeah, in 1991. And it's been anthologized a lot since then. It's sort of my dad's most famous poem." Larry didn't respond, so I continued: "Obviously the speaker has left the person he was playing with. I always thought it was *me*, because my parents got divorced and Dad moved away, and I knew he felt guilty. But what you described . . ." I reached across the table and pointed to the first stanza, the way my father might have demonstrated for a student.

"He starts the poem with *but* and then describes a betrayal. So the betrayal comes before the poem even starts. Like whatever it was was too bad to put into words. Which now I know . . ." I trailed off. "Maybe the poem is about"— I paused, realizing it only as I said it—"maybe the poem is his atonement."

Larry picked up my father's baseball. "You say this poem was anthologized?"

"Yes—"

"So he made money off it."

"Poets don't really make a lot of money, but I guess—"

"It benefited his career," Larry said matter-of-factly.

"I guess," I said miserably.

"And you say he kept this baseball next to him all his life. That he used it."

"Yeah."

"For luck."

"That's what I think."

"Well."

I thought for a minute. *Keep your eye on the ball,* Dad used to say when we'd play catch. *Eye on the ball, Ellie. You can't catch it if you don't see it coming. You can't catch it if you don't follow its arc.* What a poor token the baseball had been. If it was a symbol of his steadfastness, it was a broken symbol; if it was a reminder to avoid betraying those he loved, it had failed.

"Maybe it wasn't for luck, actually," I said. "Maybe it was to remind him not to do anything like that again. Not to hurt the people he loved. To remind him what he was capable of. It didn't work, though. He went right on hurting people until he died. But maybe he left you this baseball as a way to apologize after all this time."

"Eleanor," Larry said, "I already know what he was capable of. He could have apologized to me when he was alive. Any number of times. Any number of ways. Instead, he waits until he's dead?"

"He must have been ashamed," I said.

"I'm sorry, but it's too little too late. You can imagine, I don't want anything to do with this. You can keep the baseball. It's yours." Larry put the ball on the table and let go. It wobbled and rolled unsteadily toward me. For a moment it seemed like the ball would fall off the other side, into my lap, but then it came to rest in the center of the table.

Eighteen

I had no memory of the drive home. Suddenly I was parking in front of 1938 House. My idea of who my father was shimmered and changed before me. It ducked down in a baseball cap, pulled away in a car, left a best friend, a wife, children. Gone. I wasn't any different from all the others. My legs were pulsing with energy; I had to move.

I was too jittery to sit at home, so I unlocked my bike and set off up the hill. I would bike up 1st Street, where the houses were painted jaunty colors, baby blue and magenta, and wore pointy hats. I'd loop around the city reservoir and back down through the Howard University campus. Hard and fast, I overtook the hill, cleaving to the reservoir's chain-link fence, trying to outpace the feeling that something was rotting away on my insides.

"The Catch" wasn't about me. My father had been cruel to Larry when they were young, had behaved like a coward. He'd never had any close male friends, I realized, or any friends that stuck. Was this early betrayal of Larry the reason for the pattern? Why had he never apologized to him? And then he'd betrayed Romley Cass, a poet he'd envied, chasing his wife. He'd cheated on my stepmother Colette with Linda, wounded his family. Now that I had the answers to my questions about Larry Taylor and the baseball and my father, I wanted them surgically removed. I tried to work up a different version—the baseball was a relic of a happy time, when children played catch on a wide green field in summer's perfume. They adored one another. My father had been a good boy. He was a good man. Good boy, good man, I chanted softly, as if it might help.

I pedaled in the direction of Lucas's house. The R Street bike lane took me all the way to 18th Street NW, where I swung onto Dupont Circle. The office buildings were dark, but people were coming out of bars and restaurants, loose from alcohol, stumbling in the humid air. I scanned the crowds for Lucas and his wife. When I reached their street, I got off my bike and stood on the sidewalk. The lights were on in their house, but the curtains were drawn. As I stood watching, a shadow passed behind the living room shade. I drew a breath, imagining Mina on the other side. The shadow paused. I wheeled my bike toward the dark side of the street, out of the streetlamp's warm orbit.

I wanted her to know the truth. I thumbed a text to Lucas. *No matter what happens with us, Mina deserves to know.* I looked back at the window. The shadow was gone.

When I arrived at *Apogee*, just after 9 P.M., the office was truly empty, computers locked away in staff lockers, the Conveyor Belt long and bare, shining under the brass lamps. No bikes but mine at the communal rack. My father had cheated, he'd lied. He had betrayed his friend, his wives, all of us. He made feeble amends only in death. I poked at each fact with a stick, but each fact still lay there, dead. In the office kitchen I poured myself a beer, drank it fast while pacing.

I opened a fresh email, addressed it to Jane and Steve. In order to explain why I couldn't write about the osprey protests, I had to fess up about my connection to Larry. And that required telling them that I'd obscured who Larry was and why I'd wanted to write about him in the first place. Also that I'd lied to Larry about my identity. And, of course, that I'd failed to complete the "front page" assignment Steve had given me. It was all mixed up inside me, knotted together. My cursor blinked, urging me on.

Dear Jane and Steve, I regret to inform you that I have not reported the osprey piece . . . I wrote.

But that didn't sound right. I erased it and started again. *Dear Steve and Jane, I need to apologize for my behavior . . .*

My father had said that poetry was a way to ask endless questions without answers. He'd kept the baseball near him all his life, used its presence to compel him to write. Why? I'd always thought it was inspiration, but maybe the truth was it was guilt. Maybe all his poems were expressions of self, of remorse. Now that Larry didn't want it, the baseball was mine again. What new meaning could I give it? I considered the poems my father had loved while I swigged down another IPA, feeling it buzz in my scalp and the backs of my knees.

Whose baseball this is I think I know.

Quoth the baseball, "Nevermore."

I, too, sing of the baseball.

Tell me, what is it you plan to do with your one wild and precious baseball?

I'd have to start at the beginning, tell my bosses the truth. *Dear Jane and Steve, This is a story about osprey, but it starts with my father.* In a great gush of words, I told them about Larry, how I'd lied to get their approval in order to meet him and learn about his connection to my father. I apologized and pushed send.

Then I went on, writing for myself. Maybe for my sisters and Van, one day. I wrote about my father's will and Linda and Romley's marriage. The wives. I typed out the story Larry had told me about my father, the hardware store, and the baseball, trying to remember Larry's words and his intonation. How he'd passed the baseball back to me. I excoriated my father. I excoriated myself. I would try to scrub us clean by telling the truth.

A tender shoot of understanding was growing through me, and soon I couldn't recognize it as new—it was as if it had always been there, mixing with my own guts and hot blood. The great, indiscriminate lovableness of my father that had wounded Larry had also wounded Linda and Romley, my mother, my stepmothers, my sisters, Van. Me. He had walked out of the hardware store; he had walked away from his families. He hadn't left Colette before he died, but maybe he would have. Could there have someday been a new lover who would have become the fourth wife? My father had never been held accountable for what he did to Larry, for the privilege that allowed him to act out that betrayal. Wasn't it that very same privilege that enabled him to behave the way he had with all the women and then to haphazardly parent the children that resulted from those different unions? Summer Thanksgiving wasn't a wacky, offbeat celebration of his love—it was a way to manage a careless life. And yet I loved him. We loved him. The love was the catch. It made no sense on one level. It just *was*—intractable, unwavering, an actual thing, almost an object.

I wrote feverishly while the sun rose, a palm print of light in the sky. Morning. I had been awake all night, like during finals week in college, when I would emerge from the computer center in the early-morning hours, my throat buckled, my head jackhammering, and follow the line of undergraduate all-nighters toward the diner that opened at 5 A.M. to serve construction workers about to start their days and college students who had waited until the last minute to write their papers. In uneasy fellowship, we sat together, chewing. Crunch of bacon, sweetness of the flapjack.

Jane and Steve had my email in their inboxes. They would see it as soon as they woke up. My head began to throb like it did when I stood up too quickly. What if the email was a mistake? But there was no going back now. I put the beer cans in the recycling bin, shut off the lights. Outside, the sidewalk stretched and contracted like putty. I forced myself to walk toward my bike, my face hot and tight, just as a long shadow rounded the corner into view. Fear folded over in my stomach like a classroom note—the approach of an unknown man on a deserted street. I wondered if there was time to get back into the building, or if I should make a dash to unlock my bike. I froze in indecision.

The man came closer, peered at my tears. "Why are you crying? Who is he? I'll kill him," he said.

"He's already dead," I said.

Nineteen

I was fired! I texted Lucas. I'd cleared out my locker and had a small bag of my things slung over one shoulder: a stack of notes, printed interview transcripts, pens, two coffee mugs. The baseball. Outside the Baby Jake's factory, I unlocked my bike from the communal rack for the last time.

Lucas hadn't responded to the text I sent him yesterday about telling Mina the truth, but now I saw that he was writing back. Three dots flickered in and out. *What?? I need the whole story. But bottom line you will be FINE. Any news org would be lucky to have you.*

Then: *You know exactly where Colombo is;)*

"I caught you," said someone to my left.

Steve. I said, "Hey, Steve."

"I need your keycard. For the building."

I handed it to him. I'd paid for a replacement after losing the original sometime between my dad's funeral and that hazy first Monday back at *Apogee.* It had my old picture on it, with my lips-closed, new-job smile. The way I smiled before my father died.

Steve scratched at the side of his neck. "This is awkward. Do you want a hug?"

I thought for a minute. "No. But I want to know the secret of *Next Web*."

"Ha."

"Really. Tell me."

"Telling you would mean I'd have to fire you," he said.

"You already fired me. Can you un-fire me, Steve?"

Steve had been looking at me. Now he concentrated very hard on the bike rack. "Uh, no. I can't."

"I thought you were the boss. The founder of *Apogee*. You can do anything, can't you? Save journalism? Flirt with your employees? Hire and fire at will?" I was high on truth-telling. I'd never spoken this way before, and it was intoxicating.

Steve took a stutter step back.

"I want to talk to Jane," I said. "She wasn't in her office when I went to get my stuff."

"She's not here."

"Where is she?"

"She's gone," he said. "I had to let her go."

"Jane?"

Steve grimaced.

"Because of me?"

He grimaced again.

"You've got to be kidding. It had nothing to do with her."

"It happened under her watch."

"It was my decision!"

"I'm not discussing hiring practices with junior employ-ees." It sounded like he'd read that sentence off the Black-

Berry of a company lawyer. "We're building a seminal website here. We can't have employees who don't do their jobs."

Seminal. Even the word sounded sexist. "Good for you," I said. "Go ahead and fire me. I deserve it. But you're never going to get anywhere without people like Jane to guide you." I looked at him; he was holding himself tight. "In those Monday meetings when you undermined her in front of everyone—it was a dick move. We all saw right through you: She knows more than you do, she's more talented, and you were worried about her usurping your power. She's too good for you. She deserves to work with someone who respects her."

Steve pretended to yawn; what I'd said upset him, and he seemed to be hiding it behind his open hand. "I'm the CEO. That's my job. There's a hierarchy. You're the one who got her fired."

"Yeah, well. That wasn't my intention," I muttered.

"What was your intention?"

"To atone for the sins of the father," I said.

"Huh?"

I turned around first. I was proud of that.

It was sunny, and I had enough savings to last me two whole weeks. I knew my mother and Boris Gettleman would help me, but I wanted to manage on my own. If I chose to, I could reinvent myself. The sidewalk in front of the Baby Jake's factory was the color of fat on a steak. I loved steak. I wanted a steak. Maybe I would call Mal so we could eat all the steaks in Washington.

When I looked down at my phone, I realized I was in the middle of pocket-dialing James Adler. Instead of ending the call, I held the phone to my ear and listened to the familiar ring. For a fraction of a moment it seemed possible that my father would pick up from the other side of a long gray tunnel, from some unknown dimension, from the sticky inside of a flower, from a cold and distant planet. I imagined him saying, *You were fired! I'm proud of you,* in a deep and playful voice. "But what about Jane?" I asked. And then the exhilaration came up through my throat and I bent to throw up on the sidewalk.

"I'm impressed with your gall," Jane said, opening her door.

"Jane, I'm—"

She held up her hand to stop me. "I'm not going to invite you in. But I'll give you an audience on the stoop for five minutes until my husband gets home from his run."

We sat in high-end lawn chairs that had been set up on the landing beside an under-watered ficus. I'd seen those chairs before, at my mother's. Jane was wearing some kind of embroidered caftan and earrings shaped like coat hangers. I wiped a hand across my eyes, unsure where to begin. Luckily, Jane knew.

"How old are you?" Jane asked.

"I'm twenty-four." I moved my hand away from my face. "Jane, I had no idea you would get fired. I thought the only person at risk would be me. I'm so, so sorry."

Jane sighed. "That's the problem with you millennials. You don't think."

"I had this idea that reporting on the osprey was worth it, and I could find out about my dad at the same time. It feels incredibly stupid now."

"You have an editor for a reason," she said. "There are proper channels and outlets. You don't just go over everybody's heads, lying about things. That's another problem with you millennials. You don't think about other people. Only about yourselves. Honestly, what did you expect to happen?"

"I don't know. I thought I was doing the right thing. But I'm not sure what the right thing is anymore."

"Well, you didn't do it with integrity or with compassion for your colleagues or the company where you were fortunate enough to work. Steve and I aren't your therapists; journalism isn't therapy." She turned to look at me and I shrank back. "But you just lost your father. When my father died, I was a mess. I couldn't get out of bed. Losing a parent is gutting, especially at your age."

"Yeah, it is." I was flooded with gratitude but still compelled to downplay my feelings. I said, "But I'm fine."

"Well, I don't think you're fine," Jane said. "And that's okay."

"I thought you'd yell at me."

"I probably should. But I suppose I'm resigned, as I'm sure you've noticed. Steve has always wanted to fire me; this just provided a reason." Jane gave a small shrug. "In the old days, in real newsrooms, everyone would disagree all the time. It was our way of pushing one another, an internal check to make our stories the best they could be. Did they stand up to rigorous analysis by other journalists and editors? What would improve them? We scrutinized every line. It's depressing to try to bring that kind of rigor to a place that runs on clickbait."

"I hated the way Steve treated you," I said. "He was callous and undermining and awful to everyone, but especially to you. But I was too much of a wuss to stand up to him."

Jane barked out a laugh. "Don't you think I'd stand up to him myself if that's what I decided? Did it ever occur to you that I was making an informed decision about how to manage him? Lest you think I'm letting you off the hook, you should know that what you did was very selfish. It may not have been the best job, but I'm old. I was lucky to have *any* journalism job. My experience is costly. Replacing me means they can bring on three or four know-nothings from your generation, none of whom would push Steve to improve. Better that I should have stayed at *Apogee* and nudged him in the right direction as much as I could."

"I didn't think about any of that," I said.

"No. Of course you didn't."

"I'm sorry."

She sighed. "Thank you for coming to apologize in person. At least you did that. I had high hopes for you," Jane said.

I had high hopes for you. It cut me to hear her use the past tense. Her figure cast a long shadow.

"You'll find another job," she said.

"You won't?"

"I doubt it. Though I suppose now I'll have more time to macramé."

"Jane, I feel terrible," I said, and I meant it. I was used to being young and naïve. I hadn't realized how much my youth protected me. I thought once again about my father—how he'd married younger and younger women. How vulnerable

my mother, and then Barbara, his second wife, must have felt
to be alone, suddenly husband-less. How Colette was now
older and alone. My father had used his privilege as a man at
the expense of the women who were his wives, and I had used
mine as a young person without thinking of Jane.

I remembered sitting in a kiddie pool with him when I was
a toddler, pouring cups of water over his fuzzy blond knees.
My adoration was total. Then I thought about how, at our
final Summer Thanksgiving, I'd been disappointed in him for
not understanding the dynamic between Sadie and Anna,
who were putting on makeup in the bathroom and fighting
with the specific cruelty of sisters. For asking Van to play
catch without thinking to ask me to play too.

Maybe, if he'd lived, I would have gotten a whole picture,
including all the parts I didn't want to see. Was it connected
to maleness, or power, or narcissism, the ability to swim
above everything and know that other people—the women—
would sort it all out? But his death and learning about the
affair with Linda, Larry, the baseball, had shown me everything unnaturally, quickly, completely. Maybe, somehow, my
father had known that I would follow the narrow track of
journalistic good sense until I reached these conclusions. Perhaps, in a certain way, leaving me the tie rack, pointing me
toward the mystery of the baseball, had been his parting gift.
Or maybe I was wrong. Maybe it was just careless of him to
assume that we'd be able to find L. M. Taylor, that L. M. Taylor would be delighted to accept the baseball and intrinsically
understand the message my father had been trying to send
with it. The fact that I would never know meant that I could

decide which it was. I could decide, and choose what to believe, and no one could refute me.

"Is there anything I can do?" I asked Jane.

Jane squinted at me. "What can you do? Well, for starters, you might consider therapy."

"Got it," I said. "Therapy and lorazepam."

Jane looked at me with something close to fondness. "Now get out of here. My husband is about to get home, and I have to explain to him how I let such foolishness flourish under my wing."

"Is that an osprey joke?"

"Go," Jane said.

Twenty

Lucas and I went out for burgers at a new place in my neighborhood. On the way into the restaurant, he grabbed my hand. I was surprised—he was usually so careful about us touching in public inside the district. We sat at a table in the window and ordered from a menu printed on heavy paper.

Lucas's face looked shiny; his eyes were bright. "Have you noticed the names of these beers? Buddha's Revenge Lager? Pond Scum Ale? I might have to try that one next. What about you?"

"You seem happy," I said.

"I am." He craned his neck to look out the window. "The moon is so bright," he said.

"That's not the moon. That's the searchlight from the public housing across the street," I said.

"I'm happy and I'm . . . relieved," he said.

I brought my burger to my mouth, and as I did, a dollop of ketchup plopped out of it onto my shirt. It slid, comically, down the length of my torso into my lap.

"I'm leaving Mina," Lucas said.

I looked at him.

He nodded. I glanced down at the ketchup on my shirt and up at him, and we both laughed.

"You're leaving her?" I said. "Leaving or left?"

"Leaving, left. It's over," he said. "I adore you. You have ketchup all over you."

I got up from my chair and flung myself onto him. He laughed and held me. "And now it's all over me too."

We came back to 1938 House to lie entangled in my bed. I may have been fired from my first journalism job, but I had Lucas here with me, my boyfriend at last. My roommates were puttering around the house, Adrian was lifting weights through the wall—I recognized the grunting of a man with barbells—but I was removed from it all. Maybe I would live with Lucas someday, in our own apartment, and for a second I felt a touch of bittersweet sadness and loss and excitement that I was outgrowing all of this, that I would leave it behind.

"What was it like when you told her?" I asked.

Lucas tucked his arm behind his head. "Why do you want to know?"

"It must have been hard. You did talk to her about everything, right?"

"Of course."

"Where will you move?"

"I'll stay at a hotel until everything is settled."

He moved his fingers to my hip, and then he began playing between my legs. I opened my thighs to let him in. "Don't distract me," I said. "I want to hear about it."

He plunged his fingers in deeper, twisting them around in

the way we'd discovered together. "You're so wet," he breathed. "You're so special. My God. What should I get for my new apartment? Are there things you need? A bike rack?" These items came out breathy, and I felt him harden against my leg.

"Lucas?" I pushed him. "But you told her, right? You explained and she understood that you were leaving?"

"Yes."

"Yes?" I asked.

"Yes."

"I feel like there's something you're not saying."

His fingers lay on my hip bone. "Technically I didn't tell her. She found out."

"She found out?"

"Gianni told her. The man who saw you at my office. He wrote her on Facebook and said he thought I was having an affair. Mina confronted me and I told her the truth. We talked about it over a couple of days and decided we should separate and I should move out."

I looked at him. What he was saying didn't compute. Wasn't the cuddling we'd been doing in my bed, the burgers we'd eaten out in the open where anyone could see us, the new apartment he would get, stocking it with things I liked— wasn't that all because he had picked me? Because I was the chosen one?

I rolled onto my side, away from him. In fact, he hadn't chosen me. I was reminded again of that line from *The Member of the Wedding*, the Carson McCullers novel I loved most. *This was the summer when for a long time she had not been a member.*

"Ellie, what's wrong?" he said.

The bed between us was a wide river. He began to cross it, confident of my love. "Mina and I have been struggling for years," he said. "We went into therapy for a while. It didn't really help. Everything was stagnant. What I have with you is different. It's passionate. There's nothing fallow about it. It feels so real."

I turned onto my back, and he took me in his arms again. "Let's watch a movie and drink wine," he said. "Then I want to sleep next to you. And in the morning, I want to cook you breakfast and kiss you goodbye, and then tomorrow night I want to do it all over again."

I nodded. This was what I'd been asking for, hoping for, but now that it was here, it felt off. Mina had initiated the breakup by confronting him about the affair. Lucas could decide to return to her and work things out—it would probably be easy for him. Now his choosing me felt haphazard, like a backup plan he had been forced into. I had wanted Lucas to choose me because he loved me in a way my father never had. I wanted him to choose me over another woman. My father had always been picking others, leaving behind a trail of women and children, but confiding in me the whole time so that I felt special, like his peer. But I hadn't been his peer. I had been his daughter.

"I love you, Ellie," Lucas said.

There it was. That word. Like aloe on a sunburn, instant relief. "I love you too," I said.

Twenty-one

I spent the next few days looking for jobs on Craigslist. Sending applications into the void, each crafted carefully and returning nothing or, worse, provoking creepy offers about discounted apartments from users with names like Biff and lines like *free shared Jacuzzi in yard*. But it was either job hunting or asking my mother for money or losing my spot in 1938 House and having to go live with her and Dr. Boris Gettleman in Tallahassee.

After Lucas's revelation about how things ended between him and Mina, I no longer felt certain about us. I had to wait and see what would happen, whether his separation would stick and I was really the person he wanted to be with. His leaving his marriage was obviously what my father had done. If Lucas had done it once, would he do it again? Could I protect myself from that, be sure that Lucas meant it this time? Those questions hadn't felt urgent when he was with Mina, but now that he wasn't, I saw how vulnerable I might be.

Sometime during what felt like the millionth hour of my job search, I stumbled on a random link—short-term positions were being advertised for the Washington Nationals baseball stadium.

Baseball. That hit a chord. Short-term sounded good. It seemed kind of fitting, since my life had recently involved following around a baseball. Maybe working at the stadium could tide me over while I sorted everything out and applied for other journalism jobs.

The online application instructed me to list previous employment, along with references. I typed Steve's name, then deleted it and typed in Jane's. The application asked whether I could run. The truth was I couldn't remember the last time I'd run. Maybe on the treadmill in college. I didn't want to lie anymore. So I said that I was a fast learner, that I would do my best.

They must have been desperate, because I was accepted within hours.

I arrived at the stadium ten minutes before the appointed time, just as the parking lot was filling up with cars. People removed banners and giant foam hands from their trunks. They wore red and white, Nationals colors, unaware as they brushed by me that they were passing a Teddy Roosevelt impersonator, one of the stars of the fourth-inning show.

I thought of what my dad used to say about baseball, how he quoted Roger Angell, who was quoting a friend. "There's nothing like being in a stadium with thirty thousand people who agree with you," he would say.

The guy who was supposed to train me for "the Presidents

Race" appeared and lit a cigarette, introducing himself as Richard. "This is the worst job I've ever had. The suit smells like ass," he said.

"Okay."

"And I once spent a summer scooping ice cream in Ocean City."

I watched him scuff his feet against the concrete. He looked like a cool outsider, the kind of boy who was popular not because he was handsome but because he rolled perfect joints.

"What's your name again?" he asked.

"Ellie. What am I supposed to do?"

He gestured toward a side door. "That's the place."

We went to the locker room to dress in our costumes, and soon I was suited up in red felt trousers. The shirt was a Nationals jersey with 26 stitched onto the back, representing Roosevelt's number as the twenty-sixth president. Richard would run as Thomas Jefferson, and in the middle of the fourth inning we would meet Lincoln and Washington for the race. The four of us would compete as cartoonish heads of state bumbling across the outfield while the Nationals' lineup rested and drank Gatorade out of hundred-gallon coolers.

The Teddy Roosevelt head loomed easily four feet high with a fold of mesh at the neck, which provided my line of sight. Teddy's face was frozen in a giant toothy grin. The mustache was a thick pelt of orange yarn. The skin was satin. Teensy circular spectacles were perched on the end of the nose.

Richard stripped down to his boxer shorts in front of me, revealing a tattoo of a dragon on his back. "If you wear clothes underneath the suit, it's too hot," he said, by way of explanation. Below the dragon's claw was a tattoo of a scroll with the letters *R.S.P. '87.* His initials and birth year, I assumed. Did he think he might forget them? I laughed out loud.

"What's funny?" Richard asked. His shoulder muscles tensed under his skin as he slid the Thomas Jefferson costume over his head. I had the feeling he wanted me to appraise him, but I couldn't muster interest. What was I doing here?

"They'll call us in a few," Richard said through the Jefferson mask. "Do you want to watch for a bit?"

"You go. I'll stay here."

I snapped a photo of myself in costume and sent it to Lucas. What would my father think to see me dressed as Teddy Roosevelt, treading the stadium's clipped grass and the horsehide-colored dirt? I was pretty sure he'd never felt the grass of a major league stadium spring beneath his feet, never bent down to feel the white rubber peel of the base. It was becoming a litany for me, the things my father hadn't done. I could start listing now and never finish.

I found my way out of the dark tunnel and into the blinding white light of the stadium. Richard was lined up behind Washington and Lincoln. Lincoln reached behind him and bumped me on the shoulder. "Hey, man, gonna eat my dust today?"

I remembered Dad saying that baseball diamonds were the most American shape. "You can see them from space," he'd said. Like so many things he said, I'd never questioned it.

Richard swung into position in front of me and I followed. We trotted onto the enormous field, flat and fuzzy in the heat.

As we moved past the home-plate seats, children slid their arms through the handrails to touch our masks. I jerked away, making a wide circle out of their reach. Richard flung his hand above his head to wave at the crowd, and I did the same. Over the loudspeaker, the announcer cued us up, his voice all low rumble and flash. "And now, ladies and gentlemen, the Presidents Race! Will Teddy Roosevelt's luck turn around this time? Tonight could mark the 488th straight loss for Teddy."

Lincoln swiveled his giant head around to goad me, pumping his arms in the air. George Washington bumped my hip with his hip. Thomas Jefferson leaned toward me until I saw the blur of Richard's face through the mesh. "Remember, you're coming in last. Pretend to stumble when you get to the infield, and wait for us to pass you."

"You suck, Teddy!" a voice yelled from the stands, and there was a smattering of laughter that came from all directions. I felt the words sting beneath my costume.

Right before my father went off to Wesleyan on a scholarship, then moved to Baltimore for a job at a community college, got married and had one child (me), transferred to a larger college in Easton, then a third college, got divorced, wrote a semi-famous poem, married for a second time and had two more children, divorced again, went dogsledding in rural Minnesota, faced custody disputes and near-bankruptcy, went on dates, married a third wife and had a fourth child, danced to Van Morrison, wrapped Summer Christmas presents, and died on the floor of his bedroom—right before all of this, there was a photo of him in *The Castle Hill Moat*. It had been taken after one of his high school baseball games, and he was sweaty and smiling, his hair shaggy beneath the brim of his cap, his teammates' arms reaching for him but not quite touching.

The photograph shifted and gleamed before my eyes just as the siren wailed, signaling the start of the race. Had Larry taken that photo? Was there any sign on my father's face of what he'd done to him? Or what was to come? The children, the wives, the poems? The early death, the gifts, so much left undone. My skin prickled and my limbs flooded with heat. *I don't think you're fine,* I heard Jane say. *I love you, Ellie,* Lucas said. *Gianni told her,* Lucas said. *She found out.* He'd established a whole life with this woman, his wife, Mina. I thought of the home they'd made together, the blue teddy bear in their bathroom.

The stadium lights buzzed and bled. I was Teddy Roosevelt, a big-game hunter and a statesman and a racist with a satin face. I could no longer feel my grief, only the lingering heat from a faded summer afternoon. *Summer afternoon— summer afternoon.* The skittering of leaves on faraway trees.

I began to run, dimly aware of the other presidents behind me, surging forward. The crowd was silent and then started to roar. They came together like a pointillist canvas, a composite of bodies in a stadium, dulled to circles of similar size. I saw my father in the front row, eating a hot dog. I saw him in the second row, waving at me and raising Larry's binoculars above his head, a smile on his face. Then he was holding Luna around her great wings as she struggled to break free. "Go, Teddy!" he screamed. And I ran and ran, suddenly frightened of myself. Inside the costume, I heaved deep, guttural sobs that felt like they'd never end. My lips stung and my eyes burned and I gulped down sweaty air. I crossed the finish line ahead of all the other presidents. I wasn't supposed to win, but somehow I did. I heard my father say, "And the crowd went wild!" in his baseball announcer's voice, his hand up as if holding a microphone on Summer Christmas.

I kept running. I ran and ran to get away from him, until I'd left the field and ripped off Teddy Roosevelt's head, and then I was outside the stadium gates, weeping on the concrete.

Twenty-two

The first thing I noticed was a mug of peppermint tea emitting steam. The sweet smell went straight to my belly, igniting a nauseating hunger. I sat up. The sun was yellow, poisonous. A line of sweat was cooling at the neck of my pajamas. Reaching for my phone, I hit a wicker tissue-box cover. I never bought tissues; my roommates and I used toilet paper. Furthermore, had I gone to the trouble of purchasing tissues, I would be hard-pressed to imagine the state of mind required for me to own a tissue-box cover. I lay back down, exhausted. From the distance came the echoing sounds of dishes being unloaded from a dishwasher, first the clatter of plates, then the hollow plink of bowls nesting inside one another, and finally the metallic clanging of silverware, a domestic rhythm I had internalized from the time I was a collection of cells. That's when the tissue-box holder made sense and I remembered: I was in Florida at my mother's.

After I'd gone downstairs, and she'd finished unloading the dishwasher and offered me an egg-white omelet, and I'd declined and taken out Boris's carton of ice cream and a spoon, and she'd said what kind of thing is that to eat in the morning, and I'd said, *Mom, leave it,* and then had submitted to a brief lecture on the health benefits of egg whites, after that we didn't talk about what happened—not about me losing my job at *Apogee,* or the meltdown at the Nationals stadium, or about Mal picking me up, or how Mal had called my mother and my mother had called me and told me to come home, that she'd found a flight for me that same night, and I'd surprised myself by saying yes, and Mal took me to the airport.

We stood together at the kitchen island in her big tropical house. She had two dishwashers and a leather sofa that looked virginal; shortly after marrying Boris, she had adopted the bourgeois attitude that furniture wasn't for sitting on. Out the window, a lizard climbed the garden wall in the sun. I dug into the carton of chocolate ice cream, scraping the sides with my spoon, and watched my mother's lower jaw make a series of nearly imperceptible twitches, which I knew from years of experience meant that she wanted to tell me to use a bowl and was expending significant effort to restrain herself.

"Are you still hungry?" she asked.

"Nope."

"But you're eating a lot of ice cream."

"It tastes good."

She smoothed down her sherbet-colored tunic. She would never eat sherbet, but she wasn't opposed to wearing it. "You didn't used to like ice cream," she said.

I waved my spoon. "Dad bought a brand from this local

place that had wild flavors like ricotta raspberry and avocado salted caramel. We'd eat it for breakfast."

"Your father was always impulsive," she said. "When we first met, he showed up at my apartment in the middle of the night, just to play me a Van Morrison song he loved. Did I ever tell you that story?" My mother opened the cabinet and took down a small glass bowl. She put it on the counter without looking at me.

"Nope."

"There's a downside to impulsivity."

"Which song?" I scraped a sweet mound of chocolate from the carton. My mouth puckered. *We need a bigger size in dressing room 4.*

"I can't remember," she said.

" 'Astral Weeks'?"

"Maybe."

" 'Into the Mystic'?"

"I don't know, sweetie."

"Clearly it didn't make a big impression on you."

She shook her head disapprovingly. "I remember it was two or three in the morning. Your father pounded on the door and rushed in with a record under his arm. He looked wild and drunk, but he swore he hadn't been drinking. I remember his expression when the needle hit the record and the song began—it was like pure joy."

"But what song was it?"

"What does it matter what song?"

"Because he could have shared it with anyone and he chose you."

My mother rested her hand on the counter. A chunky turquoise bracelet slipped down her arm and came to rest on her wrist. "Let me ask you something," she said. "Do you think your father would have remembered this story?"

"Yeah."

"No. I don't think he would." She picked a crumb off the counter with one finger and reached under the sink to put it in the garbage. "Anyway," she said, "I'm going to work out."

I put the ice cream carton back in the freezer. My mom poked her head around the doorway. "By the way, I left a box of your stuff in the living room. Can you go through it and decide what you want to keep? Boris and I are decluttering. We need more space for the humidifiers we bought for his deviated septum."

Long after my mother went to sleep that night, I lay on the sofa, the ceiling fan ruffling my hair. Nothing in this house smelled like her. It smelled of the lemony furniture polish, the tropical foliage that crept up the side of the house, the success of a middle-aged man in a prestigious, lucrative field. Boris was right now in Tennessee, delivering the keynote lecture at a conference of allergists. I tented one hand over my eyes. Through my fingers I made out his medical tomes crowding the bookcase, evidence of his big science brain prominently displayed, except for the bottom shelf near the floor, which held a row of my mother's paperback thrillers. I felt angry that her possessions were minimized, laid out barely above the ground, but quickly this dissolved into cool sadness and recognition, because of course Dr. Gettleman wouldn't have arranged the bookcase in this way. It would have been her own doing. My mother had always felt it necessary to suck up to men. Even her obsession with barely eating and with constant exercise—her very body—I saw as a way to do this.

I got off the sofa and crawled over to the bookcase to look at what she had read. There were crime dramas, thrillers, romance novels, what my father had called "junk books." I ran my fingers over their cracked spines, the dusty frill of pages she had read. Beside the bookcase was the cardboard box of things my mother had packed up for me. Below faded cards and letters, and a piggy bank that clanked with nineties-era coins, was my father's first book of poems, the one that contained "The Catch." I knew it wasn't my copy, since I had mine in D.C. I flipped it open and saw an inscription on the title page in my dad's handwriting.

For my darling Rachel and our little tie rack.

I was so startled that I let go, and the book fell to the floor pages-first. "Mom?" I climbed to my feet and took a dozen unsteady steps across the hushed living room. "Mom? Mom?" I opened her bedroom door.

"Ah!" she bolted upright. "You scared me, Ellie."

"Look at this." I pushed the book into her lap.

"What?" She switched on her bedside lamp. "Hand me my glasses."

I plopped down and leaned against the headboard beside her. "Where did you find this?" she said.

"You put it in the cardboard box. Look at the inscription."

She opened the book. "Oh. The tie rack." She smiled. "That's you."

"Me?" My heart sped up.

She let the book close. "I had totally forgotten. That was a nickname he had for you when I was pregnant."

"But you said you didn't know why Dad had left me a tie rack in his will."

Her face fell. "You're right. I did say that. I think when you told me your father left you the tie rack I kept focusing on the gingerbread part. Not the tie rack part. Like, why did he leave Ellie something having to do with gingerbread? Also, I guess I don't like to think about that time in my life. And honestly, it was just so long ago."

"Why did you call me . . . tie rack?"

"Oh, it's a long story," she said. She seemed casual about the whole thing, not understanding how much I needed this from her. "It wasn't that you were an accident exactly. I mean, this is probably TMI, as you kids say, but your father and I couldn't stay away from each other. And those diaphragms back then were so annoying."

"Yeah, that's definitely TMI."

"Well, all I'm saying, Ellie, is that I wasn't too surprised when Dr. Goldfarb told me I was 'with child.' He actually said that. But your father was shocked. And he wasn't happy. At first," she added quickly, her finger in the air. "When I told him I was pregnant, he said, 'I don't want this, I don't need this, I swear to God, Rachel, it's like when you're given a tie rack for your birthday and you have to be, like, *Why, thank you!* But I don't want this tie rack.' Then he ran out of our apartment, and I sat there crying for hours. Or what felt like hours. Finally he came back with a bunch of wilting flowers. It was all that the store had that late at night, he said. And I remember he held them out and he said something like, 'Rachel, I'm sorry. I will love our tie rack. I will love it and love it and love it.' And you know what, he absolutely did love you."

By now I was crying, though I didn't want her to see, because then maybe she would stop talking. And I didn't want her to stop talking.

"For a couple of months of my pregnancy," my mother went on, "we joked about our little tie rack and how loved it was. And how necessary. And how loved and necessary *you* were. And are. I guess he figured, when he left it to you in the will, that eventually you would ask me about it and I would remember and tell you. I'm so sorry it took me so long."

"Oh," I said softly, holding the book close, wiping my face. I was a little tie rack. The littlest tie rack, which sounded like the name of a children's book no one would ever read, except for three people: my parents and me. I was a tie rack; I was my father's tie rack. My mother's tie rack. I had belonged to both of them, back when they were a couple and we were a triple. Back in a time that no longer was.

She smiled. "It was a sweet time with your father. Before everything changed."

I studied Dad's author photo on the back flap. I'd looked at it hundreds of times, and I almost had it memorized—how he peered into the camera, his face broad with youth, his eyes full of love. He wasn't any one thing, was he? No one ever is. Behind him to the left was a blur of green trees. I squinted at the photo and saw the text below: *Author photo by Linda Tapscott.*

Linda Tapscott. The lagoon woman. Romley Cass's wife. Then I registered what my mother had said. *Before everything changed.*

"Wait, Mom, why does it say his author photo was taken by Linda Tapscott?"

She turned to study me. "You know who Linda Tapscott is?"

"No," I said. "It can't be."

She nodded.

"Linda Tapscott?" I said. "I thought Dad had left Linda something in his will, but it turned out he hadn't. I went to see her. She told me about the affair. I just assumed it was recent! I mean, Linda was crying at his funeral."

"No," my mother said. "Why did you think that?"

"I have no idea. Maybe because it all seemed so present." I hadn't lived long enough to have a history, as my father had. "I thought it must've happened when he was married to Colette. Linda talked about how hard it was on her marriage as though it happened yesterday."

"I can imagine," she said. "It was hard on me too."

"He cheated on you with Linda?"

She sighed. "I knew early on your father was a seductive guy. My parents told me not to marry him, but I couldn't resist." She laughed a little. "Young love. Or lust. Other women couldn't resist either. It was very hard to be with him, because he couldn't help being alluring to other people. And by that time—it was 1988 when he had the affair with Linda—I was pregnant with you, and I wanted you to be charmed by him too. I just hoped he would never hurt you."

"Mom, why didn't you tell me?"

"Eleanor, how could I turn you against your father? How could I tell you that he was out gallivanting with other women while I was at home with morning sickness?" Her voice had no anger in it. For my mother, unlike for Linda, I realized, this wasn't an open wound.

"I'm sorry you found out this way," she said.

"You didn't think about leaving him?"

"I wanted you to have a father. And he assured me the whole Linda fiasco was over."

"Then when I was three—" I started.

"He left me."

"Did he ever apologize?"

"He did, actually. After the divorce, he wrote me a long, heartfelt letter. It helped."

That was something. He hadn't been able to bring himself to reach out to Larry in his lifetime, but he'd tried to make amends with my mother. I turned my head to the pillow. It was warm, yeasty, edged with geranium face cream. Unlike the rest of the house, it smelled like my mother.

"I didn't understand," I said into the pillow. "I thought he was sort of disinheriting me, but instead he was being sentimental. And I guess he thought I'd feel sentimental about it too."

We were quiet for a long time. Then I started to laugh.

"What?"

"This insane shaman Colette dragged me to. She said my mother would have all the answers."

"I've always known I was an oracle," she said sleepily, taking off her glasses.

"Since when do you wear glasses?" There had been a time

when I could detect changes in her on a daily basis. Now months went by when I didn't see her, and I was missing things.

"It's been a while now. Old eyes."

"Mom?"

"Yeah?"

"Can I stay in your bed?"

She yawned again. "Neither of us will sleep well."

"Just for a minute."

She shut off the bedside lamp and lay back down.

"Mom?"

"Hmm?"

"Thank you."

"You're welcome, my little tie rack."

We laughed. I felt the words shiver down my arms. I wanted to hear him say that name too, but when I closed my eyes and heard it in my head, it was still my mother's voice.

Twenty-three

I stayed three more days, sleeping, walking around the back-yard, and watching HGTV with my mother. I even did a push-up or two with her. No more mysteries to solve. On an early-morning flight to D.C. from Florida, I ate two teeny packages of peanuts in the airless cabin and thought about what I wanted to say to Lucas. When I got off the plane, I took the yellow line eight stops home and FaceTimed him from my stoop before I unlocked the door.

"You're back," Lucas said happily, from inside my phone. I asked him to meet me.

"Now? What about dinner later? I'll cook at your place."

"Now," I said. Time was an issue; I had to do this before I lost my resolve. I needed to talk to him in public, outside, where my feelings wouldn't be muddied by desire.

He seemed about to protest but then agreed with his eyes only.

We met at a bench in Potomac Park, near where we'd kissed for the first time.

"How was your trip?" He was reserved, distant, bracing himself for whatever I was about to say.

I told him what I had learned from my mother about the tie rack. "Working myself up over this mystery meant I didn't have to let go of him," I said. "It meant I still had a relationship with him, even though he's dead, you know? I was the one who knew him well enough to solve it. But on the plane, I started reading the in-flight magazine. It was weirdly enjoyable! And then I thought maybe it was because there was nothing in it about my father or the whole mystery. It was sort of a relief to not be thinking about him."

"You got the closure you needed. I'm happy for you," Lucas said.

"Yeah." And then, with anxiety, I added, "But I think we should talk about us."

"You're scaring me," he said softly.

A prism of sunlight flashed against his cheek, and I saw that his face had flattened with fear.

"Mina's pregnant, isn't she?" I said. "You have a teddy bear in your bathroom."

"No! Ellie, is that what this is about?"

"Come on," I said. "Tell me the truth."

"She was pregnant a few years ago, but she had a miscarriage. We were talking about trying again." His voice was halting, tentative. "But our marriage wasn't in a good place. And then I met you."

I didn't know what to say. Should I tell him I was sorry? I didn't want him and his wife to have experienced pain. But, also, I wasn't sorry he had met me. Both were somehow true. "When I was in Florida," I said after a moment, "I learned that my father was having an affair when my mother was pregnant with me. She kept that secret all those years. She said it was to protect me. She didn't want me to hate him, and she knew I would've if I found out. Or maybe I would have hated *her* for telling me."

"What are you saying, exactly?"

"I don't want to be the . . . alluring seducer," I said. "Katherine said, 'This isn't going to end well.' I still think about that all the time."

"Why does it have to end?" he asked. "You're tying me in with your father's history, which I have nothing to do with."

"This began with an affair," I said. "And if it continues, it's going to be because of a dissolved marriage." I corrected that. "A marriage I helped dissolve. That I participated in dissolving."

"You sound like you're talking about a crime," he said. "Like you're an accomplice."

I didn't want to be someone who always related everything to her father. When I looked up, Lucas was patiently watching me. The day was clear and calm. I couldn't endlessly pull him into this, couldn't free-associate in front of him about my father, and about my mother, myself, the past, and how her life had changed irretrievably, how she'd spent all those decades in the gym and on the scale. And Linda too, who had been crying at my father's funeral over a twenty-five-year-old relationship that had nearly cost her her marriage. Nor could I obsess to Lucas or anyone else forever about Romley, whose fury had flared up in his kitchen, as if no time at all had passed. And finally, there was teenaged Larry, with his cheek pressed against the counter of the hardware store. He had watched his friend, a man he loved, slip down the aisle and fade away. My father had chased after success, after women, the wrong things. Maybe, I thought, I was chasing after the wrong thing too: a need to be chosen in order to be healed. I didn't want to be a person who did that. Was I too much like my father? But how could anybody really know, as it was happening, if they were following a pattern they were determined not to repeat? I probably wouldn't find out until time had passed and I was looking back on it all.

Lucas gazed into the distance the way a person looks at the sea. "I want to be with you," he said. "Without the complications of my wife or your father. We could see where we end up. Can we do that? Can we try?"

I knew he was saying that he wanted to move forward and not always be looking back. I didn't have an answer, but I hoped so. We sat without speaking, facing forward on opposite sides of the bench, just as we had many months ago, at the tidal basin on the night we'd first met. The nights were lengthening, the planet tilting toward fall. At points all over the earth, people were advancing toward each other and away from each other, and this was just one instance in the vast history of these moments. I thought that the collection of all such trajectories must make up the most complex atlas in existence.

Twenty-four

At summer's end, Mal and I left 1938 House at five in the morning with coffee mugs and extra pairs of shoes. We complained about the hour, but it was exciting and almost mystical to be up this early, in the slowness and silence, driving toward the pale-blue fingers of dawn.

Mal told me about a date she'd been on with a union organizer who'd moved to D.C. from Boston. She mentioned that Nick and Adrian wanted us all to go to the Korean day spa in Centreville next weekend and that Katherine was about to leave for her annual trip to Morocco for the embassy. I listened intently, filing details away. It had been a long time since I'd been a good friend to Mal—to any of my roommates—and now I wanted to make up for my selfishness. I was grateful to Mal. I imagined us, years in the future, living in our separate, grown-up row houses nearby. I'd go over to her place for a glass of wine on my way home from work, and we'd laugh about the time I took a job playing Teddy Roosevelt and had a breakdown, running out of the stadium in costume, and Mal had to swoop in and save me, putting me on a plane to my mother's. We'd tell the story over and over, until it was seasoned properly, the way cocktail-party stories marinate over time, the high and low tones perfected, the predictable pauses for laughter. Until we had to work hard to make it seem fresh each time. *Tell us that one again,* someone would say, and we'd link arms and remind each other how it went.

When we were done, I'd walk up the front steps of the house where I lived—a proper house, no roommates. I'd drop my keys with a clink in the bowl on the front hall table, and maybe from somewhere deep in the house Lucas would call out to me. *That you?* And I'd say, *Yes, it's me, I'll be right there.*

Now, from the parking lot at the halfway point, Mal and I collected Van from Colette. We were headed to the marina to meet the osprey watchers. A half-dozen birders were already there when we arrived, binoculars around their necks, all of them several decades older than any of us but polite and curious about our connection to the Maryland Birders' Association.

When Larry joined the group, there was a small but eager round of applause for him. The protesters were long gone, just as I had promised. Luna's chicks had died in July, and Larry had carted them down his ladder and brought them to the university lab for study. The rest of the Choptank River osprey would soon begin their long migrations south.

Larry and I had exchanged several emails, mostly about birds, but in one he'd enclosed a copy of "The Retort," the photograph he'd taken long ago of his parents at the county fairgrounds, the one my father had praised, and I saw the depth of feeling in their faces—neither of them noticing the camera or their son behind it, who, untutored and yet possessing a gift, would place them down forever on coated paper.

Larry came toward us. "Good to meet you," he said to Van, shaking his hand and looking him in the eyes. My father may have been an irresistible performer, but Larry was alluring in a different way, sincere, with a quiet kindness.

Soon Van and Larry were examining the binoculars I'd brought. I'd gotten them with my first paycheck from my new job, as an assistant at a nonprofit that advocated for press freedom. It wasn't a journalism job, but it paid decently, and everyone there seemed on their way somewhere else, grateful for this good waystation and plotting their own big futures while they did. I had begun writing at night, by hand, various starts of personal essays. Lucas wanted me to show him one that I'd just begun, and after saying no a few times, I thought I would let him see it one of these days.

Larry explained to us how to identify what kind of fish an osprey had caught: A deeply forked tail meant a menhaden; a thin yellow flash was bay anchovy. We took turns holding the lenses to our eyes, scanning the riverbank, and I saw that the nests had become smaller as the chicks grew to fill them. We trailed the Maryland bird-watchers through the quiet morning. The water was high from the summer's rain, a gray murmur above which gnats mated in columns, forming new cities in the air.

"Larry says there's a nest down there with birds," Van signed.

"Let's go," I signed back.

I'd been learning ASL through an online course and practicing with Van. Little by little, I was getting the basics. Colette had even said she'd get Sadie, Anna, and me lessons for Summer Christmas next year. I wondered how much longer we'd keep celebrating these holidays out of season. Maybe we always would, or maybe they would come to an end. But if I was invited, I would go. I thought I would always go.

Van led the way, venturing down the slim spit of grass. Then Mal, Larry—who carried a big stick—and me. We passed an empty nest, where twigs had begun to fall and chicks had died or never hatched. Or perhaps the chicks had survived and flown south, where they'd stay for several years before making their first migration north, alone, instinctively knowing how to come home. Patchy the nest stood, high above the ground, and I wondered whether, if I could have seen inside, there might be one black plastic garbage bag, shredded. One ice cream sandwich wrapper.

More pieces of the nest would be swept away when winter came, when wind and snow and sleet would return the materials to the bay. But for now we pressed our feet to the marsh, beach grass pricking our legs. Dragonflies lit out over the channel. I took my father's baseball from my purse and held it in my hand. Scuffed white, stitches faded to pink, a symbol of betrayal, of regret. Of love. A testament to the possibilities that existed between two people, the conversation that was passing a ball back and forth.

"Hey, Van!" I signed, and my arm went up into the air and swan-necked to release. We tossed our father's baseball back and forth, until Mal and Larry joined in.

"Van, would you like to have this ball?" Larry asked, looking to me for approval. I nodded. "I think it should belong to you. If you'd like it, it's yours."

I did my best to translate what Larry had said. "Gift," I signed. "Belongs to you."

Van held the ball to his chest solemnly, seeming to sense the gravity of the moment. Of course he should have the baseball—it should have gone to him all along. Maybe he would actually use it; he would take it out once in a while over the course of his life and play with the ball that had been his father's. Sometimes you are given a gift you don't think you want, but then you do. *The opposite of Ellie is a tie rack.*

Maybe when Van was older, I would tell him about the saga of the baseball and the tie rack. "The Baseball and the Tie Rack" had a legendary quality to it, like "The Owl and the Pussy-Cat," a poem my father had read to me when I was very young. As for the tie rack, it had been relegated to the same kind of place where it had been before my father died. Right now it was on a high shelf in my closet, above my winter clothes. I thought of the way that people who were in possession of their dead loved ones' ashes sometimes didn't know what to do with them. Maybe the tie rack would occasionally be on display and occasionally disappear onto that high dark shelf, though I would always know it was somewhere nearby. Not unlike a baseball being tossed by friends, eventually making its way back to you.

For now Van didn't need to learn about any of this. For now he would know Summer Christmas. Van Morrison records. Playing ball in summer's perfume. He'd remember our father's hands and how he shaped them to tell Van bedtime stories, how his hands caught baseballs and tucked him in and poured razzleberry fring frongs and told him he was loved.

Van pointed out an osprey nest balanced high in a tree. Two young osprey perched on the edge, flapping tentatively, testing the air. Cars passed along the road, heading west to Washington and east to the sea. The osprey took flight, one after the other mastering the air, and as I squinted to see their passage, shading my eyes from the sun, the road fell away, and all the cars did too, and the houses and streets and spires shimmered and vanished until all that was left were the rising osprey and the four of us at the river's edge, witnesses to the commotion of wings.

Acknowledgments

I must first thank Meg Wolitzer. A more brilliant, funny, and gracious person does not exist. She has taught me so much, and I could not have written this book without her.

Kate Medina is an extraordinary editor and friend. Her vision for this novel far outstripped my own, and her wisdom pushed me to think about the novel in new ways. I will always be awed by and grateful for her passion and insights.

Thanks to Suzanne Gluck, the most perfect agent, whose belief in my work has been a buoy.

Endless gratitude to the gifted team at Random House, including Avideh Bashirrad, Maria Braeckel, Carrie Neill, Barbara Fillon, Madison Dettlinger, and Noa Shapiro. I am lucky to work with each of you.

The production team did a superb job and I am grateful for their expertise: Benjamin Dreyer, Maggie Hart, Evan Camfield, Rebecca Berlant, and Dana Blanchette.

My amazing friends offered me their encouragement, counsel, and couches, including Nina Ridhibhinyo, C. Lee Cohen, Caroline Mailloux, Emily Ardolino, Kristofer Barr, Kristin Frontiera, Masha Westerlund, Katie Bradley, Harvey

Prager, Ron Berney, Harmony Hazard, Martina Clark, Ikwo Ntekim, Nora Decter, Pamela Mendelsohn, Yaeli Bronstein, Paul Selker, Jen and Stan Dalton, Donna and Robert Trussell, and my dearest DC family—Bonnie Goldstein, James Grady, and Nathan Grady.

Special thanks to the faculty and staff of the Stony Brook MFA. The BookEnds program was invaluable, as was Mira Dougherty-Johnson's generous feedback. Emily Smith Gilbert is the most incisive reader I know, and I cherish her friendship.

I have been nourished by many brilliant teachers, including the astute and kind Susan Scarf Merrell, Susan Minot, Keith Brown, Cornel Ban, Tony Bogues, Roger Rosenblatt, Karen Luten, Elizabeth Richards, and Jill Stein, whose early encouragement I will never forget.

I'm indebted to my colleagues and mentors at Riverhead for their guidance and generosity, particularly Sarah McGrath, Geoff Kloske, Jynne Dilling Martin, and Delia Taylor.

My deepest thanks to Susie Bedsow Horgan, my beloved neighbor and my guide; Ben Dalton, who taught me most of what I know about life and partnership; Joanna McClintick, my best friend and truest reader, whose brilliant feedback on each draft of this novel was a gift; and Isaac Fried, a wonderful human and a delight.

I'm humbled by the support of my family, including Marcos (and the Pomona Writer's Colony), Gabe, Patience, Eliza, James Carter, Ivy, Richard, Caroline, Grover, Graylen, and Annabel. My gratitude, love, and admiration to my grandparents Helen and Edgar. To my mom, Jenny, a terrific editor: thank you for your ceaseless support of my writing, your wisdom and care, your insistence on my education, and all the salmon pasta I could eat. And to my father, James, my greatest champion, who left too soon, but always knew that I could: I love you, I miss you, goodbye.

THE CATCH

Alison Fairbrother

A BOOK CLUB GUIDE

"The Catch" by James Adler

but,
if time could kneel, as a catcher
shifts to his knees when the pitch is wild

For the summer we played in ruffled green grass,
or indoors if the sky shivered with rain,

Tossing the ball from end to end
In dusty store aisles.

Would the solid walls still echo with the hollow
slaps of our hands to leather mitts,

Or would I leave you there
your arms outstretched

as if to receive me.

Questions and Topics
for Discussion

1. How did you interpret Jim's poem, "The Catch," when you first read it? (If you need a refresher, turn to the previous page of this guide!) How did you interpret the poem by the end of the book?

2. Describe Ellie's relationship with her half-siblings. What traits do the kids share? How are they different?

3. In what ways does Ellie look up to her father? As she learns more about him after his death, how does her opinion of him change?

4. What does the baseball symbolize for Ellie? How does its meaning evolve over the course of the novel?

5. "When you were a child of divorce, you had to be two versions of yourself, one at your mother's house and one at your father's. But neither one was your real self," Ellie says. Who is she with each of her parents? How would you describe her "real self"?

6. Discuss Ellie's grieving process. Where does she turn? What does she think will make her feel better? What does she find that actually does?

7. Ellie says of her grief: "That was another thing I was learning—I had to read how much people could handle; I had to tuck in my sadness when too much of it showed." Have you ever experienced this? Why do you think topics like death and grief are so difficult for people to face? How could the people around her have supported her better?

8. Discuss Ellie's relationship with Lucas. Do you think they belong together? Why or why not?

9. How did Larry's story make you think differently about Jim? Do you think Jim did regret his actions, decades later?

10. How does Ellie feel when she finally talks to her mother about the tie rack? What revelations does this bring?

11. Is this a coming-of-age novel? If so, how does it confirm or challenge your understanding of what it means to come of age?

12. What do you think the title "The Catch" means, besides it being the title of Ellie's father's poem?

13. What do you imagine Ellie's life could look like after the end of the book? Who will she be?

ALISON FAIRBROTHER is an associate editor at Riverhead Books. She worked as a journalist in D.C. before getting her MFA at Stony Brook University. She lives in Brooklyn.

ABOUT THE TYPE

This book was set in Sabon, a typeface designed by the well-known German typographer Jan Tschichold (1902–74). Sabon's design is based upon the original letterforms of sixteenth-century French type designer Claude Garamond and was created specifically to be used for three sources: foundry type for hand composition, Linotype, and Monotype. Tschichold named his typeface for the famous Frankfurt typefounder Jacques Sabon (c. 1520–80).

RANDOM HOUSE BOOK CLUB

Because Stories Are Better Shared

Discover

Exciting new books that spark conversation every week.

Connect

With authors on tour—or in your living room. (Request an Author Chat for your book club!)

Discuss

Stories that move you with fellow book lovers on Facebook, on Goodreads, or at in-person meet-ups.

Enhance

Your reading experience with discussion prompts, digital book club kits, and more, available on our website.

Join our online book club community!

f g randomhousebookclub.com

Random House Book Club ™

Because Stories Are Better Shared

RANDOM HOUSE